REBECCA RAISIN is a true ~~bibliophile~~ ... ks
morphed into the desire to write them. Rebecca aims to write
characters you can see yourself being friends with. People with
big hearts who care about relationships and, most importantly,
believe in true, once-in-a-lifetime love.

Also by Rebecca Raisin

Aria's Travelling Book Shop

REBECCA RAISIN

ONE PLACE. MANY STORIES

HQ
An imprint of HarperCollins*Publishers* Ltd
1 London Bridge Street
London SE1 9GF

21 22 23 24 25 LSC 10 9 8 7 6 5 4 3 2 1

First published in Great Britain by
HQ, an imprint of HarperCollins*Publishers* Ltd 2020

ISBN: US 9780008444976 CAN 9780008456979

Emoji(s) © Shutterstock.com

Printed and bound in the United States of America by
LSC Communications

This one is for you, Jax. You are my sunshine.

Prologue

The globe is spinning in front of us, countries blurring before our eyes. All Rosie has to do is stop it with her fingertip, but I know she won't. She won't make such a big decision based on something as flimsy as fate.

'Come on, Rosie, what are you waiting for?' I can't help but tease. She averts her china-blue eyes. 'It's just . . . this feels too risky. What if I stop it on Antarctica or something?'

I grin. 'Surely Antarctica needs a pop-up book shop as much as the next place? And wouldn't they adore your house-made tea blends, enough to warm the very cockles of their hearts!' I say, laughing. The whole joy of living in our campervans is we have the freedom to go anywhere. But Antarctica might just be a little too far . . .

Before I can say anything else, Rosie dashes to the back of the van. 'Wait!' she says with a backwards grin, and I know she's had this next stage planned out all along. I'll bet my last pound she's got a notebook with a full schedule about where we go next in our little campervan-cum-shops. In truth, I trust Rosie to lead us down the right path. She's the sensible one, while I am far too whimsical to make proper life decisions. I'd have trusted the globe for sure, and probably after too much wine.

'Ta-da!' she exclaims, jumping from behind the pink curtain that separates bedroom from living room.

I shake my head and laugh. Atop Rosie's immaculate white-blonde hair is a fluffy blue beret. I'm sure she'll also have a matching scarf and a phrasebook hidden away. 'We're going to France?'

'Oui, oui!' she takes a second beret from behind her back and throws it to me. 'Call me crazy, but I have a feeling good things will happen there. It's such a *romantic* country. I can imagine love *blossoming* there.'

I roll my eyes. '*That's* your reason for choosing France? You think I'm going to fall for some broody Frenchman?'

She shrugs. 'I've done a bit of research—'

'This should be good.' When Rosie says she's *done a bit of research* it means I'm not getting out of whatever crazy notion she's got without a fight.

'—and those broody Frenchman you speak of love literature!'

I wait for further explanation, like our businesses will flourish, but none comes.

'That's it? Because some French men like reading, you think it's a great place for us to spend a year as Van Lifers? Your *whole* decision is based on that?' This is out of character, even for Rosie.

Colour rushes up her cheeks. 'When you say it like that it sounds preposterous! But they don't just *like* reading, it's in their blood, same as you! They live and breathe words and they celebrate their creatives. And also there are fromageries, and who doesn't like fromageries?'

I arch a brow. 'I do like fromageries. And patisseries.'

'Especially patisseries. OK, so we're doing this? Leaving the festival circuit and all we know behind and trying our luck in France . . .?'

'What have we got to lose?' I say. 'If it doesn't work out, we'll come home . . .'

But there's no way I'll be falling in love unless it's with a three-course French meal. *That* I can open my heart to.

Chapter One

Southwark, London

In the filmy shadows of a cosy pub in London, my tipsy nomadic friends and I squish together, oblivious to the noise, the body heat, anyone besides ourselves. As we form a tight circle our laughter mixes with tears. Max starts singing 'California Dreamin" and we all follow suit, warbling one of our favourite songs from the past year, one we sang as we huddled around a campfire while someone strummed a guitar and we sat under the soft light of the moon. Now we link arms and sway, undaunted about how cheesy we must appear.

This constellation of wild and wonderful nomads have plans to scatter across the world like so many marbles, and despite our best intentions, the likelihood of meeting up again is slim. From past experience I know a few will grow tired of van life, sell up and go back to the nine-to-five. Others will fall for a person or place and make a home on foreign soil. Some will keep going, to the edges of the earth, seeking that elusive thing they can't quite name. Goodbyes are always hard, but this one has a deeper finality to it. Everything we've held dear travelling the same festival circuit is falling away.

Maybe it feels that way because I'm taking my van, the Little Bookshop of Happy Ever After, to France for an epic adventure, alongside my best friend Rosie with her tea shop van, and Rosie's boyfriend Max with his lean, green café. A few other nomads have expressed an interest in joining us too, but only time will tell.

We're a fickle bunch.

Well, everyone besides Rosie, that is. Rosie's already trying to knuckle down a timetable, lock in dates and places, write a bullet-point list that covers every contingency, but it's just her way, even though she knows it's virtually impossible to schedule van life. Still, it's a habit of hers that's hard to break. I adore Rosie's eccentricities but she's slowly learning the art of letting go of the things that hold her back.

Besides, you can't really plan when you're a nomad. Vans break down, festivals are cancelled due to inclement weather or celebrity no-shows, money runs out, there are so many variables to daily living.

Now our gathering grows maudlin, as we break apart and refill drinks. Promises that won't be kept swirl in the air above like the glittery trail of a sparkler extinguished before the word is written. I smile sadly, wishing things didn't have to end but knowing that they do.

That's the journey.

I find a quiet perch and sip my wine, mentally counting how many I've had (too many) before figuring gloomy goodbyes warrant a tedious hangover as much as anything.

Rosie, with cheeks pinked from drink, glides over to me before plonking herself down with a long sigh. 'I didn't think it would be this difficult,' she says, leaning her head on my shoulder, white-blonde hair falling down like ribbons.

I tilt my head to rest atop hers. 'I know.' I blow out a breath. 'I swear it's getting harder each year.' Feeling safe in our little nomadic bubble, our group had shared their pasts and confided in one another. Laughed so hard our bellies ached and bickered about petty things that seemed important at the time. Almost as quick as the click of fingers, it's over and we'll go our separate ways.

Rosie is quiet as she toys with her beaded bracelet, winding it round and round. These goodbyes are harder for her – this is her first year as a nomad. 'I suppose when we're old and grey and looking back we'll have all these incredible memories of people who stepped into our lives, changing them in some indelible way, before stepping out again.'

'I love that.' I picture an elderly Rosie and Max on some weather-beaten porch, fragrant homemade tea in hand, still in love. And then I picture my future silver-haired self. Driving never-ending roads, alone. But I'd still have my books, wouldn't I? Rollicking romances to fill my days and inspire dreams, fictional friends to see me through . . .

But as I gaze around the room at loved-up couples, loved-up *non*-fiction couples, I feel a pang of loneliness despite being surrounded by people who care about me.

Deep in thought, I'm jarred back to the present by an elbow to the ribs from Rosie. 'What?' I ask.

Her eyes are fixed on a man standing by the bar; even from this distance I recognize those broad shoulders of his, and the way he stands, hands deep in pockets. He seems contemplative as he waits patiently, as if he's half elsewhere, lost in thought.

'It's *Jonathan*!' she says far too loudly. I clamp a hand over her mouth, ignoring the fact I'm probably smearing her lipstick. I feel her laugh reverberate through my palm.

'Will you shush! We don't want to get his attention.' My heart pounds as I try to make sense of him being here of all places. Now of all times.

She battles free, her lipstick only slightly smudged. 'Why wouldn't we want to get his attention? Aren't we going to say hello, at least?' Her eyebrows pull together. Rosie only sees black and white, there's no grey area for her.

While I struggle with how to explain, I turn back in his

direction and sneak a peek at the guy who has stolen into my thoughts far too often since we met. His dark hair is longer and curls around the nape of his neck. He's lovely even in side profile. There's something sensuous about his mouth, and before I get lost to it, I shake the traitorous thoughts away. Seeing him again after all this time has given me a jolt, that's all. I wiggle sideways trying to hide behind Rosie, who frustratingly wiggles further away.

Jonathan and I met at a music festival last year, and he'd been endlessly fascinated about the way we lived our lives on the road. It'd been effortless chatting away with him, almost as if we were long-lost friends, reunited. He'd *listened* when I talked, as if he weighed every word that fell from my mouth. It'd been the first time since my husband died that I'd felt a teeny tiny little spark in my heart, but I soon pushed it away. And rightfully so. I made a promise and I'm sticking to it.

Seeing Jonathan here though, spotlight shining on him as if a direction to act, has quite knocked my legs from under me. Thank god I'm sitting down.

'Well?' Rosie prods.

'Well what? We're not going to say a single word, Rosie! We're going to hide in this corner and hope he leaves.' I sip my drink and pretend to be completely disinterested.

'Why?' Confusion muddies the icy blue of her eyes. 'Admit he made your pulse race, that he caused your bodice to rip, made your bosoms—'

Who even uses the word bosoms these days?! I shake my head at her teasing my love of romance novels and the clichéd way non-believers describe them. 'Made my bosoms . . . what?'

'Erm . . . bounce?' she says, searching for the right word and coming up short.

'Can you hear yourself? He made my bosoms *bounce*? Where do you get this stuff, Rosie, honestly?' I laugh, in spite of it all.

She breaks into a fit of giggles and then her face lights up as if clarity dawns. 'He makes your bosoms *heave*! That's the phrase, isn't it?'

'If my bosoms *were* heaving, Rosie, I'd be off to get medical help, for goodness' sake!' I hide behind my hands, sure she's attracted the attention of the entire bar, and not just lusty-looking Jonathan. Our Rosie doesn't quite have the same filter the rest of us have, so I should be used to it by now. But, by golly. I peek between my fingers and sure enough all of London is staring at us yet somehow Jonathan is still facing the other way. Small mercies and all that.

'You're lucky he didn't hear you, Rosie!'

She elbows me. 'Oh, for crying out loud, Aria. You *can* say hello to the man at least! I'm not proposing you marry the guy.'

I shake my head, no. I can't trust myself. There's something wildly appealing about Jonathan and I haven't felt that spark with anyone other than TJ which is such an alien feeling and one I know that I should run from.

Suddenly he turns and our eyes meet; for a moment time stops. I hold his gaze for too long – what am I doing! 'I've got to go . . . to the loo!' I say to Rosie as I jump up and flee. She follows close behind.

'Wait, he's coming over,' she says breathlessly behind me. 'You're going to be the death of me!' Rosie is not a runner.

Of course there's an impossibly long queue, so we tag on to the end of it when all I really want to do is to race into a cubicle and hide behind the door for all eternity.

'You did say before that you liked the guy, so why not say hello?' She stares at me as if I've lost my damned mind.

'I said no such thing!'

'You did so!'

'Did not!'

'Did.'

'Not.'

She harrumphs. 'You don't even need the loo, do you?'

I shake my head, contrite.

'Come on,' she sighs. 'Let's at least use our manners and say hello to him *if* he walks over, OK? He might not have even recognized us.'

I make a show of huffing and puffing. 'Keep your voice down to a dull roar this time, Rosie, OK?'

She stops me. 'I've never seen you so scattered like this.'

'Scattered?'

'I swear I can hear your heart pounding from here.'

Am I nervous? And if so, why? It's true Jonathan and I spent the better part of twenty-four hours together and time raced by – we could have continued talking for weeks and not run out of conversation. But when I think back, it was all about books and being a nomad, nothing personal. So it's not as though I really know the guy, is it? And haven't I had millions of connections with people as a Van Lifer? It's just part of everyday life – so why am I acting this way?

Time to gather my senses. 'Right. Let's just pretend we didn't see him and act surprised if he wanders over, OK?'

She laughs. 'Good plan.'

We head back to the corner and I can't help but sneak a glance at the bar. He's not there. Despite my reservations, my heart sinks. I scan the rest of the pub but he's nowhere to be found. I've scared him off by running away.

'He's vanished, just like that,' Rosie says, her voice tinged with sadness.

Have I lost my only chance . . .?

Chapter Two

Southwark, London

Rosie does a quick reconnaissance but comes back, her mouth a tight line. 'Maybe we imagined him.' She flops beside me and deflates.

'We *have* had a lot of wine,' I say, trying to fool myself I don't care. Around us Van Lifers are quietly huddled together, the earlier *joie de vivre* gone after so many lengthy goodbyes.

Tori – the owner of a pop-up Pimm's van – zigzags her way to us, and I groan under my breath. When Tori approaches, it's a sign she's up to something and it's usually no good. Right now I don't have the energy for her.

I can't find it in me to like Tori. She circulates rumours about people and then denies doing it. According to her, I'm a fraudster on the run (which she believes is why I won't talk about my past) and Rosie and Max have an open polygamous relationship (hence Tori encourages women to approach Max!) when they have nothing of the sort. Why she does it is beyond me but if she can stir the pot, she will, by god. It's all so unnecessary and immature. We're a mixed bunch of apples so there's always bound to be a few rotten ones, but Tori is poisonous right down to the core.

I narrow my eyes, steeling myself for whatever ploy is afoot. With one hand on her hip, diva-style, Tori blurts, 'This party is turning into a sob-fest; time to lighten the mood! We don't want our last hurrah to end like this.' As she talks she stabs the air with a cordless microphone to make her point. 'So, who's going to sing karaoke, inspire the masses?'

Beside me, Rosie stiffens. The limelight is not her thing – despite the amount of liquid courage she's consumed.

'Why don't *you* get up there?' I ask, knowing it's futile. Tori's concocted some crazy plan and we won't hear the end of it unless she gets her way. I've managed to avoid her most of the route but I guess tonight my luck has run out.

'I totally would,' she exclaims again in her characteristic screech which is like nails down a chalkboard, 'but . . . I've got a touch of a cold.' Her eyes dart all over the place. 'I'm too *nasally* with it or I would be the first one up there.'

Rosie scoffs. 'Yeah, right.'

I cast my gaze around one last time and still can't see Jonathan so I say, 'Fine, give me the microphone,' and shake my head ruefully. In truth I'd rather remember our last night together as a happy occasion, and not everyone crying into their wine glasses. And I'm used to hiding behind laughter and pretending life is grand. It's what I do best. 'What should I sing?' I ask Rosie.

Tori shoos me away. 'I'll choose something appropriate, don't you worry, but make sure it's a real performance – dance, sing and really *rally the troops*.'

Could it be as innocent as all that? 'Fine.' It might be the wine, but I feel completely at ease. It's just singing and swaying to a little music, right? Something we've done almost every night around the campfire anyway. I hop up on stage, and wait for the music to start, grateful I chose to wear skinny jeans rather than the short skirt and black tights I'd been toying with, so those below don't get a flash of anything they shouldn't.

Tori gives me a thumbs-up and bellows, 'Make it count!'

As soon as the familiar tune starts I want to wring her scrawny little neck. I should've known she had some ulterior motive that involved making me look ridiculous. I can't exact my revenge from up here so I settle with shooting a poisonous look her way.

She smirks. 'We had to get their attention, somehow!'

Jittery, I sway to the opening bars of 'Pony' by Ginuwine while desperately wondering how I can dance to it without looking like I've come straight from the strip club. A chair appears and I burst out laughing. 'Is that my prop?' I ask and the stranger nods, grinning.

What the hell, I figure I'll look sillier holding myself tight, so I let go and channel my best inner Channing Tatum and use that chair in the most lascivious of ways. The nomads go wild, they wolf-whistle and clap, their screams drawing a bigger crowd. My heart pounds, and the music thumps. I'm not sure if it's the way I'm dancing or the eyes on me, but my body feels electrified and I find I'm actually enjoying it.

Some of the girls jump on stage with me, and before long I'm totally lost to it, enjoying every single syllable I belt out. I smile even more when I see Tori's thunderous expression because her plan backfired.

More people spring up to join in; it seems 'Pony' speaks to them on some wild primal level and I'm shoved forward. I stumble and the chair tips over, before I right myself just at the edge of the stage. The show must go on, but the gyrating behind me reaches fever pitch and there's no stage left and suddenly . . .

I'm flying, arms out ready to soar . . .

Until reality hits and holy mother of cliff hangers, I'm not flying, I'm *falling*! As the ground comes screaming into view, I let out a yelp and brace for a hard landing. I scrunch my eyes closed and hear the softest of *oomphs* as I land, not on the parquetry, but into the pillowy bed of someone's outstretched arms. I peel an eye open – the man holding me is none other than Jonathan!

'Is this heaven?' Maybe I hit my head on the way down and this is a prelude to the pearly gates?

He laughs, exposing his shiny white teeth, like he's the hero in my very own romance novel. *Of course.* 'It's so lovely to see you again, Aria.' His voice is like velvet.

I can feel the strength in his arms as he cradles me. Exhilaration sends a shock down my spine, a sensation I haven't felt in such a long time, it stuns me quiet. He stares so deeply into my eyes the noisy room falls silent and all I can see is him. My very own hero sent to save me from an untimely fall, just like in the books.

He lifts a brow ever so slightly and somehow I sense it's an invitation to kiss him, so I don't overthink it – I just follow my heart. I press my lips against his and let every delicious sensation wash over me. It's electrifying, as if I've been zapped back to life after a long slumber. We kiss as if we're the last two people on earth. It's everything I imagined it would be and I'm only disappointed by how woozy I am. Is it him, the fall, or the wine making me feel such a way? Really, I should be more . . . The thought floats away as our kiss deepens. He's stealing the breath from my lungs in the most enchanting way but worry pushes at the edge of my subconscious which I duly ignore, instead revelling in the touch of his lips against mine. When our lips finally part, the room spins and I'm quite lost for words. I double blink, as the noise slowly returns and the spell is broken by people jostling past.

Woozy, I see Tori glaring at me, revenge written all over her face. I still haven't forgotten she chose 'Pony' of all songs for me to 'rally the troops' with, thus practically making me catapult off the stage and into the arms of this delectable hottie – evil thing she is!

'Jog on,' I say to her. 'Before I blurt out that secret you shared not so long ago.' I arch a brow and try to look fierce.

Her eyes widen and she says, 'You wouldn't!'

'I would!'

As far as secrets go it's not very juicy; she's in love with musician Axel but won't do a damn thing about it – strange since she's so keen to meddle in everyone else's life.

With one last withering glare at me, she taps Jonathan's shoulder and says, 'Don't listen to a word she says, Aria suffers from *liar*betes . . .' With a cat-who-got-the-cream smile, she saunters away and if I wasn't bound by Jonathan's strong arms, I probably would have given her a word walloping. What *is* her problem with me?

'Did she say . . .?'

'Sorry,' I say as all reason falls away and I picture myself the heroine and Jonathan the gorgeous hero. He did just save me from all manner of broken bones and bruises. I realize he's still cradling me in his arms – he must have the strength of ten thousand men!

'Why are you sorry?' He probably thinks I'm regretting the kiss. I can't remember why. 'You can put me down if you want?'

'Do you want me to?'

Yes. No. I don't know.

His deep blue unfathomable eyes mesmerize me. I could get lost in them but that niggle is still trying to break through the haze. Rosie's been onto me about opening my heart – as if it's as simple as putting a key to a lock. And staring into Jonathan's twinkling eyes, I wonder why I haven't even tried? There's a good reason, but it's ephemeral, whisper-thin and just out of my grasp – I must be punch drunk, or love drunk or maybe just *drunk* drunk?

Rosie wanders over, her skirt swishing. When she sees us she lets out a gasp, a sharp odd sound. She gives me a look I can't decipher, but I gather I'm acting strangely, still being held aloft in his arms like he's just rescued me from a burning building or something, so I wiggle my way out, still feeling wobbly. This whole scenario has *bad choices* written all over it.

'I fell,' I say, my voice too loud. 'Off the stage. Jonathan caught me or else . . . I'd have been seriously injured. Possibly dead, in a very bloody gory way.' I picture CSI chalking the outline of my body and know a gruesome picture will distract Rosie. She's always picturing her imminent death.

'I'm glad you're alive,' she says. 'I'm ah . . . going to find Max. Back soon.' She flounces off but not before acting out a bunch of dramatic charades meant to imply *what the hell is happening, I leave you for two minutes!* or thereabouts.

Jonathan and I stand close and silence descends. I can't form words; I can't even *think* of any. My mind scrambles with the inane, but I don't want to look completely socially inept. Well, more than I already do, that is. 'It's cold outside.' *Way to go, Aria!* 'What I mean to say is, we're having a cold snap.' *Brilliant!* 'But it's warm in here.'

He grins and it lights up his lovely face. 'Spring in the UK, eh?' He's teasing me. Of course it's spring, and of course it's cold. We're bloody well in England.

'Quite.'

He saves another painful silence by saying, 'Are you staying in London for a while?'

I shake my head. 'No, not for long. France is next for us.' Surprise lights up his eyes, but it's not like France is the edge of the earth, is it? 'This is our goodbye party. What about you? Do you live in London?'

What do I really know about the man? Could I have been so selfish I didn't ask him a single question back then? As I recall we got very animated about books, and I know I can lose days when that happens, literally *days*, but we didn't delve much past that.

'No, I live in St Albans. I came to London for a meeting.'

'A meeting for what?'

He doesn't get to respond as the room darkens and that can only mean one thing. Max. He's big enough to block out the light. 'Jon, my man!' He takes his hand and does that macho, fist pump thing, and I internally cringe thinking he's going to break every bone in poor Jonathan's hand. 'What brings you to the Squeaky Pig?'

'I had a meeting near London Bridge. Got the shock of my life when Aria literally fell into my arms. What timing, eh?'

'You *fell* into his arms?' Max doesn't hide his surprise.

'I was *pushed*.'

Max shrugs. 'Let me get you a beer,' he says to Jonathan and then does the big, manly backslapping thing.

Can he not just use his words to communicate? As much as I like Max, we bicker like warring siblings half the time. He's an enigma and I'm still figuring him out but one thing I adore about him is his love for Rosie and the way he treats her like she's a goddess come to life.

'So, your meeting was for—'

Rosie interrupts as she walks back over. 'It's so lovely to see you again, Jonathan!'

I roll my eyes. 'So I was just asking Jonathan—'

'Here, my main man.' Max hands Jonathan a beer. 'Get that down you. Looks like you've had a long day.' I'm never going to get an answer and suddenly I find the whole situation hilarious.

I give up and listen to my friends instead. They met Jonathan that same evening way back when, and it was a raging success. That night raced by and before we knew it, it was over. As the best things always are.

And here we are now. I do love the fact that Max acts as though it's totally natural to run into Jonathan again whereas for me it's feels like I've been struck by lightning.

Though, I suppose Max hasn't been thinking about him off and on like I have. Jonathan and I made a connection back then and I haven't forgotten him no matter how hard I've tried to.

Max pulls Jonathan away to introduce to him to someone and Rosie takes that as her cue to grill me.

'Did I see you *kissing* him?'

I let out an awkward laugh. 'He stared into my eyes like we were long-lost soul mates and I just reacted. Wow, that boy sure knows how to kiss. This is going to sound ridiculous but it gave me the strangest feeling, as if I've been in a daydream for years and suddenly with his lips against mine . . . I'm awake again.' I touch a finger to my lips, remembering the sensation.

'Wow, that's great, Aria. That's really great. Great.'

'Why are you saying it like that?'

She blinks. 'Like what?'

'Great. Great, great, great.'

She hugs herself and says, 'It's just that you were so adamant you'd never fall in love again. I think this shows real courage.' Her eyes go glassy. Poor Rosie has been secretly worried about me and my spinster status more than her jokes have let on.

'Are you crying?' I ask. Rosie doesn't do tears. Especially not in front of people if she can help it.

'A little. You guys just look so perfect together. Like a couple on the cover of one of your romances. Except he has his shirt on.'

'That's very sweet, but I'm *not* falling in love.' I remember my husband TJ's sweet face, his big laugh. I remember my promise and I curse white wine and its bad-choice-making qualities from here to kingdom come. That was the god damn niggle!

I forgot about my own bloody husband!

My gut roils with my betrayal but I try to remain cool. 'It's nice to know that my heart isn't frozen over, but nothing can happen with Jonathan.'

Time to run. Time to change the subject swift as anything.

'And stupid Tori said I had *liarbetes* while insinuating that I liked him, and as you know I most certainly do *not* have liarbetes . . .'

A frown appears. 'She said you had liarbetes?'

'Because her plan backfired. And then I got distracted and now I'm confused and I need to leave.'

Rosie tuts. 'Come on, Aria. You're the one always looking for signs and here's a big, fat, flashing neon one. It's Jonathan, in the flesh! *Jonathan!* A man who you admitted made your heart flutter and then he was gone and you didn't swap numbers or contact details, and he just so happens to visit this bar and save you from untimely death falling from a stage . . . I mean you've got to admit this is even better than any of your romance novels because it's real!'

She's so animated my heart tugs, even if she is being far too loud. 'So?' I'd have never confided all that to her if I thought I'd see him again. And if anything, the chemistry we had before has ramped up a notch. If I didn't have any baggage, I'd still be in his arms now.

'So . . .?' Her eyebrows pull together. '*So* what now? What happens in chapter two?'

I shake my head. 'Now I depart back to the Little Bookshop of Happy Ever After, make a steaming pot of tea that will hopefully ease tomorrow's enormous hangover and then I sleep like a log.'

Her mouth falls open. 'You won't even exchange numbers with a guy who previously spent almost twenty-four hours in your company listening to you talk about *romcoms* like they were the most fascinating thing on *earth*?'

'You can stop with all the *emphasis* because romcoms *are* the most fascinating thing on earth.'

She tuts. 'You know what I mean.'

I consider Jonathan as he stands off in the distance with Max. 'Last year he really did seem enthralled about the many nuances of romance tropes and the paths to happy ever after.' It's not often you find a guy like that, is it?

We sip our wine thoughtfully as we study him and once again confusion bubbles up to meet me.

'He's lovely in a very bookish sort of way,' Rosie says.

'What does that mean?'

Gesturing around the room she says, 'Well, he's so different to all the other guys here, isn't he?'

Jonathan stands out among my nomadic friends, dressed in what looks to be high-end clothes, not as shabby as the rest of us who live in tiny spaces and don't own a lot of anything because there isn't room. But it's more than that – he gives of an air of being slightly aloof and lost in thought that makes him instantly fascinating.

'He looks like an accountant,' I say. 'That's what you mean, isn't it?' Hide behind humour, isn't that the way?

We fall about laughing because he most certainly *doesn't* look like an accountant. 'I bet he's a creative of some sort,' I muse, agreeing with Rosie's earlier description. 'It's the way he listens, as if committing things to memory. And those eyes, those deep reflective pools, hold a sort of sadness, an angst. He gives off the vibe that he's a little lost among so many people, don't you think?' I recognize that trait because I am the same except I can put on an act that will fool even the most discerning.

'Wow, Aria, is that all?'

I blush. 'Well, I guess I prefer the types who fly under the radar rather than ones who spectacularly announce themselves.'

'Yeah, yeah I can see that. But what *does* he do?' she asks.

I think back.

'I don't think he mentioned it.'

'He's got a Kit Harington vibe, right?' she says, surveying him.

'So now we've got Jason and Kit? How lucky are we!' I laugh. When we first met Max I was convinced he was Jason Mamoa, the big hulking star from *Game of Thrones*. I put the question to Rosie but she'd never heard of such a beast. I soon fixed that by making her binge watch *GOT* and even she admitted the resemblance was uncanny. Now I look to Jonathan and see if she's right about the Kit thing. She is – it's the broody eyes and the sensual pout.

I double blink myself back to reality. *Leave, Aria, before you regret it.*

With a deep sigh I say, 'He's too lovely for the likes of me. I'll just end up hurting the poor guy when I decide this is all a mistake. Which it is.' I kiss Rosie's cheek. 'I'm going to head off. I'm too wobbly to make any sense of anything.'

Her forehead furrows. 'But . . .'

'No buts. I'm done.'

As a romance novel aficionado, I know it's always safer falling for the boy in the book.

'I'll walk you to the tube at least. Or I could ask Jonathan to?'

I give her a nudge with my hip. 'Kajri wanted to leave half an hour ago, so I'll catch the tube with her.' In truth I want to be alone – my ears are ringing, my head pounding and I have this overwhelming feeling I've made a mistake.

Before Rosie can talk me out of it, I turn on my heel and get swallowed by the crowd. I need to be by myself. And I vow in future to swap every second glass of wine with water . . .

Chapter Three

Greenwich, London

The next morning, I awake slowly, delicately, mouth dry as a mathematics textbook or something equally lacklustre. As I stretch, my taut muscles ache and I briefly wonder why, until the previous night comes crashing back, like a movie reel playing at agonizingly slow speed.

Oh good lord of the rings, please tell me I did not gyrate to a chair on a stage! I squint as if that will make the memory easier to deal with, but it doesn't help. I can see myself in all my 'Pony' glory, singing and dancing (and gyrating!) as if I were being paid for it. Well, Tori can't say I didn't give it my all – but then another heart-stopping memory forms.

No, no, no, *nooo*! I talk myself down. There's no chance I could have kissed anyone.

But the memory is stubborn and plays out achingly slowly. Me literally falling into Jonathan's arms. Kissing him passionately, over and again. The feel of his soft lips against mine. The heady sensation of desire, something I haven't felt in such a long time. *For very good reason*, I berate myself. Mercifully the memory ends with me snaking my way out of the pub with Kajri's arm linked through mine.

There's a knock at the door and Rosie's face appears, a question in her eyes.

'You're awake!' she says, looking bright as a button despite the late night, and enters the van bearing a plate with two slices of delicious-looking lemon-scented cake.

'I might be awake but I'm in the midst of "the remembering" and it's not good, not good at all. And I'm hoping when I confide in you, you're going to tell me it was all a dream . . .' I put a hand to my banging head and claw back panic.

'Let me make a pot of tea,' says Rosie, avoiding my eye. She places the plate on the coffee table, which is not so much a real piece of furniture but a small square of clear Perspex perched atop a stack of hardbacks.

I edge from the bed and throw on a robe as dust motes dance. There's not much room in my little van, and it's not neat as a pin like Rosie's. But I love the comfort it brings me; every nook and cranny is stuffed with books, candles, keepsakes. Even my bed is full of books, leaving me only a small sliver to sleep on, which Rosie assures me is a death trap and swears she'll wander in one day to find I'll have suffocated.

Aria Summers tragically killed by her girl squad, Nora Ephron and Kristan Higgins . . .

Despite my full body throb, I manage to settle on a chair with tea in hand. 'Tell me I didn't kiss Jonathan?'

She blows steam from the top of her tea. 'So what if you did, Aria?'

I groan. 'And you just let me?'

'Why wouldn't I?'

I cock my head. 'You know why, Rosie.'

She gives me a hard stare which I return. Eventually she sighs and says, 'There's times where you've just got to listen to your heart, Aria, and this is one of them.'

'It clearly wasn't my heart doing the decision-making, it was

21

the copious amounts of white wine. Urgh. I bloody well *forgot* I was married!'

'Widowed.'

'Same thing.' It's getting harder to spin that line though as the idea of love blossoms inside me more because I'm surrounded by loved-up couples at every turn. *I had that* – I want to scream – *and I miss it.*

Her scoff rings out. 'You can keep lying to yourself, but I won't go along with it.'

I frown. 'I'm doing no such thing.'

'No?'

'No, Oprah. I'm not.'

'So what did you kiss him for then? I've seen you tipsy before and you've never shown the slightest interest in any other man, despite several trying to make a play for you.'

Cue the dramatic eye roll which hurts my brain. 'What? As if. You make it sound like I've got men falling at my feet.'

'You do! But you never see it, Aria, because you don't *want* to see it. Men circle you, their tongues practically hanging out like lost puppies, tails wagging, hoping to get a moment of your attention.'

My laugh escapes at the preposterousness of such a thing.

'Don't laugh like that, it's true. And things are different with Jonathan. Out of a *sea* of men, he is the only one who stands out for you.'

'A sea of men!' I snigger at her exaggerations. Sure there's plenty of men about but they're Van Lifers, more like protective big brothers than anything. 'It's not that anyway, Rosie. He could be bloody Prince Charming and it wouldn't matter an iota. I've had the greatest love affair of all time, that's enough for me. It's not very fair to TJ for me to be acting like a floozy, is it?'

Her brows knit. 'A floozy is pushing it. Would TJ want you to act like a martyr? I think not. It's hard for me to see you so down, Aria, writing The End after TJ left.'

I sigh and sip my tea my while my head pounds with self-recriminations. 'It's not The End, is it, Rosie? I'm still alive, I'm still here. I'm getting on with my life as best I can. And I enjoy it just the way it is. I really do.' These protestations come naturally, I've been saying them so long, but part of me wonders if I still believe it myself.

'You left without saying goodbye to Jonathan.'

I slide my gaze away. 'So?'

'You're not fooling me.'

'I'm not trying to.'

She lets out a frustrated groan. 'You're going to let a great guy slip through your fingers, Aria and you might be able to lie to everyone else including yourself, but you can't lie to me. I can see the loneliness in your eyes when you think no one is looking. Last night I saw your face drop when you scanned all the couples in the room and then *light up* when you were with Jonathan.' She pats my arm and says gingerly, 'It's OK to want to be loved. TJ would want that for you.'

What would TJ think if he could see me now? Waking up hair a bird's nest, eyes red from lack of sleep, having kissed a guy I barely know? It smacks of a life lived teetering on the edge and once again I doubt my place in the world. Just what am I doing?

'Whatever it was last night was just a momentary slip. There are millions of women out there with fulfilling, happy *single* lives. Why am I any different? I don't need a guy to complete me like the last piece of a jigsaw puzzle. I'm fine just as I am.' *Lies, lies, lies.*

There is something endlessly fascinating about Jonathan but my guilt-plagued heart can't give in to such temptations.

'I'm not saying you *need* Jonathan, I'm saying you *want* Jonathan, there's a big difference. And it doesn't even have to be romance, it can simply start with friendship.'

'I'll take your comments under consideration,' I say making a moue. This badgering about boys was a lot more fun when it was me pestering Rosie and not the other way around.

She puts her hands on her hips and does a sigh so theatrical it's worthy of an award. 'When you go into job-interview mode, I know I've lost you.'

I stand and fold the throw rug.

'And pretending to tidy. The conversation really is closed,' she says and laughs.

I laugh too, knowing she's picked up on it. I never clean the Little Bookshop aside from vacuuming. Even the dust bunnies are my friends. That's the appeal of the tiny space. It's full to bursting with romance novels, the air perfumed with the lemony scent of preloved books and rose candles. Ruby and teal velvet cushions give it a Gatsby feel and plush throw rugs litter the space for customers who find a tome and settle in for the day.

Books line shelves and lie in disorderly alphabetical piles from the floor up making it a warm cosy little haven, lit by fairy lights and the odd candle when Rosie doesn't blow them out with wild protestations about fire hazards and cinder boxes.

'What's the plan then?' I cannily reroute, breezy as anything.

'If you're insisting on your own spinsterhood, then I guess we pack up and get ready to head off for France tomorrow? We've got that fete and a few festivals lined up already.'

I raise a brow. 'Let me see your bullet-point plan, Rosie and don't pretend you haven't scheduled our every move.'

A blush creeps up her cheeks and she takes a notebook from her bag. 'OK, OK, I have made a very simple plan, we don't have to follow it precisely' – she lifts a shoulder – 'but it's rock solid and I think we should.' The book falls open and I see pages and pages of notes.

'Bloody hell, Rosie. France is not another planet, you know that, right?'

There's no accounting for some. Rosie's a planner and always will be.

'I know, but we only speak basic French and I wanted to make sure every possible contingency was catered for.' She flicks the pages with a worried sigh. 'I think I've covered it all.'

I take the notebook from her hands; it's heavy with ink and angst.

'Rosie . . .' I struggle with what to say. 'This must have taken you weeks.'

She tries to laugh it off. 'Yeah about six all up. I guess I'm a little more nervous about leaving the UK than I once thought.'

Anxious Rosie's researched every possible thing that could go wrong and then found potential solutions. I skim through the notes before landing on one that makes me smile. 'Haunted places to avoid in France . . .?'

Surveying her nails as if they're fascinating, she says offhandedly, 'Better to be prepared for everything. It's an old city and I think it's best if we go in with eyes wide open.'

I struggle to contain my mirth because I know she's serious but it's almost impossible as I feel my lips quiver with it all. Rosie's such a hoot and has no idea how funny she is, probably because she truly believes in such things.

Composed, I say, 'You think we're going to be killed by ghosts?' Rosie's got this weird obsession with envisaging her demise, often in a gruesome way. Escaped convicts with white-blonde hair fetishes (coincidentally the colour of her hair), spontaneous combustion, vampires, Ebola, packs of wild animals . . . you name it, she's imagined it.

'It's possible.' Her face is a picture of solemnity and I can't tell whether she's winding me up or not. Rosie's foibles are many and varied which is what makes her so great, but it also makes her hard to gauge at times.

'Right, well, I'm glad you've made note of so many places to avoid. Who wants to see glamourous old chateaux anyway?'

'You're being sarcastic?'

'I am.'

'You're evil.'

'I am.'

'OK, now that's cleared up, are you ready to make a move, tomorrow morning about ten?'

'There's nothing keeping me here, if that's what you're asking.'

Best to run away like you always do, Aria . . .

'Mm-hm.'

'Well, I guess all I can say is toodle-loo England, and *bonjour* France.'

'*Oui, oui.*' She gives me a peck on the cheek. 'Get cracking and we'll meet for a late lunch, yeah? One last meal of proper fish and chips before we leave the motherland?'

'Is there anything better to soak up the effects of the night before?'

Her eyes sparkle. 'Well, only if you're Max. He's already insisted I have kombu kelp juice, whatever the hell that is.'

'Tell him seaweed is a living breathing thing too.'

'Will do.' She grins. 'I'm going to wash Poppy and check all my kitchen accoutrements are packed away ahead of the long drive. Meet you out front at two-thirty and we'll walk down to the pub?'

I nod. 'Perfect.'

I wave her goodbye and flop back into my chair to contemplate it all. France, Jonathan, TJ. The epic journey ahead. I've managed to live over a thousand days without my husband. *One thousand days*. It seems like forever and yet just like yesterday too. With him in mind, a new man turning my head seems so foreign.

The spark with Jonathan has been ignited no matter how much I deny it, but a drunken kiss isn't exactly a relationship, is it? I can still protect my heart and forget all about it.

Whenever I'm conflicted, I picture myself the heroine in a love story to make sense of it all. That's the problem with being obsessed with romance novels, you see everything play out as one, including your very own life.

Hopeless romantic Aria vowed never to love again after losing her husband, TJ, but fate seems to have other ideas and keeps throwing mysterious Jonathan in her path. Is this a test of her commitment to her husband, or is it a sign she should open her heart and her mind to the possibility of falling in love once more? Nomadic by nature, Aria can't see the point when home is always at the end of a new patch of road . . .

Chapter Four

London to Calais

After a much better night's sleep *sans* alcohol I'm packed and ready to go. I take my pot of tea and sit on the tiny deck outside the Little Bookshop, marvelling at sunshiny clear skies while I wait for Rosie to appear. The swollen fat grey clouds of the previous day are long gone, and instead all I see is an expanse of bright blue above. Birds chirp and butterflies frolic as if trying to woo me to stay.

Spring has been as dull as dishwater up until now. London, the wily beast, puts on a great show when we're about to leave these familiar shores.

Before long Rosie joins me for our usual morning ritual – I hand over a cup of tea which she swaps for a chocolate chip muffin. She chats away nineteen to the dozen while I come slowly awake, mainlining tea in order to be able to communicate. Our Rosie is one of those annoying *early bird catches the worm* types.

'What's with all this glorious sunshine?'

'It should be criminal,' I agree, taking a bite of gooey chocolatey goodness waiting for the sugar to jumpstart my body into another day.

Pretty flowers add pops of colour to the expanse of garden. 'It's a false spring. It'll go back to grey as soon as we hit the border, you know.'

I laugh. 'I know. The homeland trying to lull us into a false sense of security.'

'Bloody outrageous.' She takes a bite of her muffin.

'I'm not fooled for a minute! Where's Max?'

'Securing the perimeter,' she says, her voice deadpan.

I grin at her explanation. 'Jogging?'

'Yeah, I guess. I'll never understand his need to exert so much energy first thing in the morning.' She looks guiltily at the rich calorie-laden sweet treat in her hand and then shrugs and continues munching away at it.

'Gotta keep up that physique somehow.' Max is buffed and bronzed, a real mountain of a man. It's a mystery to us how he maintains said physique subsisting on a sugar-free, processed-carb-free, vegan diet. Rosie of course is the exact opposite; she bakes old-fashioned comfort food (carbs loaded with sugar and spice and all things nice) and doesn't run unless some mythical terror is chasing her.

Rosie and Max are my favourite 'opposites attract' romance trope come to life. While Max is a carefree, save-the-planet pacifist, Rosie is a highly efficient over-planner who doesn't read social cues too well. They're the perfect balance for one another and proof romance novels are truly a guide to life and not just a fun way to pass the time.

'While we're talking about healthy choices and diet and exercise, could I tempt you with some scones and lashings of jam and cream?'

'My arm could be twisted.' I swipe the crumbs from the chocolate muffin I've just demolished out of sight. Rosie says I've got hollow legs and she'd hate me for it if she didn't love me so much. She's curvaceous and I'm straight up and down – I know which I'd rather be, but Rosie doesn't believe me.

'Stay right there.'

Within minutes she's back with a plate bearing freshly baked scones, still warm to the touch. 'Golly what time were you up?'

'Four,' she says sheepishly. 'Couldn't sleep. Big day.'

Poor Rosie. Any change does not come easily to her and I know she struggles with it more than she lets on. Pre-dawn, she'd have been scrubbing the inside of her van, Poppy, and then baking up a storm until it was light enough to wash the outside of Poppy. When she's in turmoil, she cleans. She cleans and cleans and then cleans again. And then bakes. And the whole cycle of cleaning starts again while the rest of us sleep like the dead.

'All set though?' A small part of me worries that Rosie will pull the plug and decide leaving is too great a risk for her. She's changed so much over the last year, but part of her will always carry that fear that the unknown is not safe.

She rubs the back of her neck. 'It's going to be an adventure and while I'm nervous I know I'll have you and Max, so what's there to be worried about?' Her words wobble but I smile encouragingly at Rosie trying so hard to be brave. 'Once we're finished here,' she says, 'I'll check Poppy over once more and then we're good to go.'

I lean into her. 'That's the spirit.'

As we chat a couple of remaining nomads come to say one last goodbye. 'Stay for morning tea?' Rosie says to them before dashing back to her van for more plates.

Leo, who runs Rollerskating on the Road, gives me a big hug. He's off to run his retro skating tours in Cornwall to catch the hordes of tourists who flock there over spring and summer.

'I'm going to miss you,' I say, giving his hair a tousle. He's one of my favourite people on the festival circuit for his ever-present megawatt smile. A twenty-something with the world at his feet and his whole life ahead of him. What's not to be happy about when you've got wheels strapped on and the day is but young?

'Keep in touch, yeah?' he says, squishing the breath from my lungs as he hugs me tight. 'And I mean it, I want to hear all about France and the wild exploits you lot get up to.'

'Sure will. You be safe, please? Don't go careening down hilly streets and around blind corners. I want to see your big smile with *all* of your teeth in place when I get back.'

'I'll try.' He grins flashing those pearly whites. 'But I can't promise anything.'

'Daredevil.'

'Bookworm.'

I laugh. 'And proud of it!'

'I'm going to miss you two so much,' he says and moves to give Rosie a hug. I can tell she's trying not to be as stiff as a toy solider but our Rosie's not one for displays of affection.

'You remember to wear that helmet I got for you. It has the highest rating safety specifications out there. I tested it myself,' Rosie says.

'I sure will, Rosie, and I won't listen to anyone in future who calls me a namby-pamby for wearing such a thing.' I struggle to hold myself in check. The helmet Rosie bought for Leo resembles something worn on the Apollo 11 mission and I wonder how on earth he can see out of the damn thing, but you know Rosie, safety first, always.

'A namby-pamby? But it's for safety, I don't understand?' Rosie asks, bamboozled by others not being as safety conscious.

He shrugs. 'Jealousy is a curse. Be kind to the herbivore, won't you?' he says to Rosie about Max, the resident plant-eater. Rosie is trying her best to keep up with the conversation, confusion shining in her blue doe eyes because she's probably picturing Leo and what other safety gear she should have bought him.

I move to her and swing an arm over her shoulder. We exchange a glance and I give her an almost imperceptible nod to spill that we know his secret. She whispers, 'Look after Lulu too!' We cover our mouths to stop giggles from pouring out – how child-like we are at times!

He raises a brow. 'It's out then, is it?'

'Imagine keeping that from us,' I jokingly admonish him. But we all know love on the road is delicate when it's new. Eyes on your every move doesn't help and the gossip spreads like wildfire, so it's best to play it coy until those feelings are certain, and that much I do know . . . from watching on the sidelines, all the damn time.

Lulu joins us smelling as always like the purple flower she loves so much. She owns Lavender at Lulu's, a pop-up shop that sells homemade natural bath products, from soaps to shampoos and everything in between. She wears her heart on her sleeve and is the true peace-loving hippy of the past, reincarnated.

I take a step back to drink in the lovebirds one last time, my heart doing a little happy dance for them. They're both salt of the earth, big-hearted wanderers who tread gently on this planet.

We take time over our scones laden with jam and cream coupled with freshly brewed tea. It's a wonder I'm not the size of a house since Rosie walked into my life, but I suppose I've stopped eating from a packet these days, whatever charred mess I'd previously managed to consume in order to stay alive. Cooking is not my forte and I had little interest in food until Rosie came screaming into my life.

Everything she makes is from scratch and even if it is laced with butter and sugar, there's a homeliness about it, conjuring Sunday visits to Gran's house where you'd leave with a warm heart and a full belly.

Maybe I can grow a food baby, that will give me something to love . . .

After sharing their travel plans, Lulu and Leo thank us and offer another round of hugs. We watch them walk off together, hand in hand. 'No more goodbyes, my heart can't stand it,' I say, resting my head on Rosie's shoulder.

Rosie gives my arm an affectionate rub. 'We'll see them again, surely.' It's a strange game this wandering lark. You'd think it would be easy to keep in touch, but it never works out that way. Patchy Wi-Fi, days spent driving from one place to the next, busy festivals and fairs and those people who once owned a corner of your heart slowly get pushed out for the people you meet on the next part of the ride. These special people may dart out of our lives but I will always remember them for the easy open friendship they offered.

'I'm hoping there'll be a wedding invitation in the inbox soon!' I nudge Rosie and motion to Leo and Lulu who kiss in the distance under the shade of an oak tree.

'Won't she make the most beautiful bride?'

I sigh, picturing it. 'Stunning! I can see her with long blonde plaits, wearing a gauzy cheesecloth dress.' I'll never tire of seeing love bloom. Never, ever, ever. 'Barefoot, a beach wedding . . .'

'A bouquet of bluebells and forget-me-nots.' Rosie's face shines, as we lose ourselves dreaming.

'Daisy chains for the flower girls.'

'Cream linen for the ring bearer, a lavender filled cushion a bed for the quartz wedding ring.'

I smooth down my shirt. 'If we mentioned all this to her do you think she'd freak out?'

Rosie laughs. 'It might be a little presumptuous since they've only been dating for a week.'

'But when you know, *you know*.' They catch us staring and we both yelp and wave enthusiastically as if we're proud parents. 'OK, Cupid. Let's just stalk their Facebook pages and if we get any hint marriage is on the cards then we can bombard her with our suggestions.'

'Bombard?' Rosie queries.

'Gently make myriad helpful suggestions . . . Perhaps I'd better stick to fictional weddings.' Wedding season, you'll find me attending all sorts of *fictional* weddings; from historical to modern-day romances, there's not a single one that doesn't make me shed happy tears.

'For the time being stick to the books,' Rosie says. 'You can blubber until your heart is content and you don't have to worry about wearing waterproof mascara.'

'True, another reason reading beats real life. Waterproof mascara is impossible to remove.'

I turn to her, suddenly enamoured with the thought of weddings, babies, good, solid strong futures. 'What about you, Rosie? Have you and Max discussed the next stage much?'

A blush creeps up her neck.

'You have!'

'Don't be ridiculous!' Her voice rises with each syllable.

I fold my arms. 'What's ridiculous about it? I've never seen a couple so besotted before.'

Playfully she swats at me, a sure-fire sign she's embarrassed discussing it. 'So why do I need marriage to cement it?'

Hands on hip, I say as if it's obvious, 'So I can plan the wedding!'

She dissolves into a fit of laughter. 'That's it?'

'Well, I want to be an aunty too. Can you imagine your little brood of curly-haired beauties who roam wild and free, climbing trees and speaking four different languages?'

'It screams pathetic, but yes I *have* pictured them, a little boy and a little girl two years after . . . and I'm already in love with them, even though the boy is a bit reckless and the girl always hangs off Max and insists on speaking in an American accent like her daddy. Isn't that a little cuckoo?'

I waggle my brow. 'What are their names?'

She gives me a hip bump.

'I know you have it all planned, Rosie!'

Our peals of laughter punctuate the day. It feels so good to celebrate these little wins my friends are having. To think of the way love can blossom into real-life miniature humans blows my mind and I'd love to be part of their family, as the eccentric word nerd adopted aunty who lives next door and teaches them to read.

'Fine, their *tentative* names are Alchemy and Huckleberry.'

My laughter dies and dries into a hard lump in my throat which I semi-choke on. 'Wow . . . Rosie, they are, erm, certainly unique names. Won't forget those in a hurry.'

'I thought you'd especially like the literary nod to Huckleberry.'

I swallow my shock. 'Ah, wonderful! I'll order in *The Adventures of Huckleberry Finn* just as soon as I get a free moment.'

She gives me a hard stare. 'Do you really think I'd name my children Alchemy and Huckleberry?'

'You're not?'

'No, I'm not.'

'Oh thank god! I wasn't sure what to say! You know as well as I do that nomads have a tendency to name their offspring all sorts of wacky and wonderful things, I thought you'd been bitten by the same bug. Don't get me wrong, I love Sage's son Quest, and Ziggy's daughter Freedom—'

'You hate their names.'

'I do *not*! Their names are as adventurous as their little spirits. What if Quest grows up to be an explorer? Quest going on a quest! And Freedom might become a human rights lawyer and how handy will her name come in then?' OK, I don't love their names, but I'll never tell.

'You're a hopeless liar, Aria. My chosen names if you must know are Indigo for the little boy who is destined to arrive first, and exactly two years and six months later little Aria Rose will be born into this world. You've ruined the surprise.'

'Aria Rose?'

'It's got a nice ring to it, you have to admit.'

'It's beautiful. And I'm honoured. So when do these little cherubs plan on gracing the planet?'

She huffs and takes out her ever-present notebook with a long sigh as if I've pushed her patience to the limit, knowing (as I do) that everything is planned no matter whether babies can be or not.

With supreme confidence, she says, 'Indigo should arrive

around June 2023, and baby Aria in January 2026 or there about. It's not too soon, is it?' A frown appears.

'Not at all.' Knowing Rosie, she'll figure out a way to make babies happen exactly as her schedule decrees. 'What does Max say?'

She scoffs. 'He says let nature take its course, and if it's sooner then that's all the better.' She pinches the bridge of her nose as if Max's carefree nature pains her. 'But I'm not ready, not yet. I'm still adjusting to life on the road.'

'Me too,' I say and feel the truth in my words. 'It's an ongoing learning curve.'

'What about you, Aria, would you ever consider babies?'

I baulk. 'By immaculate conception?'

She purses her lips.

Noting the time so I can distract her, I say, 'Wow, we'd better push off if we want to stick to your schedule.'

There's a tap on the van door. A courier stands there with a package in hand. 'Aria Summers?'

'That's me,' I say. Had I placed a special book order I'd forgotten about? Or a blindfold so I won't see myself walking into any more bad choices? Maybe a chastity belt for those times when I forget I'm resolutely single . . .

'Sign here, love.' I do and he hands over the package. 'Have a good day.'

'Book order?' Rosie asks.

I tap a finger to my chin. 'Must be but I can't remember who for? I'm sure I got them all sorted already.' A big part of my business is ordering in rare books for my customers and then shipping them on for a small profit. I also have an online shop with a romance cult following. Anything to keep the wolf from the door. Van life is a constant state of hustle to be able to continue the journey.

'Open it up.'

I tear it open to find a handwritten note and what looks to be a diary.

When I see the name at the end my heart stops. 'It's from TJ's mum.'

I fold the letter.

'Aren't you going to read it?' Rosie asks, eyes enquiring. 'Oh . . . privacy, right? I'll go and give you a few minutes?'

I nod. 'Thanks, Rosie.'

When she's gone I take the letter and sit on the edge of my bed, trying to slow the rapid beating of my pulse. Surely TJ's mum wouldn't write to harangue me? I'd always hoped we could mend bridges but part of me is still angry about the way the family ghosted me after TJ died. His mum, Mary, led the charge, ignoring me at his funeral, not inviting me to family birthdays or Christmases after he'd gone. It was as though I didn't exist to them anymore. I'd gone from favourite daughter-in-law to public enemy number one. It hurt. It still hurts. And despite being treated horrendously by them, I still miss them, especially Mary who was like a mother to me once.

> Dear Aria,
> I hope this finds you well. Although if you're anything like me, you're just plodding through every day on autopilot. The world isn't the same without TJ. Don't you find that colour has been leached from everything? The sun isn't as bright and even the sound of laughter sounds strange to me these days, but I endure. What else can one do?
> He left this diary with instructions to send it to you, but I'd misplaced it. For that I am sorry.
> Mary

She had this precious keepsake for almost three years and forgot? It's that same old game-playing and to what end? I expected better from them, but grief is a wily beast so I stretch my limits trying to sympathize to justify her behaviour, find any reason why she'd keep this from me and come up short. She blames me for taking TJ away from her when he got sick, and she won't listen to reason about it.

My hands shake as I tentatively open the diary. I slam it closed when I see the loops and scrawls of TJ's neat writing. I'd never seen him write in a diary, not once. I blink back tears at having a relic so treasurable – his thoughts, his words, trapped inside. There couldn't be anything sweeter for a word nerd like myself. But when did he write in it? What if it's some terrible secret he's chosen to confess?

There's no time to ponder now. We're about to leave and the very last thing I want to do is read it in haste. I kiss the diary and put it in my bedside drawer wishing my husband had been sent back to me but knowing that his words are the next best thing.

Chapter Five

Calais

The diary is on my mind as we say goodbye to old London town and start our journey. It's nice to be alone in the front of the van and let my mind wander. I'm following Max so I don't have to worry about the route. Instead I spend the next couple of hours reminiscing about TJ and some of the amazing adventures we shared. He was the type of guy who was up for anything. Rock-climbing, chick-flick marathons, sailing, and my favourite – walking in the rain hand in hand with me. He loved his life and I hang on to that.

After a long drive we arrive in Calais, park up and stop to stretch our legs as gloriously warm sunlight bathes our stiff bodies. French accents bounce around, and I smile listening to such poetic language. *Ooh la la*, it's theatre come to life as men gesticulate wildly over tiny cups of café crème and women with broody eyes sit smoking cigarettes.

'Not too keen on doing that drive again. Poppy was all over the road,' Rosie says, her face white. Driving a big rig like Poppy is no easy feat, just keeping her on the road requires a certain kind of concentration. Like the Little Bookshop, pink campervan

Poppy has a mind of her own at times and will pull this way and that to get your attention. They're grand dames who've had long, illustrious lives before they stepped into ours.

'That's the first leg done, Rosie. You did well. We've got less than three hours to go to get to Rouen.'

She blows hair from her eyes and Max takes her in his arms. He doesn't say anything, he's always just there for her when she needs it. A calming presence who never speaks in platitudes to Rosie, because who likes platitudes? I love *love* and seeing it jump from the pages and come to life with these two gives me the warm and fuzzies.

But I can't let them know that. 'Get a room, you two.'

Rosie's anxious mood is soon replaced by wonder as, wrapped in Max's arms, she takes in her surroundings. The parading of their love is probably half the reason I'm suddenly consumed with Jonathan fantasies – the two of us reading side by side with only the flickering glow of candlelight. OK so it's not exactly a wild, passionate imagining but baby steps, and all that.

Rosie's happiness is infectious so it takes me a minute to take in the view and that's when I spot them. 'Look!' I point. 'You can *just* see the white cliffs of Dover from here.' They are so spectacular, the white of them is luminous even this far away. 'I can't help it; the song is playing in my head.' I start humming Vera Lynn's classic hit 'The White Cliffs of Dover'.

'Wow,' Rosie says. 'I'd love to take the ferry past them one day, see them up close.'

'Me too.' There's so much world to explore, I'm hoping this French trip inspires us to keep going as far as we can in our vans. 'But for now, adventure awaits. And that is *Le Phare*, the lighthouse on the point.'

Rosie groans, not being one for heights. 'How many steps?' Or exercise.

I feign ignorance.

'Don't try that look on me, I can see right through it.'

'Fine. Two hundred and seventy-one teeny tiny little steps.'

She harrumphs. 'I'll never understand why you two like hurting your bodies in such a way. Where's the fun in having your thigh muscles burning?'

I grab her elbow and lead the way. 'The view of course, silly.'

We find the lighthouse and buy tickets, Rosie muttering the whole time, more so when we're halfway up and our legs are wobbling with effort. 'Remind me again why I couldn't see the same sea from the ground level?'

I laugh. 'You've got a point there.'

Max sprints ahead of us, and again I idly wonder if he is some kind of closet superhero. The man never runs out of steam. Poor Rosie is grunting, grumbling and ruing the day she met us.

We climb on, somewhat slower, chests (*dare I say it, bosoms!*) heaving. We're eventually rewarded with the magnificent view from the top of the lighthouse. Max is at the rail and motions us over.

'Say it . . .?' Max goads her, his face split with a grin. I note he's not out of breath, not in the slightest.

Hands on hips, Rosie grins back and manages an out-of-breath, 'Wow!'

Waves crash and we're assailed with the briny smell of the sea. It's enough to rejuvenate us after sitting so long in our vans, and fills me with energy for the next stage of the drive. 'In my next life I'm going to be a lighthouse keeper,' I say, imagining myself sitting up here, wrapped in a throw rug, book in hand, with waves lapping at the shore.

'You might have noticed they're not really in use these days,' Rosie says.

'That's even better, I don't want to work, I just want the view.'

Rosie smiles. 'Rapunzel, hey? Hiding away in her own castle.'

'Something like that.' I picture future me: Aria Summers, lighthouse recluse, teens running to the door and knocking before they shriek and leg it away like I'm the modern-day Boo Radley. *Le* sigh.

'Coffee and then we'll begin the second leg?' Rosie asks, taking a quick look at her notebook. 'We're tracking right on time.' Her grin is triumphant.

We find a little French patisserie, where fragrant jasmine climbs the walls and perfumes the breeze. We find some cane chairs that all face the street and sit side by side like soldiers. I find it strange the way the French don't sit around a table but rather facing outwards. I've been admonished before on a previous trip to Paris when I turned my chair to face TJ. That is not the done thing, I soon found out. The memory makes me smile and some devilish part of me is tempted to try it now to see what would happen, but I rein it in.

A few minutes later the waiter takes our order of two *café au lait* and *tartelette fraises* while Max settles with herbal tea and fresh air. How the man is still alive with what he subsists on is beyond me.

We do the usual nomad café etiquette and all take out our phones and connect to the free Wi-Fi to see what we've missed since our last break stop. Nothing my end, it seems. The world has continued to spin with nary any need from me. I try not to take it to heart.

I stretch my arms above my head, relishing being out of the van when Rosie pipes up. 'Tori wants to know where we're staying in Rouen.'

I groan. 'Are you kidding?'

'Nope, she says if the offer still stands, she wouldn't mind joining us.'

I cross my arms. 'What offer?'

Max gives me the ghost of a smile. 'We did give a blanket statement to everyone about joining our French sojourn.'

'Yeah, that might be so, but I didn't mean her!' I sputter out.

He shrugs. Max is one of those people who gets on with everyone, everyone wants to be his friend. If he were any more laid back, he'd be dead. 'She's OK in her own way, isn't she?'

Tori hasn't once set Max up to fail, played practical jokes that backfired or any of the number of things she's tried on me and Rosie. He doesn't know about the polygamy rumours she started about him and Rosie – no one wanted to be the one to tell him. Max is a pacifist but when it comes to Rosie all bets are off.

'She's a bit of a closet viper,' Rosie says.

His face darkens. 'She seems so harmless.'

'Spoken by a man who doesn't understand feminine wiles,' I say, envious that Max can float through every day never once picking up on such a thing. We're almost predisposed to it just being in his bloody limelight. Women flock to Max, and he doesn't seem to notice or care one jot.

'I don't think I want to know, if that's the case,' he says, his leonine eyes ablaze at the thought someone might be under-handed with Rosie.

'Are you going to tell her where we are?' I ask. But I know Rosie, and her moral compass which always points true North. It's not her way to leave anyone out, she knows from personal experience how much it hurts – even if Tori does deserve it.

She lifts a palm.

'It's fine,' I reassure her. 'If Tori starts, I'll put a stop to it, simple as that.' The strawberry tart explodes with flavour and I debate ordering a second serve. How do the French get their fruit to taste so sweet? I make a mental note to hunt out a fresh food market and buy a bucket load of seasonal fruit.

'What's the worst she can do?' Rosie says, scrunching her nose.

'We're all going to be busy once the festivals and fairs start anyway, right?' Max says.

'I hope so,' I reply, munching away and trying to put Tori far from my mind. I've never travelled abroad before *and* tried to pop-up at the same time, so I'm a touch apprehensive that things might not run as smoothly as they did back home. We've got each other though, and if the bottom falls out of our plan, we'll make a new one, right? It's not as if we're in Antarctica.

'Right. Speaking of,' Rosie says, glancing at her watch. 'We'd better head to Rouen. We want to find the campsite before it gets dark.'

I drink the last of my coffee. 'I can't bloody wait!' I've always wanted to travel around France, stopping at as many little provinces as possible, finding gems off the beaten track. I love Paris – who wouldn't, with it being steeped in literary history – but there's something magical about going the long way around the country, choosing places that aren't as big and as bustling as the city of light.

What treasures will we find?

As we leave the café Rosie sidles up to me and whispers, 'Was the letter OK?' She's one of the only people who knows the story behind it all. I don't usually tell anyone about TJ, it's an awkward thing to throw into conversation and it usually freezes up those new interactions before they've started. It's easy to pretend to be a carefree nomad whose great loves are all fictional. Rather than admitting I'm a broken-hearted girl running from her past.

I debate whether to go into it now and decide I'll give Rosie a brief rundown so she doesn't worry. 'His mum, Mary, misplaced a diary of TJ's and it's only just been found. She sent it along with a short letter. All it says really is that life has been hard for her too.' In truth, I haven't been able to think of anything but the diary and what it might contain but I need to read in solitude when I won't be interrupted.

'Oh, Aria, I don't know what to say. Are you going to write back to her?'

I contemplate it. 'It's hard to know whether that will just stir it all up again, you know? Both of us are still bruised from it . . .' I *should* write to her. She deserves that at least. But whether it would help or hinder, I'm not sure yet.

Rosie's eyebrows pull together. 'But at one time you loved your mother-in-law.'

I fold my arms against the breeze that blows from the sea. 'And she loved me. But things changed, Rosie. And I don't know if it can go back. There's a lot of resentment there.'

With a nod she says, 'Read the diary first, see if that makes things any clearer.'

I consider it as I look back towards the deep blue of the ocean, just visible from the café. 'Yeah, for sure. You'd think I'd devour it in one sitting, that's what I'd normally do, but I want to make it last. It's like a gift from him and I need to savour it.'

'I totally get that. It really is the most beautiful surprise and she did send it eventually . . .'

'Yeah, you're right. I don't think she'd ever be truly malicious. She's not that kind of person. She's heartbroken, and that I understand. I just wish I could call her and explain, but it's not that simple.'

'I'm always here if you need to talk, you know that, right?'

'Thanks, Rosie. Once we've settled in, I'd love to.' I give her a squeeze. Rosie is all about fixing family rifts after learning the hard way there's not always all the time in the world to do so.

Revived from the caffeine and cake, we huddle checking the map before getting back into our respective vans and heading for Rouen. We drive in a convoy of three with Max leading the way, and Rosie following behind me.

A few hours later the spires of Cathédrale Notre-Dame de Rouen pierce the skyline and my mouth falls open in awe. A little while after, we drive through the medieval town and I'm astonished at its beauty. The old buildings look almost Shakespearian, Tudor style with colourful wooden cladding. It's a postcard come to life but there's no time to ogle as I do my best to follow Max, hoping that Rosie is OK behind me. We park up at the campsite and Max gestures that's he's going to the office to check us in. While he's doing that Rosie and I take a moment to stretch our legs and check out the park.

'Right.' Max returns and points to the far end of the park. 'We're back there, right by the river.'

'Nice.' We're only staying in Rouen a couple of weeks but already I know it's a place I'll want to return to and spend time meandering hidden laneways and tiny alleys. 'It's a vibrant energetic town from what I gathered driving through.'

'Yeah, it's a pretty place,' Max says. 'The manager, Antoinette, has given me directions to the fete which is only a hop, skip and a jump from the campsite, so that'll make it easier on the day.'

Our first French fete and it's a big one, well known for hosting exotic vendors from all over the country! We managed to secure an allotment because of Max's connections. His mom, Nola, is Van Lifer royalty, she basically created the movement way back when and knows how to survive on practically every continent. We sorted out a range of places to pop-up and applied for permissions and paid whatever fees so we'd be one step ahead when we arrived.

'We've got a week to explore before the fete,' says Rosie. 'Though I'll have to start preparing as soon as I can. I need to make another batch of jam and also some literary tea blends.'

Once we've moved our vans and are connected to the power, I shower and change into comfier clothes. I check my online shop and am happy to note a big order for Maeve Binchy books. It takes me less than thirty seconds to find them buried behind an ottoman that's seen better days. I wrap them in butcher paper and pen a quote by the icon herself, that we are nothing if we're not loved . . . I'll get them in the post tomorrow.

Once I'm sorted I go to Rosie's van to discuss the plan for the next day (OK, and also because she will feed me a dinner big enough to send me right into a food coma).

I knock on Rosie's door and enter to find them sitting side by side at the dining table. Max looks ginormous in the space, as if he's being squashed inside a doll's house. 'So, lovebirds . . . tomorrow, what do you want to do?'

'I need some supplies for the fete,' Rosie says. 'But aside from that I was just going to follow you two. I'm absolutely beat today. I'm hoping the fog will clear and when I wake up I'll be energized.'

'A good night's sleep will be just the ticket, Rosie.' We've had a big week, all those goodbyes, all those glasses of wine. 'I thought I'd wander into town after breakfast tomorrow. I'm sure there's a bookshop calling my name and there's a big chance that I might find Narnia and never return.'

She laughs. 'In that case I'd better supervise. I'd love to find some French patisserie cookbooks. What about you, Max, what did you want to do?'

He runs a hand through his leonine locks. 'I'd planned to head off alone to arrange a little surprise . . .'

'A surprise?' Rosie's face turns puce, actually puce, and that quickly too. 'Not for me . . .?' Max's surprises are usually of the high-octane nature and safety-first Rosie is still coming to terms with life in the fast lane.

Max cuts her off with just a look.

She cradles her head. 'Why am I picturing my imminent death, a fireball, a knife skirmish, being shot out of canon into a deep body of water . . . urgh, I need to sit before I fall. Oh, god I *am* sitting. Flip.'

He tries his best to contain his smile but his lips quiver in rebellion. 'Right. You wouldn't *be* Rosie if you didn't think of the gory, terrifying, bloodcurdling way in which you'd leave this mortal coil whenever any new experience crops up.'

She looks aghast. 'That's simply not true.'

'Isn't it?' he probes.

I laugh. It is very true!

'What did you say before you tried abseiling, rally driving, zip lining? And don't forget driving the quad bikes through the forest a few weeks ago,' Max reminds her.

She guffaws. 'It's not unreasonable to imagine the quad bikes could very easily roll over, spill fuel which catches alight ripping through the dense forest in mere seconds causing wildfires and . . . I still can't understand why the manager of that death trap of a place took offence?'

'No?' Max grins and raises a brow. 'When you started throwing out statistics about the amount of people injured on quad bikes and his customers halving in thirty seconds flat, you don't think that might have rubbed him up the wrong way?'

'That? You think that's why he got so uppity? I was doing him a favour, he should have been thanking me!'

'Yeah, right. I guess it's just your way to fantasize your own grisly death.'

'OK fine, I do always picture my imminent death, but that's only so I can prepare ahead: what to do in the *likely* event of an emergency. I wouldn't call it a fantasy, god, Max. You make me sound like I'm eagerly awaiting such a thing when in actual fact it's the exact opposite!'

With a laugh he says, 'Well either way, I'm proud of you, Rosie, and you're going to love this surprise. It includes you too, Aria.'

'Great! I wouldn't call myself an adrenalin junkie but I'll give anything a go at least once . . .'

'Almost anything,' Rosie says. 'Love is off limits, right?'

'That old chestnut?'

'Slipped out,' she says, her voice sheepish. 'So that's sorted, let's have a dinner feast and an early night . . .'

Music to my ears.

Chapter Six

Rouen

Refreshed after an early night, I go to find Rosie, hugging the prepacked Maeve Binchy books tight to my chest, not wanting to part with them. #BooksellerProblems. Maeve has always been one of my favourite writers; hers are the sort of novels that you gravitate towards on bad days when you want to curl up with some old friends who've also hit bumps in the road and are just the same as you.

Rosie's deep in conversation with the campsite manager, Antoinette, and a youngish man with a stern face. She motions to me to join her.

'Hey,' I say, noticing that Rosie is standing stiffly, her eyes glazing over – the usual signs she's uncomfortable and is very close to doing a runner. I put a hand to her arm to ground her.

Introductions are made and Rosie haltingly explains the fete vendor fee is a lot higher than we'd thought. Why has this man tracked us all the way to the campsite instead of emailing? It screams of some kind of intimidation tactic. 'Oh, why is that?' I ask, confused. 'We had the email weeks ago about the fee. We agreed and we've paid already.'

The man, Jean-Pierre, shrugs and Antoinette speaks rapid-fire French to him. He shrugs again and she sighs. Whatever is going on, Antoinette seems to be in our corner but it's not going our way. 'Jean-Pierre says there are more vendors now so the price will increase.'

I'm sure we're getting the *tourist tax* that we hear so many tales about and I'm not having it. 'If there are more vendors surely the price should go down, not up. Otherwise he's taking advantage. And is he going to personally visit every other vendor to demand more money or just us?'

He folds his arms and mutters belligerently at Antoinette. Jean-Pierre's gaze turns steely and mine follows suit. Poor Rosie darts her eyes this way and that looking for an escape route.

'Let's just go,' Rosie says. 'We'll find another fete.'

'Oh no we will not. We organized this weeks ago and I've spread it all over social media that we'll all be there, so be there we will.' I turn to Antoinette. 'Thank you for helping us translate, we appreciate it very much but I can take it from here.'

Confusion dashes across Antoinette's face and the man cocks his cocky head as if urging me to argue. I pull myself up to full height like they do in the books and say, '*T'es une poule mouillée!*'

They stand gawping at me, their mouths hanging open.

'What did you say?' Rosie whispers and takes out her phone typing hastily.

I ignore Rosie and focus on the belligerent man before me. 'We'll be at the fete, and we're not paying one euro more than the agreed price!'

Antoinette nods and tries to hide a smile. I storm away, hoping this is not a sign of things to come, being ripped off simply because we're new and they think we don't know any better.

'Wait!' Rosie struggles to keep up with me. 'According to my translation app you just told him: *You're a wet chicken!*' She bites down on her lip before laughter gets the better of her.

I stop and put my hands on my hips, chest heaving with

adrenalin, but I manage to continue throwing daggers back his way in case he's still watching us. He is. 'The only other phrase I know is 'Your mother is a prostitute' and I don't think that would have gone down too well.'

'How?'

'Well, who wants to hear their mother is—'

'No, no.' She holds a hand up to stop me. 'How do you know those phrases?'

'From a romcom set in France that I've read so often I've memorized it, and look how handy it's turned out to be.'

She rolls her eyes. 'I should've known it would be from a book. I can't believe you called him a wet chicken out of the blue like that. I nearly died, his face . . . I thought his head was going to explode.'

'Apparently it means that the person is a coward or something. I love French insults, they're the very best.' Our Rosie isn't one for confrontation, but I am if the cause is just. 'We can't let him walk all over us. If we let one, then we let them all and it becomes a pattern. Plus I really dislike smarmy men like that. Makes my skin crawl.'

Her wide eyes are serious. 'I'm sure they're not all like him. He tried his hand, he lost.'

I pretend to flex my muscles and say, 'And we have a backup plan if he tries to stop us at the fete.'

'Weapons! What . . . a spatula? A whisk? No, a frying pan to the head!'

My eyebrows pull together. 'What? No! We have Max!'

'Of course! Six-foot-four muscle man. How could I forget.' She slaps her forehead.

I lift a palm. 'So he's a gentle giant? No one needs to know that.' As much as I'm capable of standing up for myself, sometimes I miss the fact I could shove my husband to the fore and let him deal with slimy men like Jean-Pierre. Although TJ would have killed the guy with kindness until he eventually gave in . . .

We head into our new town, chattering about the beauty before us as we wander down narrow medieval streets. The brisk morning air is like a tincture and I feel refreshed after the long drive the day before and I soon forget Jean-Pierre.

'I didn't even consult my maps for a bookshop for you,' Rosie says.

I raise a brow. 'Progress.'

'No, it's not that. I know you'll sniff it out, you're like a bloodhound when it comes to books. Is it something you learn, or does it just come naturally to bibliophiles like yourself?'

I knock her with my hip. 'Very funny.'

We zigzag our way through the streets full of colourful buildings before Rosie stops at *un* épicier to stock up on baking essentials for the fete. The figs are lush and ready to burst and will make the most delicious jam for her French twist Devonshire teas. The grocer promises to deliver her haul to the campsite in a few hours' time.

Onwards we go, stopping at the *fromagerie* which is ripe with the smell of exotic cheeses. Rosie gets to talking to the fromager about all the various types. She's a wealth of information about French cuisine from her fifteen years at Époque, a French restaurant in London. He offers us a taste of an aged comté that is so delicious I'll die if I don't eat more. Next, he cuts a wedge of gooey camembert that's so creamy and lush I vow to only eat French cheese for the rest of my natural born life. I spend far too much money but leave the *fromagerie* happier than when I came in.

And I put all thought of a budget to one side. *The universe will provide*, isn't that the Van Lifer catch phrase?

The hair on my arms stands on end and that can only mean one thing. I'm close to a bookshop. I can almost smell it, the heady scent of adventure trapped between parchment. Eventually I spy it. The most beautiful bookshop I've ever seen; the curved old stone building that leans slightly to the left as if seeking tentative rays of sunlight that eke in from the open square. Pale-blue weather-beaten shutters are thrown open, ivy snakes through the wood.

Rosie sees the excitement on my face and with a sigh glances at her watch. 'No more than one hour, Aria.'

I scoff. 'It depends on how many floors it has.' I gaze up at the windows, sheer curtains flutter in the breeze as if welcoming me in: *We've been waiting for you, Aria . . .*

'One and a half, that's my final offer.' I grin as I pull her inside. 'OK, nope, I take that back. I'm going to need two hours,' I say breathlessly. Tiny fairy lights blink in the shadowy space, dark wooden shelves curve around the room in an arc, snaking from the floor all the way up the ceiling.

It's my kind of bookshop, shelves full to bursting, novels spilling over, double and triple stacked. In the centre of the room sit two antique French chaises in pale pink and ruby red, chenille throws draped over the arms patiently waiting for a bookworm to plonk down and relax for a time. Magazines sit atop a coffee table, all that's missing is a pot of tea and a tin of biscuits and then no way would one and a half hours suffice.

A staff member wanders over and asks in perfect English, 'May I help you find something?'

'Where are the cookery books, *s'il vous plaît*?' Rosie asks.

'Back there to the left.' She points to another rabbit warren of rooms. 'Let me know if you'd like any further assistance.'

'Thank you.' We watch her walk away on sky-high heels. Even booksellers are glamorous in France. I dip my head to my own outfit which could be described more as bookworm chic. Jeans and a literary tee is about as fancy as I get these days. I don't think I can even *walk* in heels anymore.

I nudge Rosie. 'She could tell on sight we weren't French.'

She gasps with the realization. 'How? It's not like we're wearing rainbow-coloured happy pants like Lulu does!'

'Maybe it's the way we hold ourselves?' The opposite of shoulders back, proud, the way French women seem to master from a young age.

Rosie holds up a finger. 'We're not wearing scarves! It's French fashion etiquette 101. You must always wear scarves. And there's a particular way you wrap them depending on the fabric.'

My eyebrows shoot up. 'You studied French etiquette before we arrived?' This is Rosie's way of coping when she's in an unfamiliar situation – she studies whatever it is to the nth degree. My guess is she knows every French rule about etiquette there is to know, including the more bizarre ones.

She gives me a look that says I'm obtuse. 'Of course! And you should too, you know. There's a lot of unwritten rules that we'd do well to follow if we want to fit in here.'

I hadn't thought about the need to fit in. 'Wouldn't that just happen naturally?'

'Urgh, you and Max with your sunny, winning personalities don't have to work at it as hard as the rest of us. But still, the French have so many rules, it's been fun to study them. Do you know that if they serve grapefruit juice at the end of a dinner party it's a sign that your host is ready for you to leave? The wine disappears and *voila*, you have a glass of juice that signals it's time to go. Isn't that *magnifique!* I abhor it when guests overstay their welcome. I think I might be a little French on the inside.'

'Well, you studied French gastronomy, so you're practically French, Rosie.'

'*Oui,*' she says seriously.

I shake my head, again unsure if Rosie is joking. 'Come on my little *ingénue*. We've got treasure to find.'

But she doesn't move, she's frozen to the spot.

'What? What is it?' I swing my gaze to where she's looking and I spot it. A black-and-white picture of Jonathan with that lovely mysterious smile of his. We stumble closer. What on earth is a picture of his face doing tacked up to a wall in a bookshop in France? I hastily try and make sense of the French words.

'No!' How, how could I have missed such a thing?

'Yes!' Rosie says, her face alight.

My stomach seesaws in surprise. 'I can't believe it. How did I not put two and two together?'

'You didn't ask him what his surname was, did you? Jonathan is no other than the incredibly famous writer, Jonathan Chadwick!'

'How can that be?' Rosie knows more about the guy than I do, it beggars belief!

'We've *just* missed a talk he gave here!' She's one step away from jumping up and down.

'Whaaa . . .' I'm trying to make sense of it all but my brain is stuck like a scratched disk. 'He's an author and *my* Spidey senses didn't pick that up? Boy, am I slipping!'

'Maybe we'll run into him somewhere in France?' Rosie is so excited she's practically yelling. 'Writers of his calibre usually become reclusive, don't they? They don't drop in to gorgeous little bookshops like this. That's saying a lot, don't you think?' Rosie's babbles continue like a run-on sentence.

'Yeah, it's saying *huge marketing budget.*'

She tugs on my arm. 'Oh, golly even I've read one of his books, and I'm not a voracious reader like you! I can't believe it's him and he never mentioned a word. He didn't tell you he was a writer, did he?'

I shake my head, bewildered by it all. 'No, he didn't! We talked about romcoms for hours, and he never mentioned it. Don't you think that's odd?'

With a swift shake of her head she says, 'No, I think it's lovely. It shows he doesn't have a massive ego.'

'It's a lie by omission. I feel so foolish!' I say wringing my hands. 'Banging on about books like I'm an expert, when *he's* clearly the expert. I must've looked like a prize idiot to him.' My brain rattles at my stupidity and I slap my forehead to settle it.

She puts her hands to my shoulders, her big eyes round. 'Not at all! He's the writer, you're the reader. You *are* the expert!'

Maybe. Possibly. No.

Hilarity takes over as I sift through the memories of our time spent together. 'I spent the better part of an hour explaining to him what the word trope meant!' *Way to go, Aria!*

'Jonathan is as popular as Lee Child, Nicholas Sparks . . .' Rosie says.

'And there I was giving him lessons about writing – kill me now!'

She clucks her tongue. 'It shows how sweet he is that he let you "teach" him.'

'How did I not pick up he was a writer?'

'Well, how *would* you know? It's not their bio picture you're interested in, it's their words. Have you read one of his books?'

'No, I haven't. I haven't really even heard of the guy to be honest.' My voice trails off as another memory forms, this one of my husband, TJ.

'What is it? You look like you've seen a ghost or something.'

My heart stops. For a fraction of a second I'm stuck in limbo, half in the present, half in the grainy sepia of the past. 'He *knew*. How though?'

'Who knew?' she says, giving me a puzzled look.

With wobbly legs, I say, 'I have to sit down.'

She guides me to the chaise, her forehead furrowed. 'Do you need water?'

'I need wine, lots of wine.'

She tuts. 'That's not going to help.'

'It will blot out reality for a while.'

'What is it?'

I take a deep breath and debate whether to tell her, but Rosie won't let it go now I've cloaked it in mystery.

After a deep steadying breath I say, 'I just remembered something TJ said and it's given me goose bumps. I'll tell you but you have to *promise* you won't overreact.' She's going to overreact. I steel myself for it.

'You have my word.'

I narrow my eyes but press on regardless, 'TJ and I were in the Lake District – we knew at that point we didn't have much time left. He kept insisting on me finding someone else after he'd gone, he wouldn't let it go. I kept changing the subject because who wants to even consider such a thing at that point? Just before he drifted off to sleep that afternoon, he said he'd had this vision of the guy I'd move on with and said he'd be *a lover of words* . . .! At the time I didn't think anything of it, I couldn't even contemplate it. Do you think he meant Jonathan?' I gasp. '*Could* TJ have known such a thing?' My head feels foggy with it all. No, it's ridiculous, it's a stretch, it's wishful thinking on my part.

Rosie stands up and bounces around as if she's a puppet being pulled by strings, her face ablaze. If there's one thing Rosie loves, it's a plot twist when it comes to my life. For the last year she's been at me to date, to at least *try*. And now I've virtually handed her this on a platter.

'Sit down, Rosie. And don't give me that look.'

When she drops back down, I put a finger to her lips. I can practically see the words threatening to bounce off her tongue. 'Don't say it.'

'But—'

'No buts,' I admonish her.

'But, but, but, Aria, that's not fair! You gave me so much grief before about Max.'

I tut. 'That wasn't grief, that was good solid advice.'

'Semantics.' She lifts a shoulder. 'It's only fair that I can offer my own kernels of knowledge in such a situation.'

'No.'

'Yes,' she says.

'That's unfair.'

'*Life* is unfair,' she says with a harrumph. 'And we could do this back and forth all day. But you're a complete fool if you don't see that the universe is showing you the way, and that it's time to think about your own happiness for a change.' She does jazz hands before I shoot her a look and then she snatches them back as if they're acting of their own accord. 'TJ *has* had a hand in this somehow,' she says. 'You have to admit, the timing of Jonathan being here a day before us is uncanny, or some would say, a *sign*.'

I let out a long sigh as if she's speaking nonsense but secretly wonder too. 'How can TJ have had a hand in this, when there isn't even a *this*? Listen to me, gah! Also it stands to reason the biggest bookworm on the planet would be drawn to a lover of words. Anyone could guess such a thing, or else he was just holding out hope, but god knows why.'

I've done an about-turn so fast even Rosie is shaking her head at me.

'Geez, Aria, you are all over the place!'

'You should see inside my brain right now.' It does give me pause though. Is TJ rewriting my life from wherever he is . . .? No, impossible! I need more sleep, and less wine. I need to meditate, do yoga, become one with the earth! *Or something* . . .

'Well, I highly doubt he was holding out hope. TJ *knew!* He was halfway between this world and the next and there's a lot we don't know about such things.' Her face is so serious it breaks my heart for some reason.

I do what I do best and deflect. 'Honestly, Rosie. He was heavily medicated, more like.' But part of me wants so desperately to believe such a thing is possible. That those feelings I'm developing for Jonathan are natural, that it has been written in the stars.

Rosie concedes defeat and flops back against the chaise. 'You've got to admit that Jonathan keeps popping into your life in the most unexpected of ways. What for, if not love?'

'Meet-cute style too,' I admit. 'But it feels wrong, still. Like I'm not ready and never will be. I don't know.' There's that guilt again, creeping up and tapping me on the shoulder like the friend who won't take no for an answer.

Rosie's shoulders slump. 'Well, it can't hurt buying his latest book, can it?'

'Sure, I'll take a copy of his latest book. I'm intrigued actually.' Books are so *safe* compared to the real world.

Her eyes twinkle like she knows a secret and she goes to a display shelf stacked with his latest book titled *The Quiet of Loneliness* and hands it over to me. The cover features a blurred black-and-white picture of an entwined couple sitting in a park.

'Their faces are obscured but the image manages to conjure the feeling they've been through a lot and are rekindling a love affair, don't you think?' Rosie asks.

I search their body language for clues – the way they clasp hands seems fragile as if they've just made up. 'Yeah, it feels as though they lost their way for a while but they've realized what they needed was right in front of them all along. Aren't cover designers the unsung heroes in literature?'

She nods and gives me one of her unfathomable Rosie looks.

'What?' I ask.

'Nothing. I think I might buy myself a copy *of The Quiet of Loneliness* too.'

'Good plan, and then we can unpick every chapter and look for meanings that aren't there.'

'My favourite way to spend an afternoon.' She grimaces. Rosie reads sporadically and doesn't tend to enjoy disassembling books as much as I do. But for me that's half the fun of it, going back and searching for clues the author cannily left us, sneakily woven into the fabric of the story if only we take a moment to consider the order in which the words are placed.

We spend the next hour in paradise, hunting high and low, and leave the bookshop a little dustier than when we arrived. I resolutely turn my head the opposite way when I pass Jonathan's poster.

'Let's retrace Joan of Arc's footsteps,' Rosie says.

'Starting where?'

'The Church of St Joan of Arc on the *Place du Vieux*.'

Anything to get my mind off the two men who are intent on scrambling my thoughts despite them both being absent. I sure know a thing or two about *The Quiet of Loneliness* . . .

After Aria Summers' husband died she made herself a promise.

She'd never love anyone again. Easy, right? After all, she had her romance novels to see her through and so she fell in love with fictional characters instead. Sheiks, princes, and even the odd billionaire or two were enough for her. But that all changed when the past merged with the present and suddenly it felt as though her life was being orchestrated from above, as though it was written in the stars. But Aria knew a plot device when she saw one, so was it simply a matter of being faithful to her promise or was it a sign from above?

Chapter Seven

In the old market square, there's an enormous gold clock above us that captures our attention. Rosie points up to it and then takes out her guidebook. 'I've read about this.' She finds the page. 'It's called *Gros Horloge* and it was handcrafted in the fourteenth century.'

It blows me away how these relics are still around after all this time. 'How many eyes have gazed up wonderingly at it through the ages? Thousands of people, some gone from this world and *still* the clock ticks.'

'God, you should write song lyrics,' she deadpans.

'Very funny, Rosie.' I laugh as we continue to the church.

'This church is newly built for French standards, completed in 1979 in honour of Joan of Arc. Isn't it a thrilling design?'

'Is it meant to look like a fire-breathing dragon?' As far as churches go it's like nothing I've ever seen before. It's contemporary and artistic and I love it on sight.

'It's meant to reflect the flames that consumed her.'

'Wow. She was burnt at the stake here?'

'Close by in that little garden bed. People confuse the cross at the church as the spot, but it isn't so.' We find the location and the plaque that confirms it, and a shiver runs the length of me imagining Joan's demise but how brave she had been standing up for her country.

'She was so courageous. Can you imagine?'

Rosie shakes her head. 'A woman leading the French Army to victory back then is almost unheard of. I wonder how she managed it. But then to lose her like that. She was only nineteen.'

'She left one hell of a legacy.'

We go back and tour the church and get a history lesson too in which we learn more about Joan of Arc and how much she packed into such a short life. 'I need to read more about her,' I tell Rosie as we wait for an interactive display to start.

Once we're finished in the church, I stock up on biographies of Joan in the gift shop before we wander around the old town square marvelling at the ancient town, rich in history and beauty.

'Lunch?' Rosie says.

'Do you even need to ask?'

We find a little café called *La Couronne* that Rosie claims was established in 1345. 'There's signed photographs of Salvador Dali and Bridget Bardot who visited here,' she says as a teaser to tempt me in, but just the smell of creamy French food is enough for me.

We're seated by the maître d' who wears an elegant black suit and bowtie. He pulls out chairs for us and places linen napkins over our laps. When he rushes away to get who knows what, I lean over and hiss to Rosie, 'Are you sure this place suits our budget? We don't usually eat in establishments with proper napkins . . .'

Patrons are glamorously dressed and I feel downright shabby in comparison. The thing about van life is money rules, and it's always at the back of our minds, every penny accounted for. Food is always the last thing we splurge on, and Rosie feeds us all anyway. And I've just spent a few days' worth of takings on books, which is typical of me.

Rosie nods, and looks up as the waiter returns with two leather embossed menus. 'I checked already. The basic three-course lunch menu is twenty-five euros and I've made allowances for this in my daily expenditure since it's for research and all.'

'OK. I guess we can splurge if it's for the benefit of your business.'

My willpower is also fairly weak, and I'll follow anyone anywhere if there's fun to be had, money be damned.

The menu has a selection of mouth-watering options. 'How amazing does the Normandy Cheese platter sound?' I have no idea what the cheeses are or how to pronounce them, but any cheese is always good in my opinion. 'What's the Neuf . . .'

'Neufchatel,' she finishes for me. 'A delightfully pungent cheese that will blow your socks off.'

'Well, we'd better get through entrée and main first!'

As we slowly consume our body weight in rich, French food, Rosie builds up to another inquisition. I can read her like a book – she begins by sitting straighter, fidgets with her napkin, looks everywhere but me while she rages an internal battle about how to begin.

'Just say it, Rosie.' She feigns confusion but Rosie is a hopeless liar. 'You're acting like you've got ants in your pants and that can only mean one thing, so just get on with it.'

Her mouth opens in protest but then she notes my steely-eyed gaze and drops the farce before it truly it begins. 'Well if you must know, I was just hoping you'd be amenable to catching up with Jonathan at some point? We could easily find him online now we know who he is.'

'What for?'

'I'm thinking Cupid might be around and can sprinkle a little love dust over you, so shoot me.' She puts her hands up in surrender.

With a sigh, I say, 'Truth be told, I can't stop thinking about the guy, which fills me with the *worst* pangs of guilt, because TJ is still with me' – I tap my heart – 'so how can I even consider such a thing?'

'It's just – don't take this the wrong way – but I can feel your sadness, Aria. It comes off you in waves. It worries me sometimes, that you're going through life with a big smile plastered on your face but inside you're screaming. Tell me to shut up, but that's the impression I get.'

I thought I'd acted my part so convincingly. 'You're right, Rosie,' I say with a sigh.

'Tell me more about TJ, and what made him so great.'

Where to begin? 'He treated me as if I was his every wish granted. How to explain without sounding cheesy?'

'It's me, Aria,' Rosie says softly. 'You know you can tell me anything.'

Doesn't everyone think their love affair is unique and special, as if no one else has ever loved quite as hard, quite as much? 'TJ's love was palpable; I could *feel* it as soon as he walked into a room. I'd get that fluttery feeling and that never waned. He made me feel like every person on the planet paled in comparison to me, it was such a heady love. I hope I made him feel the same way. To me, he was a prize and I felt so lucky he was mine. And that he chose me.'

'He sounds like a wonderful man.'

'He was. The best. So full of life that it seemed so cruel that it had to end. Who'd ever be able to live up to him, and why would I want them to? Wouldn't it be greedy of me to expect someone else could love me as much as that?'

'Why greedy? Why shouldn't you have high standards for love? We all should! And if one man can love you like that, then why can't another? You don't get a quota in this life, Aria. It's not like you've used your voucher and it's now expired.'

TJ's face flashes into mind, and then Jonathan's face too. Both men are similar in their reflective and gentle ways, their expressive faces unable to hide every emotion they feel. I love those kinds of people, the ones who aren't closed off, who relay every thought and mood keenly in the shape of their face, in the complexity of their eyes. The way they worry their hands, expressive whether they mean to be or not.

'Yeah, I know, Rosie. And I'm happy for those who manage to fall in love again, and find a sense of peace after loss, but I feel like I'd just compare the two men and as lovely as Jonathan is, I'm guessing he'd come up short to TJ. Everyone would. And that's so unfair of me.'

'Even as a friend?'

I shrug. 'I think so. Maybe it's the fact the diary turned up but I feel like TJ is right beside me, walking along these cobble-stoned avenues marvelling at this and that. It's so *wrong* that he doesn't get to have any of these experiences. I feel robbed and bitter at the world. I try so hard not to fall down that dark hole but sometimes it just swallows me up and I think I'll never find my way out. Without him . . .' I stop as tears pool in my eyes, and silently berate myself. Once they start though, there's no stopping them. Like a floodgate, tears and emotions rise to the surface. 'Life isn't the same . . .'

'I get that,' Rosie says, laying her hand on mine.

I choke on a sob, willing patrons to look the other way. Magically they do. 'It's just that we had this full life planned, you know? Renovations on the cottage for the big brood of children we were about to start trying for. TJ would quit his teaching job eventually and open up a centre for kids with special needs so he could focus solely on them. Imagine the amount of lives he would have changed. TJ saw his students as kids with unlimited potential, a puzzle to solve, so they'd have the best chance of the future they deserved if only he could translate their needs, especially for the non-verbal kids in his class.'

'I wish he'd got to fulfil that dream.'

'Me too. That was his number one priority, and I loved that about him. We wanted to travel.' I take my napkin and swipe under my eyes. 'Bare bones style, like we do now. Hike, help build wells in developing countries, show our kids the real world, not

64

the resorts and theme parks, and then one day, we'd retire, we'd be sitting on our front porch on our love swing, stars twinkling above, reminiscing about our full and happy lives, how our kids grew up to be kind, and that's all you can ask for, right? And none of that can happen without the man himself. Don't get me wrong, I'm grateful for the time I had with him but it's *broken* me for anyone else. I admit, I've toyed with the idea of finding love again lately but then I get cold feet and realize it can never be. There was only one man for me and the love we shared will remain in my heart for the rest of my life – it has to sustain me, right?'

Rosie's eyes well up and she swallows hard. 'Right.'

I've upset Rosie but I feel like a weight has been lifted explaining just how my husband fulfilled me and why I can't just carry on as if everything is OK. 'Sorry, Rosie, I didn't mean to unload all of that on you.' I've shared snippets before with Rosie but never in as much detail as today.

She dabs at her eyes, trying desperately to compose herself. 'Don't apologize, I'm crying because it's beautiful in its own tragic way. Not many people find a love so strong, and it's shattering that you lost TJ. I guess I've never thought about the *future* that you lost too, you know? When I think of TJ, I think of the man who'd be by your side, I never thought of the father, the special education guru to generations of kids, the grandfather. The guy who'd grow into the grey-haired man on the front porch sitting with the love of his life while she reads yet another book. It makes me to want to weep for you.' Rosie colours. She's not one to display emotions, always keeping them bottled up tight. I try to comfort her, knowing it's a lot to take in. She's probably picturing herself without Max and thanking her lucky stars it's not the case.

'Yes, that's the crux of it, Rosie. Jonathan has made me realize my heart works just fine, but that's all it can be. Just the *knowing*. The broken pieces aren't ever going to mend, they're just barely holding together. And it's enough, truly, it's enough, to know that I caught Jonathan's eye, that I mattered to him for that brief moment we shared. Trust me, if I wasn't married – widowed – if I was someone else, I'd be beating down his door. But it's not fair to either of us to start something I'd eventually run away from. I've already made some rash decisions there under the influence of sauvignon blanc.'

'I hate it – I can't argue, you've tugged at my heartstrings and made the robot cry.'

I laugh. 'Well, wonders will never cease, eh?'

A silence descends so we do what millennials do best – take out our phones. The mood lightens when we check Facebook to see what our fellow Van Lifers have been up to since we parted back in London. As promised, they've scattered around the globe. Rosie checks on Max's parents, Nola and Spencer, who're spending the warmer months in the Czech Republic. They've tagged us in numerous pictures, including the Idiom Installation, a cylindrical well of books, stacked like a game of Jenga. It's impressively long and makes my belly drop thinking of the depth.

'Oh, and there's Kafka's head, spinning for eternity!' Rosie says, delighted by the moving sculpture. 'It's meant to reflect his torment. He was somewhat troubled, it says.'

'Aren't most writers?'

She raises a brow. 'I know one you could ask . . .'

'A great conversation starter, if there ever was one.' Is Jonathan troubled though? There's something wildly enigmatic about the man. He's full of fictional stories, but what about his own? Is there any point wondering? Probably not.

We get to the third course and groan once the waiter has walked away. 'We ordered too much.'

'No such thing,' Rosie says, spearing a candied strawberry.

'I guess I can always try.'

'It would be rude not to.'

Is there anything better than eating your body weight in French food? I think not. Especially when love is *not* on the menu . . .

* * *

After helping Rosie make fig jam in preparation for the upcoming fete, I finally escape to the comfort of my van.

PJ clad, I squish myself into bed, and take the diary from the drawer. What will it contain? My heart thrums at the thought, but I know my TJ and I trust he's penned this for a very special reason.

If you'd asked me a year ago, I'd have said a diary is a strange pursuit for a thirty-something-year-old man – after all, who wants to hear about my innermost thoughts, fears, secrets? I'm just a regular guy with a regular job who just so happens to be married to my dream girl.

So why now? Why commit anything to these pages? It's nothing concrete that I can fathom. I woke from an obscure dream a few days ago with this strange feeling of knowing that I had to commit some thoughts to paper for my word nerd. Strange, eh? I hope it doesn't mean I'm going to get hit by a bus or struck down by a bolt of lightning or something! All I know is, I must write to her and express my love in a way that resonates most. What to say to the woman who reveres such things? If I were to be abducted by aliens, I guess I'd want her to know that she lit up days and my heart. Not everyone gets a love like this . . .

He could have been saved if only he knew what that dream meant! But he remained physically fine until it was too far gone, too late. His words, his parting gift, lift my heart as if he's right here next to me. I'm so grateful that I got to be TJ's one great love even if our time had been cut short.

I send Rosie a quick text.

I've read the first diary entry . . .I'm all good, just wanted you to know.

Within seconds a reply beeps back.

Do you want to talk about it? I make a mean hot chocolate which is medicinal . . .xxx

I'm all good, Rosie, but thank you xoxo

I switch off the light and sit in the dark. Time can't take away the love we shared. It can't take away the memories. I hug the diary close to my chest, conjuring the man. His Oceana cologne is trapped in the parchment, bringing him to life inside my mind. I close my eyes, his face a whisper away . . .

Chapter Eight

Rouen

A couple of days later I wake up groggy after an all-night reading binge and like almost every morning I wish I'd had a little more shut eye. Needing distraction from the diary and the feelings it had produced, I'd started Jonathan's book, became engrossed and desperately wanted to finish it but my eyes kept slipping closed and that was that. #BookwormProblems.

I'm not sure what I'd expected his prose to be, but I found it the complete opposite. He too is the heart-on-sleeve type, or at least that's what my take is. I know it's fictional but I kept picturing him as the hero.

Like your typical bibliophile, I'm counting down the hours until I can get back to it and see where his love birds end up.

After a long, hot shower, I dress and head outside to find real-life love birds Rosie and Max sitting on a rug by the river soaking up the morning sunshine. Teapot in hand Rosie pours me a cup and hands over a floral-scented tea – her homemade blends are one of her bestsellers, and she has a range for every mood. Pick-me-ups, wind-me-downs and even a bouquet for the broken hearted.

'She's alive!' Rosie jokes. My sleeping patterns can best be described as erratic, while Rosie awakens each morning at exactly the same time, or two hours earlier if worry bothers her.

I yawn. 'Could have slept all day but I dragged my sorry self out of bed just for you.'

'Hashtag blessed,' she jokes. 'Max went hunting and gathering early this morning and came back with croissants and baguettes for us. Help yourself.'

'Thank you. Oh, there's fruit too!'

'A man can't live on fresh air alone,' Max says, grinning. Clearly he's heard our jokes about him.

'Not a man your size.'

I sip the tea trying to gauge the type of flowers and what healing properties it has. 'It's some kind of relaxant, isn't it?' I ask, feeling lulled somehow. Rosie is an alchemist, no two ways about it but I'm leery in case it's some kind of love potion and next minute I'm declaring my love for some broody French man. You have to be on your toes with this little tea merchant.

With an eyebrow waggle she says, 'It's a secret recipe I'm still tinkering about with. It will give you clarity for the day ahead if nothing else.'

'I'll have another then,' I say. 'Does it prevent blisters too?' Adventuring tends to shred my feet as I like to walk until I'm lost and try to find my way back. A pastime Rosie doesn't share with me.

She laughs. 'I haven't figured out a blend for that yet, but I'm sure I could make some kind of tincture . . .'

'You're starting to sound like a tree hugger, Rosie.'

She guffaws. 'Look, I hugged that bloody tree but I don't think it did any good. In bare feet! *Earthing.*' She shakes her head. 'What a notion.'

When I first met Rosie, we went to Magic Tree forest, and I made her – no, practically *forced* her to – hug the magic tree, which is well known to have restorative powers. She pretended it didn't heal her from the tippy toes up, but of course it did.

She puts all these new age things down to wackiness but I do think our little A-type is turning. 'Liar.'

Max pipes up. 'It's well known that the magic tree grants the wishes of those who hug it in just the right place.' His face is a mask of earnestness so it's hard to tell if he's winding her up or not. 'But I believe, as the saying goes, *if you don't believe you don't receive . . .*'

'See!' I say, giving her a pointed look. 'Did you make a wish, Rosie?'

Turning away, she mumbles incoherently and it's then I remember our conversation that day which had been all about Max, and how the tree resembled him in sheer size and toughness alone.

'Rosie?' I prod.

'I don't remember.' She averts her gaze.

'I believe we were talking about some hot specimen of a man, but I could be wrong . . .'

Max emits a low growl as if he's a wild man, and grabs Rosie in a hug, taking her down on the picnic rug. 'Is that true? Who is this hot specimen you speak of?'

She pushes him away not wanting to concede the point. 'Stop it, you two, you're like children at times.'

'Tell me his name!' he cries out in jest, drawing the startled attention of other campers wandering past.

'Oh my god! Fine, I might have thought of you *briefly* as I hugged the damn tree but I highly doubt that the bloody thing granted me one wish and there you were – how ridiculous!'

'I don't know, Rosie, you've got to admit it *was* all a little magical.'

'Yeah, if you believe in fairy tales . . .'

What a ride it's been! The tree *is* magic, no two ways about it.

'Well, I was going to play it all macho, but back then I *also* happened to stop in Magic Tree forest and made a wish.'

This time Rosie jumps atop him and tickles him to confess. 'Did you now?'

They wrestle half-heartedly which is quite the sight, with Max being six-four and Rosie about half his size. 'Ask the magic tree and it will provide my very own Rosie, made to order.'

'Well, maybe it's not such a fairy tale after all . . .' Rosie allows, stopping to catch her breath.

'What did you wish for, Aria?' Max asks as Rosie lies beside him on the rug.

They both turn their bright curious gazes towards me.

I gulp. 'Erm . . . for world peace.'

Rosie jumps on me, taking me backwards. 'You *do* have liarbetes!'

I push her off and stay prone, both of us laughing until our bellies ache. Once we're composed, Rosie and I munch the flaky croissants and demolish the fresh baguettes laced with salty buttery goodness. How can such simple food taste so mouth-wateringly good?

'So, I forgot to tell Max about our discovery the other day . . .' She shakes her head. 'Honestly I've been so out of it at night, I've been falling asleep before I've even cleaned the van.'

'Oh?' I play dumb. 'What discovery?' My lie is so translucent even Max raises a brow.

'That Jonathan is actually a literary legend.'

'Oh, that . . .' I say.

'How's that for exciting, Max? We had a famous writer in our midst and none of us were any the wiser.'

Max colours but keeps schtum.

'What . . .?' Rosie asks, gazing at Max.

'Max, you knew all along who he was?' I ask. 'Since right back to the music festival last year?'

'Yeah.' He shrugs in that infuriating it's-all-good way. 'I thought it was common knowledge.'

'What! This is a huge design fault when it comes to men, they don't share enough,' Rosie says, making a note in her book for some reason. 'They don't think hard enough about what women need to know – I mean this is huge, Max, and you never thought to mention it even in passing?'

He lifts his palms in apology but he can't hide his smile. He's doesn't function the way we do, and it's such a learning curve at times.

'I'm sorry. I guess I presumed you'd have talked about his work when you spent that day with him, Aria. I've been in contact with him since back then too. But isn't this good news? You'll see him more; you can read his books . . .' He peters off when he sees abject panic on my face. 'Or not? I'm not sure what to say or do. Why are you both looking at me like that? I feel like I'm being blamed, which is cool, but I'm just not sure why?'

'Poor Max,' Rosie says with a sigh. She takes an inordinately deep breath and then speaks like a TV presenter. 'When it comes to love, Aria has sworn it off. Yet she feels a twinge for our lusty writer Jonathan, and unwittingly *you* have now practically thrust them together for the summer when all Aria wants to do is hide. Don't you see?'

His eyes widen but I think it's more fear that he's stuck with two women who, in his eyes, aren't making a lot of sense. 'Why don't you just tell him how you feel?' Max directs the question to me.

Rosie scoffs and slams her notebook closed. 'Are you even *listening* to a word we're saying, Max?'

He edges backwards. 'I'm listening but I'm a little confused, is all. Wouldn't it be easier to be straight with the guy?'

I roll my eyes. 'Max, that's just not the way love works. You should know, you and Rosie had to overcome many an obstacle before you both admitted how you felt.'

'I see,' he says, clearly not seeing.

'You're not to tell him anything we say,' Rosie admonishes.

'But . . .'

She holds up a hand like a traffic warden. 'No buts, you're in the sacred circle but we'll kick you out if you can't keep our secrets.'

He does his best to remain sincere and holds a hand to his heart. 'I solemnly swear I won't break the trust of the sacred circle.'

Rosie opens her notebook again. 'Sign here.'

At that, Max's checked laughter explodes and it's hard not to follow suit. Rosie laughs too, so I gather she's joking but it's always hard to tell when her notebook is involved.

'Still, I find it strange he never mentioned it to me,' I say.

Max shakes his head, his leonine locks blowing in the wind. 'He's not one to brag, is all.'

'It's not exactly bragging when you're talking to someone who lives and breathes books, is it?'

'It's not his way,' Max says mysteriously.

Max is also a man of few words and there's probably some kind of bro code at play. I know I won't get the right kind of information from him. 'Right,' I say. 'Well, I guess we just missed out on seeing him. Shame.'

Also, phew, I can still be invisible here.

'Don't worry,' Max says grinning. 'He's on a mammoth book tour in France, so we'll be seeing a lot more of him.' Rosie elbows Max while I quietly reel in horror.

Now it makes sense why Jonathan acted so surprised at the Squeaky Pig when I announced we were all off to France. He knew he'd also be in France at the same bloody time!

'I need to change,' I say. 'I've got grass stains on my jeans and I'm coated with more croissant than I consumed.' And I'm rambling because I'm nervous quite suddenly. 'We have Max's big surprise this morning!'

Rosie groans and cups her head. 'You had to remind him.' Conversation deftly changed!

'As if I'd forget,' he says, and wraps his arms around her. 'I'll pack this up if you both want to meet at my van in fifteen?'

'Such a gentleman.'

'I try.'

'Let's go, Rosie.' I take her hand and we walk back to our respective vans.

'What do you think this grand surprise is?' she asks, her face pinched.

The gentle rippling of the Seine catches my attention and I point to the water. 'Some kind of sailing? Paragliding?'

Her eyes widen. 'OK, no need to panic. No need.'

'None at all, you know you can trust Max.'

'He didn't mention anything about life jackets, though, did he? It's just that I've done a bit of research, not all life jackets are created equal and there's certain safety aspects—'

I cut her worry off with a small shove in the back so she'll climb Poppy's stairs and focus on the job at hand. 'We don't want to be late.'

'No, we definitely don't. Not if there's a safety briefing . . .'

I dash back to my van and pull on a fresh pair of jeans and tie up my hair. When I get back to Rosie she's calmed herself and is packing things into a backpack.

'What's all that?'

'Snacks, pen light, safety goggles, a small inflatable life jacket. Just the usual.'

I shake my head and pull her out the door before she can pack her first-aid kit and a parachute. We find Max sitting in his van listening to folk songs. 'Bloody hippy.'

'You know it.' He smiles. 'Get in and let's get this adventure underway.'

We drive for half an hour or so before we stop at an airfield.

'Oh holy mother of tofu, please tell me I'm not flying a plane!' says Rosie, panic erupting from every syllable.

'Nope, not a plane. A helicopter.'

'What!' Her voice *boings* around the van.

'You're just a passenger, Rosie. Not the pilot.'

She screws up her nose. 'Why can't we just go on winery tours like normal couples?'

'Where's the fun in that?' He gives her an impish grin.

'Slightly sozzled in the spring sunshine does sound good,' I say. 'But this is so much better, Rosie! Imagine what we'll see from up there!'

'We'll see ourselves reflected in the river when we—'

I clamp a hand over her mouth to suffocate the words.

'Ready?' he asks.

'Ready,' she manages to muffle through my palm.

We meet the pilot for a safety briefing, with Rosie diligently note-taking throughout. On board we're given noise-cancelling headsets to wear so we can hear the pilot and talk to one another during the flight.

'You're going to luff it,' the man says in his sensual French accent.

'*Oui*,' Rosie squeaks, mouse-like.

He starts the chopper. Even with the noise-cancelling headphones the sound is next level, the thump of the rotor blades reverberates through the cabin, making my entire body vibrate.

Rosie gives me a shaky thumbs-up and I grin back. We take off, my belly somersaulting as we ascend.

The view is incredible and the town gets smaller as we climb into the blue sky. The pilot weaves the chopper and points out places of interest. The town has a distinct medieval feel to it even from all the way up here.

We press our noses up to the glass not wanting to miss a thing.

'Wow,' Rosie says. 'This is even better than abseiling because I just have to *sit* here and be rewarded with the spectacular scenery below, I don't have to push my body to its limits.'

Max turns from the passenger seat in front. 'Did you say you want to go abseiling?'

She throws him a faux dark look.

'Victor Hugo called Rouen "the city with a hundred bell towers" in one of his poems,' I remark idly. 'I think we could count them from up here.'

The pilot circles over the city once more. It seems miniature from this height.

I don't want the ride to end, but far too soon it comes to a close as we land just as noisily as we took off. 'Let's do that again!' Rosie says, her face alight. For someone who is so fearful she sure manages to adapt quickly, so used to Max's daredevil streak is she now.

'Yes,' I say. 'But we've got to learn how to fly one of these suckers ourselves!'

'Let's not get carried away!' Rosie admonishes me.

We thank the pilot and head back to the town proper, but I can't help feeling weightless still, as if whatever had been holding me down was left high in the sky. I'll always be grateful for finding Rosie and Max on my nomadic journey. They've opened my eyes to how exciting life can be if you just take the chance. Even Rosie knows to say yes now, when her mind screams no.

Maybe I need to be a little more like Rosie . . .? Jump out of the comfort zone no matter how scary it feels.

'What's on the cards for tomorrow?' I joke.

'Our feet firmly on the ground, that's what.' Rosie says, laughing.

But in actual fact we've made some plans for a number of quick day trips. We're meeting some of Max's old friends at Monet's gardens in Giverny, I'm desperate to see the waterlily ponds and Japanese bridge. And then if there's time, we're off to see the butterfly house in Honfleur.

Chapter Nine

Later that evening Rosie knocks on my door, one hand holding a plate of colourful macarons aloft. 'Thought you might want to talk?' she says, her voice catching as if she's not sure. Rosie still doubts herself when it comes to social cues, and I just wish she'd be herself, because her quirks are what make her so lovable.

'Sure. Come in.'

I make the obligatory pot of tea and a floral scent permeates the air.

'How's it going with the diary?' she asks.

'It's both magical and heart-wrenching having the diary turn up three years after the fact, you know?' I've read a few more passages. They bring my husband to life and remind me how he never took life too seriously. He lived for the moment, and I'm trying to do that too in honour of him.

'Do you think she held it back on purpose?'

I consider TJ's mum, Mary. 'I don't know. We were so close until we weren't, but I can't imagine she'd stoop to that level, but you never really can tell. Grief changes people. It changed her.'

'I'm sure she probably meant to send it early on but it's likely she couldn't function herself. Losing your child, there's no getting over that. When you're grief-stricken, waking up is hard to do never mind a trip to the Post Office . . .'

A burst of resentment rises to the fore. 'Part of me is angry that she gets to be excused for her bad behaviour though. Mary feels I kept him from her at the end, but that was *his* choice, not mine. Deep down, I do understand she needs someone to blame. But when I lost him, I lost them all. I felt as though I could've disappeared and no one would have missed me.'

'That's so sad, Aria.' Her face falls.

I shrug, not wanting to make Rosie sad. 'I wonder why she'd send this now. Is it a peace offering? Or did she truly misplace it?' He was the apple of her eye, her lovely son who made the world a better place every single day.

'Why don't you pay her a visit? We can catch the train back and stay a few days? Have a long overdue and much-needed chat about it all?'

I shake my head vehemently. 'No, I don't want to visit. I couldn't bear to see the grief in her eyes, or her mannerisms that are TJ all over. I'm not ready for that, and I don't think I ever will be.' TJ's family had been my family too and in the space of a few months I had no one. I'd been left with a horrible sinking grief, wondering if I'd ever function normally again. For months I struggled to leave my house. There were too many reminders of TJ everywhere. The park where we walked in the rain. The café where he always ordered eggs benedict and read the Sunday paper. The school he worked in, now mourning the loss of one of their best teachers. The tree we first kissed under. The jewellery shop where he got my bespoke and utterly perfect engagement ring made, a stack of silver books, no diamond for this bookworm. And of course, the hospital, where our lives had come crashing down.

Rosie puts a hand on my knee and gives me a watery smile. 'It *will* get better, Aria. I promise you that. But eventually you will have to face Mary and make peace for that to happen. It doesn't have to be today, next week, next month, but it does need to happen.'

'When did you get so wise, Dr Phil?' I don't want to mire Rosie in this all the time, and so I try to lighten the mood.

'Right around the time I met you.'

'Shucks.'

'So I heard Jonathan has been video-chatting with Max and your name came up.'

I lob a cushion at her. 'Really, Rosie? From TJ to Jonathan in one single breath?' Despite the weighty subject matter I do feel better having shared my problems with Rosie. Even if she insists on bringing Jonathan into the conversation every chance she gets.

'Sorry! But you've sworn off love so I won't bother telling you what he asked about you.'

'Fine.'

'Fine.'

'Good, I'm glad.'

She smiles, waiting me out.

Damn it. 'OK fine, what did he ask, not that I care!'

She lifts a shoulder. 'If you don't care . . .'

'Don't make me come over there, Rosie!'

She laughs. 'OK, OK, he asked Max if you ever spoke about him much after the music festival.'

My pulse races. 'And what did Max say?'

'Nothing. He's sworn to secrecy remember?'

'Oh . . . right.' I can't help feel a little crestfallen at the idea that Max left him hanging.

'But then I happened to walk in and I'm not bound by the same code of secrecy so I told him that yes, his name had come up, of course it had, and we're eager to see him when our paths cross.'

My heart lifts. 'And that's it?'

'Aren't you proud of me? I didn't once try and set up a double date or anything of the sure-fire alternatives that would set you on the blissful path to happy ever after.'

'You showed remarkable restraint, Rosie.'
'It almost killed me.'
'I'm glad it didn't.'
'Thanks.'
'You're welcome.'

Chapter Ten

Rouen

On the morning of the fete the sun beats down with the promise of a scorching day. It bodes well for a big turnout and I predict Rosie's going to sell out of her famous knickerbocker glories.

Rosie, Max and I drive to the grounds and park up next to each other. Edging close, Rosie says, 'You don't think the wet chicken guy is going to turn up and demand more money, do you?'

I laugh. 'No, I'm sure he won't. But if he does, just holler out for me.'

Relief shines in her eyes. 'OK, thanks, Aria.'

With a backwards wave we go about our business, getting sorted for customers who'll begin arriving within the hour.

I set up my folding table under the awning and stack summery romances and vintage bundles of Mills and Boon books that are always popular among romance readers and have become collector's editions. Inside I find my bright purple bunting and tack that onto the front of the table for a splash of colour. Dashing off, I gather wildflowers and hunt for old jam jars we use as vases.

With that done, I find our outdoor furniture and place tables and chairs in the space between Rosie's van and mine, plonk the perfumed flowers down and then root around the storage box for our shade umbrellas.

'It's hot already,' Rosie says, sauntering over, brow knitted. She still gets nervous when we're at a new location so it's best to keep her busy so she relaxes into it.

'You'd better get some more ice cream churning with a beautiful day like this on the cards.'

'It's mixing now.'

'Can you find our chalkboards?' I ask. 'And write them up?' She stops wringing her hands and gets to work. She's so much more relaxed when she's got a job to do.

Across the way, Max has his juice bar open. Brightly coloured liquids swish away in vats. His display fridge has all sorts of 'raw' treats on offer and I wonder how the French will take to his version of dessert, since they're all about enjoying life's pleasures when it comes to food.

With the outdoor area organized and our signs ready, there's nothing left for me to do except assume the position favoured of this bookworm – butt in chair, feet up, nose in a book – and wait for fellow reading enthusiasts to find me and discover the joy that is the Little Bookshop of Happy Ever After. Before I sit, I open up the small windows and hope for a cross breeze. I could sit at the folding table out front but the sun is relentless today and the shade the awning provides isn't enough for my pale complexion.

Soon I have my first customer, a young mother who wears her baby in a sling across her chest. She enters the van slowly as if unsure and emits a gasp when her eyes adjust to the light. 'Ooh la la,' she cries. '*Enchanté*.'

'Welcome! Can I get you a cool drink? Ice-tea, sparkling water?' The heat is merciless, and the young mum's cheeks are pinked from sun and the extra warmth of having the baby cocooned against her. '*Oui*, ice-tea would be lovely.' She wipes her brow with a sigh of relief.

As she unstraps the baby, I toy with which of Rosie's literary teas will most suit. She looks adventurous, so I pick French Kiss, a charming blend of rose and berries that will perk her up on even the hottest day. 'Make yourself comfortable.'

I take the glass tea pot from the fridge and add a helping of ice to two mismatched glasses. She takes a long gulp of the tea, and her eyes widen in surprise. 'The flavours are incredible.'

'My friend Rosie hand blends the tea using all natural and organic products, and I have the matching book . . . around here somewhere.' Of course, I know exactly where it is, but I like people to stay awhile in the Little Bookshop, to absorb the weight of words and peruse at their leisure.

'I'd love to see what book it pairs with.'

I find the book, *French Kissing* by Catherine Sanderson. 'May I?' I hold my arms out to take the baby, and she shoots me a grateful look as we swap warm bundle of baby for slightly dusty book.

'She gets heavy after a while for such a petite little *enfant*.'

I cuddle the baby close, marvelling at her chubby cheeks and bright-eyed gaze, so wise for one so young. I inhale that precious baby scent, sweet like the breath of a puppy. She coos and I babble in baby talk back to her not in the least fazed that I must sound ridiculous. 'She's beautiful. What's her name?'

'Marie-Claire. And I'm Lisette.'

'Nice to meet you, I'm Aria.'

'You're British?'

'Yes.' I go on to tell her about our French adventure and where we've come from.

'You pop up just like that?'

I nod. It always surprises people when we explain the Van Lifers movement and the band of nomads who travel the world on a hope and a breeze, putting their trust in the fact things will work out. 'Yes, we research ahead and make sure there's enough going on and then we hit the road and see where it takes us.'

'Don't you get scared? What if you run out of money?'

I shrug. 'It's always at the back of my mind, but we're all pretty frugal and squirrel away whatever we can for those lean times. And we have each other.'

I rock Marie-Claire gently in my arms as her eyes grow heavy. 'It sounds so adventurous. I wish I could do something extraordinary like that.'

'Right now what you're doing is pretty extraordinary.' I grin and look down at the softly sleeping baby in my arms. She's so beautiful, I pretend for a moment she's mine. Would my babies have looked like TJ? Grown-up like their dad with his endearing gap-toothed smile and impossibly long eyelashes? 'How lucky you are to have such a treasure.'

'She's the best thing that ever happened to me. But I am alone. Her papa decided he wasn't quite ready for fatherhood.' She speaks so matter-of-factly, as if it's just one of those things, like it raining when you planned a picnic – not ideal, but not the end of the world. Probably a good way to deal with forks in the road but it saddens me he left her at such a vulnerable time.

And it goes to show you can never judge a book by its cover. Here I'd pegged Lisette as well-to-do young mum who had the perfect husband cooking up a three-course lunch at home while she took in some fresh air at the local fete. 'Do you manage OK?'

'So far.' Her mouth pulls to one side. 'You know what's saved me?'

I can guess . . . 'Reading? Doesn't that save us all in the end?'

She gives me a warm smile. '*Oui*, of course you'd understand. It's the only thing that stops panic from setting in at times. I love reading about other women who've gone through the same things and come out the other side. My *maman* says I'm crazy, those girls are fictional, but I don't care if they are. They make me feel better.'

'And fiction has to come from somewhere, right?'

'Exactly. And so, like them, I know that when it's time I can dream big for us, but right now I'm just concentrating on one day a time, while Marie-Claire learns how to sleep a little longer each night.'

When life is pared right back, that's when you realize what's important. For this young mum it's the bare essentials like sleeping right now. And that's how van life is. Sometimes you go without, but in the bigger scheme of things, we're gifted with this incredible journey and we don't *need* much to survive.

Besides, a girl who finds comfort in reading can get through anything. 'You'll do great things when the time is right.'

'Maybe you'll see me and Marie-Claire on the road one day?' Lisette brushes a length of hair behind her ear. I notice she is still very well groomed for someone snatching sleep hours at a time. I imagine myself as a mum, my already messy bookworm hair a bird's nest atop my head, and the best excuse to wear PJs day in, day out.

'You never know what's around the corner, *literally*, when you're a Van Lifer.' I want to tell her about the many single mums travelling the same roads as us, their babies being raised by a village as everyone pitches in to help. The children on the circuit bring us so much joy, in the innocent, uncomplicated way they see things. But that would be Lisette's gift to find out if she chose the same life as us.

A couple of hours later she leaves with a bag full of books and a baby who is happy being wherever her mum is. I make a silent wish that she'll follow her heart and live life on her own terms, and do only what's best for herself and Marie-Claire.

A trickle of customers wander in and spend time eking out books hidden high and low, until eventually I deem the morning successful and go back to my book and shut the real world out for a time. One can only talk about books so much until reading them becomes as necessary as breathing. Jonathan's characters have a firm hold of my heart. I have this notion that when you put a book down, they pause and wait for your return. I'd left my lovers in a bar staring angrily at each other, ready to break up, and I hoped the time I'd been away they'd managed to cool down and were ready to make amends – wild, right?

I prise open the pages and plunge back into the story . . .

Later, the sound of laughter breaks through my reading fog but I'm so close to the couple finding their resolution! Begrudgingly I peek up and am startled to see a queue snaking from Rosie's van, all the way past mine. I bookmark my page and go to join her.

'There is a god,' she says, her face red with exertion. 'I've been run off my feet.'

'You should have yelled out.' I tie on an apron. 'What do you want me to do?'

'If you serve, I'll catch up on the milkshake orders.'

'Sure.' I butcher the French language as I speak to the customers patiently waiting; some give me looks of confusion, others speak in halting English. One thing that doesn't need translation is Rosie's food. It goes down a treat and people come back and order seconds. I'd have thought the French crowd would have gone for their French favourites, like macarons and madeleines, but instead they choose Rosie's simple English fare.

When I get a minute to look up, I notice that Max is busy too. His lean, green café has a long queue. He's regaling them all with some story, gesticulating wildly, and they stand enthralled. He's like an action hero come to life and I bet they don't see that much around here, by the way they're ogling him. Rosie calls it the Max-Effect.

Alongside Max, French vendors smoke in huddles and chat to Van Lifers from around the globe. They seem to find our way of life amusing and are keenly questioning them about how we manage life on the road.

'Right,' Rosie says returning, taking a deep breath. 'How's it going?'

'Great, we've almost sold out here. But . . . you look like you've run a marathon; do you want to take a break?'

'Do I? Bloody hell,' she says checking her reflection on the microwave door. 'I'll just fix myself up, be right back.'

Rosie doesn't like to appear dishevelled, whereas it's my natural state. I'm always a little rumpled like I've just woken up. Reading most of the day tends to do that to a person.

The customers ease to a trickle, ordering what's left – plates of pear and almond cake and boxes of jammy dodgers.

When I get to the last person in line, I stifle a groan. 'You made it,' I say, managing a wooden smile.

'I sure did,' she says, grinning, but as ever there's a hint of malice to it. 'Wouldn't want to miss out on all the fun, now would I?'

Pop-up Pimm's van Tori has arrived. And again, I'm struck by the *why*. Out of everyone on the circuit, she zeroed in on Rosie and me the most when it came to spreading malicious rumours. So why come and travel alongside us?

'Are you staying at the same park as we are?'

Her mouth pulls down. 'Yeah, but I've been given a space by the main road which is completely unfair. The manager pointed out your spot by the river – just goes to show it's not *what* you know, right?'

Internally I do a karmic *take that*. 'Shame.'

She waves me away. 'I'm going to ask Max to have a word with them. Surely I can fit between you guys . . .'

'We're pretty squished as it is.'

'We'll manage. We're not here for long.'

Marvellous.

'Sure you will,' I give her a dazzling smile that belies my true feelings. 'Well, I'd better get back to it. I'll see you later, yeah?'

'Yeah, tell Rosie I'll be there when she gets back. I've got a Pimm's with her name on it.'

'Will do.'

While I wait for Rosie, I go to the little outdoor eatery, collect the dishes and give the tables a wipe-down. Tori is over at Max's, flicking her hair and making a spectacle of herself trying to win his attention. He pays her no mind and focuses on cleaning the fold-out counter of his juice bar.

'Hey, thanks,' Rosie says, returning looking revived. 'I needed that ten minutes.'

'You should have called out earlier, I would've helped.'

She shakes her head. 'You're always helping but I feel bad calling you every time I get busy.'

I frown. It doesn't make sense. I've helped Rosie since day one when she joined the festival circuit back in Bristol. 'I don't mind, you know that.'

She fiddles with her apron. 'I snuck my head in at one point but you had your nose so firmly pressed in Jonathan's book I didn't have the heart to disturb you.'

There it is. 'That's why you didn't disturb me, because I was reading Jonathan's book?'

Rosie's let herself be overwhelmed in the hopes I'll fall in love with his prose and then him! She really is as much a hopeless romantic as the rest of us.

'You're disillusioned, my friend. Your cunning plan is all set to fail.'

She narrows her eyes. 'I have no idea what you're talking about. So tell me, is it as good as it sounds?'

I let a silence fall, just to keep her in suspense before saying, 'It's even better! It's all about the power of love in an uncertain world in all its messy, complicated glory.'

'It's a *romance*?' Her eyes go wide with surprise.

I consider. 'Yes, it's beautiful, a modern-day romance. You can see these two characters should be together, but they can't make it happen. They've got these complicated pasts – I'm spoiling it. I'll let you read it first.'

We take the empty milkshake glasses to the serving awning, as sun shines off the paintwork making me squint. 'No, I'll forget by the time I'm ready to read it. Keep talking.'

'It's all about chance meetings and these two people, they seem so real, almost as if I know them. He has really painted such a detailed picture with his crystalline prose.'

'Oh, they feel real, do they?' She nods as she gathers empty glasses.

'Yes, very real.'

'Familiar, even?' She gives me an odd look. Quite suddenly, all colour leeches from her face.

'Yes, yes, familiar, the sign of a good writer when their characters are so three-dimensional – are you OK, Rosie?'

'Yes, I'm fine. I just feel so lethargic all of a sudden.' Wiping her brow, she exhales. 'The heat has zapped me today.'

'Have you drunk any water? Had anything to eat all day?'

'No, there hasn't been time.'

Poor Rosie has been run off her feet and is probably suffering heat stroke from running about trying to keep up. 'Let me tidy and you can sit and have a late lunch?'

'OK that sounds good to me.' She follows me back into her van, and I dump all the dishes on the side board and fill the sink.

Our roles reversed, I plate her a warm slice of quiche and pour a glass of water. 'Drink up.'

She downs the glass of water, and stares at me for an age which means something is brewing in that complex mind of hers. You can't rush her or she starts peppering conversation with French words or turns robotic and goes glassy eyed. It's her quirky way of coping when her brain overloads. I take her glass and refill it and still she doesn't speak. Maybe she's exhausted, I bet she spent half the morning worrying Jean-Pierre would show up, but I haven't seen hide nor hair of him.

Back to the sink, soap suds rise up and I can't help but blow some over Rosie.

'You are such a child!'

'You love it.'

'I do.'

Humming, I wash the dishes and stack them to dry while

Rosie eats her lunch and then potters around her bedroom. Before long she's back and holding Jonathan's book. 'Oh, you're getting started so soon?'

'Your description got me interested.'

'Great. Oh, by the way, Tori's here somewhere. She stopped to tell me she's not happy with the allotment she's been given at the park.'

'Maybe she's anxious about being alone in a new country?'

'Yeah, maybe.'

Rosie drums her fingers on the book. 'Hopefully she's not here to cause trouble. It does seem weird though since she really didn't gel with us all that well back home. Do you think she's into Max?'

I think back to her flicking her hair and giggling like a school-girl and Max's complete disinterest. 'Even if she was, Max isn't having it.'

'You know, I'm sort of sympathetic because I've been that person on the outside, most of my life. Breaking into the robot when I'm intimidated or feel like I'm the odd one out. Part of me wonders if she's the same and is putting on this persona thinking it's her way in, but getting it wrong, you know?'

When Rosie first joined the circuit, her quirks made her notice-able but it was adorable and not cunning like Tori is. Still, I see her point and vow to be kinder to Tori in case it is as simple as that.

'Yeah, Rosie, you always see what lies beneath, I need to take a leaf out of your book.'

'Looks like you've got a few customers too,' Rosie says, pointing out the window. 'Please tell me you locked your cash drawer?'

'Where's the fun in that?' While Rosie has laser-like focus and set rules in place for her business, I tend to be laxer. I leave a sign saying pay for what you take, with an arrow pointing to an unlocked cash tin. I've never run into any problems with it, sometimes losing a book or two. And I figure if they need the book that bad, then they can have it – but this attitude makes Rosie almost break out in hives.

I go back to my Little Bookshop van and meet a cluster of newly arrived nomads who want to stock up on English books. We get talking and the rest of the day escapes.

After packing up from the fete we head back to campsite with a bunch of new Van Lifers. We agree to meet for drinks by the river later that evening so we can get to know them better. Most of them are following the same fete/festival circuit as us so it makes sense to stick together and share stories.

I'm a little annoyed to see Tori's van in my spot, blocking me from Rosie and Max but I bite my tongue and park next to her. I'm keen to read the diary and have some quiet after such a busy day. I close the curtains, turn on the fairy lights and light my scented candles. My life, while chaotic, has these blissful moments of solitude every day and I relish that I get to live like this.

It's not all Brontë and butterflies, but what is?

Falling back on the bed with a groan of pleasure, I take TJ's diary and flip it open, desperate to reconnect on some plane with my husband.

Writing this bleary-eyed and watching my bookworm as she has a lie-in late this morning. She'd been reading into the early hours of dawn, a common occurrence for my book-sprite, and the light kept me awake. I didn't have the heart to tell her though. Between bouts of restless dreaming, I woke, and caught glimpses of her glued to the pages of the novel as if her whole life depended upon it. It's one of the things I most love about her. That she can consume words like others consume food. Mundane things like life are forgotten when she creaks that spine, she loses whole days to other worlds. I guess that's why I'm writing this, in case one day she needs to remember that I loved her with every twenty-six letters of the alphabet and then some.

And I loved him just the same back.

Chapter Eleven

Blois, Loire Valley

After a glorious ten days in Rouen we say our goodbyes to the campsite manager, Antoinette, and leave with a promise to be back. Our new band of friends drive in convoy. It's like old times with a bunch of us following the open road together. A French girl called Violetta takes the lead in her lime green van, and hoots and hollers out the open window. Some kind of death metal screams from inside her cabin, it's a wonder she can hear herself think.

Sunshine beats down and soon we find our groove and the drive becomes a pleasure. The further out we get the more meadows crop up and soon it's green as far as the eye can see with only little hamlets popping up here and there. A sign announces we've entered the lush Loire Valley dubbed the 'Garden of France' by nobility in the fifteenth and sixteenth centuries. It spreads out like a blanket before us. I'm eager to explore this new area, including the famous Château de Blois, despite Rosie's warnings about 'death by haunting'.

Mid-afternoon we arrive in Blois itself. The beautiful French weather puts a spring in my step with the promise of fun to be had.

The new nomads are a chatty bunch, and we're all eager to

swap stories. In the late afternoon bottles of cheap red wine are passed around, offerings to burgeoning friendships. I get talking to Violetta. She's beautiful in that unadorned French way with pixie black locks and wearing minimal make-up that makes her big dark eyes stand out. French women are born stylish and it all seems so effortless for them. But she's definitely got a quirky side if her choice of music is any indicator.

'So where to after Blois?' she asks in heavily accented English.

I wiggle back to get comfortable in my chair. 'We're heading to Bordeaux for the wine, food and literary festival. It's not for another couple of weeks though so we have a few fairs, and roadside stalls lined up beforehand. I sell books, Rosie sells old-fashioned comfort food and Max sells the tonic to living forever.'

As the wine flows so do the words, and before long we're being told by other campers to keep the noise down.

She laughs, displaying teeth slightly marred from tobacco. 'And what about her?' she points to Tori.

I'd almost forgotten. 'She has a pop-up Pimm's van. Sells all sorts of summery flavoured alcoholic drinks. Very popular among the nomads as you can imagine. What about you?' We're down on the bank of the Loire river so none of our signposted vans are visible, and our group has grown in numbers as they have a tendency to do at campsites like these.

'I'm a travel agent, my business is called A World of Wanderlust. All I rely on is a good Internet connection so I shell out for that and then I am free to go wherever my heart desires, good, *non*?'

'Wow, so you spend your days planning other people's dream holidays while taking your own?'

'*Oui.*' She stretches her legs. 'I organize a lot of business travel too. That's my main income. I have a loyal client base so I look after their travel needs. They are mostly bankers, lawyers, foreign services, consultants. Whatever they do, they do it all over the world.'

'Do they love the travel aspect of it all?'

She shakes her head. 'They're never anywhere long enough. High-pressure jobs like that, they fly in, attend seminars or meetings and fly out the next day, often to another country, another meeting. Such a hectic, sterile way to live. But I suppose they must enjoy it, or why else would they do it?'

'Sounds dull.'

'Very dull, but they earn a lot of money.'

'But don't have time to enjoy it.'

'I do have one family who thoroughly enjoy their money, but I'm not allowed to share any details . . .' She arches a brow.

In return I playfully slap her arm. 'You can't say that and not tell me!'

With a contemplative smirk she eventually says, 'OK, the father is a shipping magnate, that's all I'll say, and he has three daughters who' – she makes air quotes – 'are ambassadors for the business.'

'Ambassadors . . .?'

'They fly their private jet around the world, stay in the most upmarket hotels you can imagine, money is no object. When I schedule their holidays I have to factor in every last detail, like cases of Cristal, Beluga caviar, a bowl full of only red M&Ms, the whole celebrity lifestyle cliché. If you can think of it, they've asked for it. Usually a scandal follows in their wake and then their PR person is all over the place putting out fires. It's impossible to imagine how much money these girls burn through; you wouldn't believe me if I told you.'

'They sound hideously fascinating.' And instantly I know who she's referring to. Three sisters who put the Kardashians to shame when it comes to being in the spotlight, and often for all the wrong reasons. They certainly live life in the fast lane and money means nothing to them, because they have so much of it. Well, Daddy does, at any rate.

She clucks her tongue. 'They are hideously fascinating! And I make a small fortune when I work for them, but it's nothing compared to what they spend in a day.'

'I suppose it keeps work exciting though, seeking out hotels where week-long stays cost the same as small houses. Not for me though, I love the solitude I find in my van, and getting lost down lonely roads and parking up with no one else about.'

'Me too. Their life certainly makes van life more appealing. Who needs all of that, really? We get the same spectacular views being on the road. I don't envy either group: the execs or the socialites, but I appreciate that they fund my life.'

To those executives and socialites our lives must seem so disorganized, so in flux. So lacking fiscally!

A man comes to join us, he wears loose-fitting jeans and a tight white T-shirt. He plonks beside Violetta and gives her a kiss on both cheeks in the French fashion. It's when he slings his arm around her I realize he's more than just a friend.

'This is Laurent, he only joined van life a month ago, and lucky for him he met me on his first day.'

He grins and kisses her. Is everyone in the whole damn world in love and I haven't got the memo? Where are all the single people at! I feel like I'm wearing a sign around my neck that says: *Solo and sad* . . .

But I shall press on, surely there're some singletons around here somewhere. 'What's your specialty, Laurent?'

'I type up love poems for five euros a piece.'

'Wow, I love it! Do you get much of a call for that?'

'*Oui*. Everyone loves *love*!'

Of course.

He's devastatingly handsome. I bet he sells poems as fast as he can type them. They make a fine-looking pair and are fun and frivolous with it.

'We're going to an author event in town now,' he says. 'Would you like to come with us?'

'Oh, who is it?'

'Jonathan Chadwick, have you read his work?'

The drink I've just taken a sip of comes screaming out of my mouth and I cough to cover my faux pas. 'Yes, yes, I have, just recently.' Rosie's not close enough to see my nerves jangle so I make a quick decision before I can overthink. 'I'd love to come along.'

'You need a ticket but I know the owner of the bookshop so I'm sure it won't be an issue.'

'I'm happy to stand at the back.' *The very back!* For obvious reasons I don't want Jonathan to see me. Part of me wants to see the author in action without him noticing me. Will his public persona be different to the man I've met, albeit briefly?

'Great, let's go.'

I stand and dust grass from my jeans, trying to spot Rosie in the group. Eventually I see her curled up with Max further down bank of the river. She senses me and turns, a question in her eyes. I dash over to them. 'I'm going into town with Violetta and Laurent. Back later.'

'Have fun,' she says. 'And lock up your van before you go, will you?'

I give her a salute. 'Already done.'

'Wow, you're learning to live safely.' She turns to Max. 'They grow up so fast.'

'My cash tin is still unlocked.'

'Well, baby steps. At least the door is locked . . .'

I laugh. 'OK, Ma and Pa, see you later.'

Sometimes Max and Rosie do feel like parent figures, even though we're all roughly the same age. Max is the protective sort and since I'm Rosie's best friend that extends to me, and Rosie is the chief worrier in our little trio, so she keeps an eagle eye on me to make sure I get through every day without getting kidnapped, robbed or burnt to death by candle. Perhaps they need a new project that isn't me . . .

Chapter Twelve

Blois, Loire Valley

Butterflies swarm in my belly like a vicious plague of locusts and I realize I have no idea what I'm doing. Luckily my two new friends don't know me well enough to notice I'm more fidgety than usual. In London I made a fool of myself lunging into Jonathan's arms and smooching him as if I'd never been kissed before so I'd rather he didn't notice me so I can hide out for say . . . the rest of my natural born life. Hermit-like. But I *do* love good fiction so it's not like I should miss out for making a bad choice or two along the way. Well that's what I'm telling myself at any rate.

Laurent goes inside the bookshop to enquire about a spare ticket, while we hang outside behind a queue of people waiting to get in. How they're going to fit such a crowd in the seemingly tiny space is beyond me and I marvel that such a famous name still tours quaint bookshops like this. It says a lot about the man. Don't tell Rosie that though.

'Don't worry,' Violetta says, clutching my arm. 'Laurent will find a way, he's good friends with the author too.'

I gulp. 'He is?' Holy mother of plot twists!

'*Oui.* They were part of the same writing group for a while when Laurent lived in London.'

Ah, of course, the poetry. Damn it all to hell and back! 'Oh?' Words fail me as I picture the French couple rushing up to Jonathan when I'd planned to remain inconspicuous. I do a very subtle side-eye looking for escape routes but find none. I'm wedged in by the crowd.

'Yes, they even shared a flat for a little while.' She lets out a small laugh. 'But as you can probably guess Jonathan doesn't need to flat-share anymore. He's got a great big house by the river in St Albans.'

'I can see why he's so successful, his writing is illuminating. Quite poetic really, but with those big doses of reality thrown in. *The Quiet of Loneliness* quite took my breath away.'

'Isn't it *fantastique*? You need to go back to the beginning and read them all. Although this book is *very* different to all of his others – a new direction so to speak and one I think he has mastered. Everyone doubted him, but once again he proved them all wrong.'

I nod, despite having no idea what she means. 'I need to get over this one first.' I lower my voice to avoid spoilers for those around me. 'It kept me up into the early hours, and by the time I'd finished I swear I could've slept for days! Their love affair exhausted me.'

'This latest is his masterpiece. It captures the very essence of matters of the heart. Every notion you have about love is flipped on its head, but isn't that how it truly is? We have such limited time on this earth and we have to grab love by the collar and shake it. We have to act! Or what's the point?' Violetta's cheeks pink as her passionate monologue comes to a close.

I cross my arms as the evening air cools. 'I agree with you but I'm leery of the idea that passionate love is all we exist for. There's the love of friendships, family, a feeling, a place even, to consider too.'

She waves me away, twisting her mouth as if I've missed the point. 'You don't believe in soul mates?'

TJ flashes into mind. 'Of course I believe in soul mates, but I'm less inclined to believe you can have two or even *three* great loves over a lifetime.'

With a scoff, she stares me down as if she's actually offended by my ideas. But it rings true for me. A soul mate is someone who shares the key to your heart, and you theirs. It's rare and it's irreplaceable.

'But that is unfair, *non*? What if your one great love leaves or stops loving you or is already married, then what?'

'Then they're not your soul mate, they're an imitation. Your soul mate can't be married to someone else for goodness' sake, that just doesn't work!'

She waves me away and gives me a look that suggests I'm naive. 'You Brits are so uptight about affairs of the heart. Of course they can be married and still set your world on fire. They might not have known you were out there, and then worlds collide and suddenly there's three in a marriage.'

My head's about to explode. *Whaaat!* 'Three in a marriage! You're thinking about this all wrong.'

She lights a cigarette and blows smoke all over the place. 'All I'm saying is you don't get to decide who you love! Love chooses you!'

I shake my head, but smile at her theatrics. 'I agree love chooses you, but love also chooses the right people, *unmarried* people. Two people who are a perfect fit.'

'Fine but if *they* leave, then the next love of your life will appear. It's just how it works and it's what Jonathan's book shows too, *non*?'

I consider it. In his book they'd both been married, but their marriages had ended before they'd found each other and realized that despite or maybe *in light of* their pasts they were perfect for each other. 'I suppose so,' I grudgingly admit. 'But whether I'd call them soul mates is another thing.'

'Why label it? It is what it is. And their love was fiery, passionate, the stuff dreams are made out of.' Laurent nudges slowly through the crowd to get back to us as Violetta says, 'True love doesn't always last forever. We have to be prepared to open our hearts again, no matter how damaged we might be.'

Thankfully no reply is expected as Laurent flings an arm around Violetta and nods to the side entrance of the bookshop. 'We can skip the queue and watch from the open gantry upstairs. We'll have the best seats in the house.'

My shoulders relax; surely Jonathan won't notice us up there? We go through the side entrance and sneak up the stairs, the air heavy with a thousand stories waiting to be read. My bookworm blood pulses and all I want to do is hunt through the shelves but I let them lead the way up a flight of rickety steps that are probably a thousand years old and settle on some beanbags that have seen better days. Laurent pulls a bottle of red wine from his jacket and a sleeve of plastic cups in true nomad style.

I laugh. 'You just happened to have those secreted there?'

With a grin he says, 'Wine and literature, a perfect match.'

I scrunch my nose. 'None for me, thanks.'

The last thing I want to do is drink my body weight in wine (again) and throw myself in Jonathan's arms and kiss him like some lost desperado (again). No, I shall be in full charge of my faculties and not the lax Van Lifer I truly am.

'Have one,' Violetta chides. 'It's not going to hurt you.'

It would take the edge off, I suppose . . .

'Just one then.' Did I mention I'm easily led if there's fun to be had?

By the time the author talk starts the bottle is almost empty. I give myself an imaginary pat on the back for loosening up and easing my angst about being here. Really, what's there to be worried about? He's an author, I'm a reader, and that's that.

But good Golem, Jonathan radiates a certain *je ne sais quoi* that sparks a strange sensation in me. No, it's probably just hunger, I haven't eaten after all. Maybe it's not him it's simply a dietary issue. That's clearly what it is. I quaff the last of the cheap wine and hope it fills the void, hunger, desire, whatever the damn hell it is, and settle in to enjoy the talk.

'Why are you holding yourself like that?' Violetta whispers.

'Like what?'

'You've got your face pressed up against the rail – you're going to fall through it if you're not careful!'

With a gasp I see what she means. I look like a prisoner pushed up against the bars, desperate to catch a glimpse of the real world. Violetta stares at me as though she's worried I'm slightly demented. Which I clearly am. 'Oh, it's erm . . . my eyesight. It's terrible,' I lie. 'Can't see a bloody thing.'

She cocks her head. 'Really?'.

'Yep.'

'You should have told us, we'd have asked for seats down-stairs. Laurent!' She shouts and I cringe as the sound echoes around the room catching the attention of the crowd below. I edge from the bannister in an effort to hide, but all I see is empty space so I lie flat and hope Jonathan can't see me.

'I'll get Laurent to sort us better seats,' Violetta says, and then frowns. 'What are you doing?'

Oh god. 'I . . . I, ah lost a contact lens . . .'

'Can you see out of the other eye?'

'I've lost them both.' I can practically feel my nose growing before me from the amount of lies falling from my lips. I sneak a peek downstairs, hoping the crowd has turned back to Jonathan, but find a of mob steely-eyed death glares instead. Violetta's voice rises as she announces, 'We have vision-challenged friend up here! She cannot see a thing!'

I want to die. I want to curl into a ball and rock. Must keep up the farce though since everyone in the *entire damn bookshop* is staring at me. I scrunch my eyes closed and pat the carpet as if looking for the meaning of life, instead of a couple of contact lenses that aren't there because I am *not* vision-challenged at all.

In fact, I have perfect 20/20 eyesight which is a real shame in this case, as I can see quite clearly the error of my ways.

The unthinkable happens. Jonathan calls out, 'Would your friend like to join me on stage? She should get a pretty good view up this close.'

My toes curl.

I cover my face in the hopes he won't recognize me and disguise my voice by speaking with a bad French accent. '*Merci*, but *non, non*, that won't be necessary.'

I peep through my fingers and see a grin on his face. And something else. Wonderment. He knows. Oh god, he knows it's me. I debate about flinging myself out the window but don't like the idea of splattering to the ground from the second floor and all.

'*Oui*,' says Violetta and grabs my hand. 'We'll be right down.'

No, no, noooo!

I'm dragged along whether I like it or not and pushed into a chair on the stage beside Jonathan. 'Thanks for being so considerate,' Violetta says. 'Poor girl can't see her own hands right in front of her face.'

The crowd softens their steely gazes out of misplaced concern.

'Welcome,' Jonathan says. 'Are you comfortable? Can I get you anything?'

An invisibility cloak would be good, right about now. My voice curt, I say, 'I'm fine, thank you. Please continue.'

'You seem so familiar to me . . .' I can hear the sarcasm if no one else can.

'I wish I could say the same, but I can't quite make you out.' I make a show of pressing my hands in front of me as if he's right here, not a few steps away.

'Allow me,' he says and moves to place his face in my hands. Talk about backfire.

I press at his face and accidentally-on-purpose stick a finger in his eye socket. 'Ouch.'

'Sorry!'

'Ringing any bells?'

'Nope, not a one.'

He grins, his face flushed, probably from the pain I inflicted digging into the soft flesh of his eye.

'Perhaps you came to me in a dream?'

I narrow my eyes. 'This is real life, Jonathan, not fiction.'

'Can't we pretend it's the same?'

'Only a pen pusher would hope for such a thing.'

'Right.'

I note the crowd starting at us intently and I wait for coughs of impatience but none come so I take matters into my own hands. 'Why don't you continue with your talk and I'll do my best to listen.'

'Sure, sure, thank you. Love the blue of your shirt, brings out the coppery colour of your hair.'

'Thanks, your shirt isn't too bad either.'

The crowd gasp.

'I can tell by the feel of it.' I say quickly feeling it. 'Burnt orange, magnificent colour on a man.'

'It's green.'

'My mistake.'

The crowd collectively sag in relief.

'Right, where was I?' Jonathan asks, running a hand through his hair. 'Ah, yes, so what made me choose two lost souls to write about in *Loneliness*? Well, who isn't lost in some way? We've all had pasts that lead us to a certain point, a sink or swim moment, and I used that to see what mettle my characters had. Their fragility is what made them so special, what drew them together, and by the time I'd finished the book I didn't want to let them go.'

The gathering nod and a few wipe away stray tears. Oh, he's good at this.

'But does that not mean those people would be wary about jumping into another relationship so soon? I mean, haven't they learned their lesson? Tread water for a while, for goodness' sake!' Why oh why did I speak out loud? I'm not doing a very good job of hiding in plain sight at *all*.

'Why place oneself in purgatory and pine for what is lost for so long?' he counters.

'Because it matters!'

'Of course, it matters but should life be put on hold forevermore?'

Like a tennis match, the crowd turns from him to me and back to him.

'Why is it on hold? Just because she's choosing not to love again? That's not exactly on hold, is it? She still goes about her everyday life.'

'But it's empty. Void of meaning.'

Is it? I'm suddenly confused who we're talking about as I put myself in place of the main character. I double blink, comprehending the book in a completely new way. It's too much, though, it's too complex a notion to process on stage in front of so many people. I feel exposed as if my own grief is pasted on my face for all to see.

Stunned, I sit mouth clamped closed while questions and answers flitter back and forth. A numbness creeps over me. Do I have the right to start over? *Could I?*

One long lonely night in a bookshop in France, widow Aria Summers has a revelation . . . Her broken heart will never truly mend, but new love just might ease the ache. That's if she'll let writer Jonathan into her life. But how can she test her theory when she's still so damaged, so unsure of herself? And what does she really know about the man except that he can kiss the pain away . . .? All she knows for sure is this limbo style life she's walking has to change, but how?

I pull myself from the daydream, hoping I didn't speak out loud. Scanning the room, I can't spot my new French friends anywhere. There's a gaggle circling Jonathan, so I attempt to creep out the side door and hotfoot it back when a voice calls out . . .

Chapter Thirteen

Blois, Loire Valley

'Watch out, Aria, you're about to walk into that door!'

I freeze, knowing I am about to do no such thing. Jonathan says his goodbyes and joins me, grabbing my arm as if helping a little old lady cross the road.

Once we're outside I say, 'You can drop the pretence now.'

With a shrug, he drops my arm.

'Definitely one of the most unusual author talks I've had.'

I groan. 'I'd planned to hide upstairs and creep down later. I got the shock of my life when Violetta called out to you.'

'Interesting charade.'

'Meant only for Violetta!'

'Your acting skills are to be commended.'

I can only imagine what my stricken face must have looked like and laughter gets the better of me. 'You're a very good sport.'

'How long are you in Blois for?'

'We leave tomorrow, this was just a quick stop along the way.'

'It seems a pattern with us.'

'The life of a nomad.'

'You ever think of staying put?'

'Never.'

'Right.'

'Sorry, I just mean that life isn't for me. Not anymore.'

'I can understand that. Who wouldn't want to go and drive off into the sunset when things get hard?'

I bristle. 'Is that what you think?'

He says, guilelessly, 'Isn't it what you're doing? Escaping?'

No one has pulled me up on that before. I'm a nomad after all but he senses it's an escape rather than a journey but still it irks me that he has the audacity to call me on it. 'If this is about the kiss in London . . .' I turn on him, because he knows the real me somehow.

'It isn't.' Head cast down, he slips his hands into his jean pockets.

'Well, that was a mistake and I'm really sorry I latched on to you like some kind of sucker fish. I don't know what came over me.' Although I haven't been able to forget how his lips felt against mine . . .

Surprised laughter barrels out of him. 'Sucker fish?'

'Urgh, don't remind me. When I relive that night I see this caricature version of myself. It doesn't bear thinking about.'

'I'm sorry the memory bothers you.'

'Don't worry. I've made a vow to drink in moderation going forward.' He must think I'm some desperado flinging herself into strange men's arms whenever the mood strikes. And then I recall I just sank the best part of the bottle not leaving much for Violetta and Laurent. Really, I can't be trusted around wine when I'm hungry.

'Lucky me.'

Colour races up my cheeks.

'Yes, well I hope you'll accept my apology.'

'No need.'

'Friends?' I hold out a hand for him to shake.

He pauses before taking my hand. 'Friends.'

We stand under the moonlight for so long it becomes awkward. 'Well, thanks for walking me this far. I know the way back, now my vision has been miraculously restored.'

'It's OK, I can walk with you. Max invited me over for a few beers.'

'Of course.' *Face palm!* Here I'd been thinking he was doing the gentlemanly thing and walking me home in the dark when really he wanted to visit Max and unwind for a while.

We carry on in silence, before he eventually says, 'You argued at the talk that we only get one true love. Do you really believe that?'

'Of course, don't you?' I feel defensive somehow, as if he's going to insist I'm wrong and then I'll have to explain about TJ which would be weird considering.

'No, absolutely not . . .'

This is the theme of his latest book so I shouldn't be surprised but just for once I want someone to side with me on this. 'I've had my one great love, and I know it's irreplaceable.' My words come out by rote, just like always, but as I say them I feel how hollow they are. Do I really feel this way still, or am I just so used to having that guard up?

'So that's *it* for you? You'll never entertain the thought of love *ever* again?' His voice seeps with incredulity and he stares at me with those mesmerizing unfathomable eyes of his. I quickly look away before I get lost to him.

'It goes deeper than that.' My voice comes out curt. I'm so confused which Aria I'm supposed to be with him. Happy-go-lucky Aria that the world sees, or the real me?

'But you're so—'

I cut him off. 'Don't you dare say young.'

He grins. 'I was about to say lovable.'

My heart stammers. 'No, you weren't.'

'You'll never know.'

He always manages to lighten the mood, and part of me is relishing this one-on-one time. His dark hair curls around his ear and for one instinctive moment I go to brush it aside, and then catch myself and snatch my hand back. Thankfully he doesn't notice, and I struggle to focus on the subject at hand.

I shake away my haziness and ask, 'Have you been in love before? Proper heart beating out of your chest, dreamy, intoxicating love.'

'Yes, of course. I'm not a priest.'

'So how did it end?'

'Badly, for me, at any rate. I didn't see the end coming, not even a hint of it.'

There's a story there but I don't prod him. 'Therein lies the difference. Yours ended by choice. Mine didn't end because I chose it to.'

'But isn't any end of love, bad?' His velvety voice is gentle, but I surmise that Jonathan is one of those people who gives it his all when he loves someone and whatever happened left its mark on him.

'You wordsmiths, always trying to twist things.' Love is such a messy subject . . .

He laughs. 'My relationship didn't end happily, but really, when do they? Not many people celebrate the dissolution of a marriage. We'd changed, both of us, as people, as partners, and you can't really change back, you know? But that doesn't mean I won't love again.'

He speaks as if by rote too, as if he's said the same line over and over. I know because I do the same thing when pressed about TJ. What happened to this lovely guy to make him stand on the edge of the world? I'm sure it's not as simple as two people growing apart. 'It must have been a shock, but I'm glad it hasn't ruined you for someone else.' Perhaps death is the difference? The shock of losing someone forever and ever with no chance to rekindle what is lost.

His face shines under the moonlight. 'I hold out hope, what if the first go was a prelude to something better? Wouldn't you agree?'

'Not for me, no I don't think that's possible.' TJ will always remain my one and only true love, otherwise what kind of wife would I be?

'Ah, but you can't actually know that yet.'

'I can.'

'You really can't.'

'I know it in my heart.'

'A fickle beast if ever there was one.'

'Maybe for you but not for me.'

He raises a brow. 'Sometimes you just have to take the plunge and see.'

We walk in silence. I can't think of an answer that he'd understand and that doesn't sound like I'm forcing myself to live in some kind of purgatory. We come to the famous Jacques Gabriel Bridge. It's yellow under the moonlight, the Loire river below gently lapping like something out of a fairy tale.

'Don't you ever get lonely?' he asks.

All the damn time.

He notes my hesitation and continues on. 'I've spent a lot of my life lonely.'

'Despite being mobbed by fans, adored the world over?' I gently tease.

He smiles but it doesn't reach his eyes. He wears loneliness on him like a perfume once you recognize it for what it is. It's the sadness in his eyes, the half-smile. The way he's always looking just off in the distance as if waiting for something to materialize. 'They love the characters, not the writer.'

'I doubt that. So why not find this grand new love you speak of?'

'I'm trying.' He averts his gaze and I don't know what to say. Does he mean me? *Pick me*, I want to scream and then correct myself, *not available – sorry*. Here we are, both a little displaced in the world – are we both running from hurt destined to don fake smiles and pretend we're living full and happy lives when inside we're empty?

Is that really it for us?

But he has the world at his feet, people scurrying after him just to get a glimpse. If anyone had a chance at love it would be him. Or maybe they only love the *idea* of him, the celebrity side and really he's all alone in this world? I feel a pull towards him, as if we're both struggling with how to live after loss, albeit different kinds. He reminds me of the hero in his book, so struck by heartbreak he can't see what's right in front of him because he's so busy looking backwards. Or is that more like me? Once again, I get that feeling it's all too much to process when I'm in the middle of a conversation so I pack it away to think about later.

'I'm curious. Why didn't you mention you were a writer back at the festival where we met last year?'

When he gazes at me my heart stops, his eyes are full of such longing. For what? Acceptance? Understanding? 'There was no expectation from you, you didn't know me, didn't ask anything of me, we just spoke like two regular people who love words. Why ruin that?'

I nod. 'Do people act differently when they know who you are?'

'Some do. It's not like I'm Bono or anything. But there's always a shift if they know my work and I don't mind that, of course, I'm the same way with authors I like. But when it's someone I want to get to know, especially a book lover . . . I found it refreshing that we just connected on a clean slate, knowing zero about one another.'

He kind of is like Bono, or at least the bookselling equivalent. Up there with Nicholas Sparks when it comes to copies sold, according to Rosie. 'I get that. So it's just you and your work most of the time?'

'*All* of the time. I get lost to it. Not so great when it comes to relationships, you know?'

I give him a wide smile. '*That* I can understand. I do the same with reading. It's what's saved me, these last few years. Having worlds to escape into that weren't my own.'

'The beauty of literature. It's always there when people aren't.'

Isn't that the truth of it? When all else fails there are worlds out there to secrete you away where real life can't intrude, at least for a little while. 'I lost my husband to cancer and I felt like I would die without him, literally die, so I escaped into reading, fully immersed myself and without that portal to another world, I wouldn't have survived. There's nothing like the magic of reading to ease the most damaged heart.'

He considers it, taking his time before eventually saying, 'There's a healing quality to reading, even to writing, I guess. I find I can delve into my characters and my own problems fade. But for you, Aria, I'm very sorry to hear you've been through such a tragedy. That kind of thing shapes the rest of your life. Now what you've said previously makes more sense and I'm sorry for making light of it.'

'Don't be sorry. I don't usually tell people about TJ. I don't want to hear platitudes like *time heals all wounds*, and *you're still young*, impossibly thoughtless remarks that are actually nonsensical.'

'People are just wired to trot out the same old lines they've heard; they don't *think* about what they're saying in times like that.'

'Yeah, I get it. They just don't know and I'm glad they haven't had to lose someone, but I can be a little defensive about it too. That's why I don't usually tell people, and they don't notice.'

'Thank you for trusting me with it.'

I wave him away as if it's nothing when really it's a big thing for me and I love how he's answered just the right way for my sensitive heart to cope with. As we turn into the campsite, I see Rosie and Max are still where I left them. 'There they are.' I point. Thankfully Tori is nowhere to be found. Rosie looks like she's fast asleep, her head resting against Max's chest.

Chapter Fourteen

Blois, Loire Valley

We approach Max and Rosie quietly. They're the only ones still on the embankment. Rosie is fast asleep on Max's chest, a checked blanket draped over her.

'Aww,' I whisper. 'She's out of it.'

Max smiles and says hi to Jonathan. 'She was mid-sentence and she dropped off just like that. Not Rosie's style at all.'

I tut. 'The last few days she's been run off her feet. Maybe she needs a proper day of rest.' Rosie has a night-time ritual and I know she'll be anxious having missed it. She cleans her already clean kitchen, sorts her fresh produce and gives the inside of Poppy a thorough going over or else she can't sleep, so this is really out of character for her.

'Yeah, I'll suggest that to her, but I don't like my chances.'

Rosie doesn't have days off. 'True. Maybe she just needed an early night.'

'Maybe,' he says. 'How'd the author talk go?'

Jonathan and I exchange glances which Max catches because his gaze soon bores into mine as if he's trying to read my mind, the devil he is. Now I've been spotted with Jonathan, I'll have to tell Rosie all about it tomorrow. When really it's nothing, is it?

'It wasn't boring, that's for sure,' Jonathan says and coughs into his hand.

'Aha, never a dull moment when Aria's in the house, eh?' Max says with a fondness in his voice.

But I groan as I remember the evening, charades and all. Max knows me too well, including the fact these kinds of disasters seem to follow me. 'How about I wake Rosie and take her to her van so you guys can catch up?' *And then I don't have to stare at Jonathan and talk myself down from the ledge.*

Max hesitates for a fraction of a second and I wonder if there's more to it with Rosie. She has been lethargic of late and he doesn't seem to want to let her go.

'Sure, sure,' he finally says. 'Maybe a cup of chamomile will help her have a steady night.'

'Has she been having problems sleeping?'

He averts his gaze. 'No, nothing like that. You know how she gets when things change. She's up before the birds, that's all it is.'

When she's worried she wakes at crazy hours and bakes and cleans, and cleans and bakes. She must be exhausted burning the candle at both ends.

I bend down and gently shake her awake. 'Rosie . . .'

With a snort she comes to. 'Oh, god, sorry!' She covers her nose as if it has offended her. 'I was dead to the world.'

'Come on. I'll make you a pot of tea before you turn into a pumpkin.'

'Jon,' she says groggily, stretching as she stands. 'It's so lovely to see you.'

'You too, Rosie. I hope we can catch up again another time.'

She gives him a loose hug. 'I'm sure we will. Sorry I can't stay, I need to sleep something fierce.'

'I hope you get some rest,' Jonathan says to Rosie before turning to me. 'Goodnight, Aria . . .'

I chastely kiss his cheek and instantly regret it. He smells like hopes and dreams, he smells like books! I double blink and mumble gibberish before I lead Rosie away – she's half-asleep and I'm all wobbly.

We go back to Poppy, and I make a pot of tea. The ritual has calmed me so now I can focus on the job at hand. I haven't even sat when the words come tumbling out. 'Rosie, are you OK? You're not sick, are you?'

Her eyes are red from being woken from a deep sleep and she looks downright dishevelled. 'What makes you say that?'

'You've been tired a lot lately.' My voice catches. 'It's nothing, is it?' My poor heart remembers how innocently it all started with TJ. How his flu-like symptoms were a lot more treacherous than we gave them credit for.

She yawns, big and wide. 'You know, I don't know what it is. Max is insisting I find a doctor too. I just can't shake this sluggishness. It's putting me so far behind.'

My heart twists, imagining the worst. 'I'm going to find a doctor and book you in for tomorrow.'

'But we've got to head to Bordeaux, it's all scheduled.'

'So, we'll be a day late.'

'Can't we—'

I interject before she convinces me to do it her way. 'No, we can't. Nothing is more important than your health, and that's that. Drink up. It's your night owl brew, so that should send you right to sleep.'

'OK, OK, wow, you're acting like me.' She grimaces.

'It's a scary thought.'

'How did tonight go? How did you end up with Jonathan?' she says with a question in her eyes. I see what she's doing though, and I won't be distracted. She needs rest.

'I'll tell you all about it tomorrow once you've had a decent sleep.'

116

Once she's finished her tea, I tidy the mugs, otherwise I know she'll be up and at them before I'm out the door. 'Into bed, Rosie.' I tuck her in and kiss her forehead as if she were a little girl then I sit at the end of the bed. Within minutes she's asleep.

Back in my van I connect to the campsite Wi-Fi and find a local doctor and book her in for nine o'clock the following day. I send Max a Facebook message and let him know.

I'm overthinking it, I know I am. It's just so unusual to see frenetic, ball-of-energy Rosie lying there so sallow and limp. I need a distraction so I take TJ's diary from the drawer and hope the passage is an uplifting one.

I found a book stuck to Aria's face tonight, literally stuck. She had fallen asleep, mouth open, face down on the page and the two became one! When I delicately peeled it from her cheek a smudge of black ink remained, a tattoo of her wild night reading. Who knows what she gets up to in these other worlds. I should be jealous of all the men she swoons over, right? But I can't help but laugh at her dedication. She'll be amused, I think, when she sees her reflection in the mirror tomorrow . . .

I laugh, imagining him finding me in such a state. Of course, I don't remember it, and he wouldn't have said, as he so often found me in various poses with books as I'd read until the very moment my eyes closed and I fell into slumber. I still do. Which book was it, I wonder, that kept me up?

A part of me feels a pang of guilt though – how can I have such precious memories like this diary while his mum is struggling so without such a keepsake? Perhaps it's up to me to reach out so she can begin to live in the light again . . . Could I be the bigger person?

Here I am surrounded by people who love me and a man I'm trying hard not to think of in a romantic way and Mary is all alone with her husband who thinks emotions are for the weak. I bet she's been just as lonely as I have.

I find my laptop and boot it up. I decide not to overthink it and instead I write from the heart.

Dear Mary,

Thank you for sending TJ's diary. It has been a revelation of sorts and such a precious keepsake. I'm only reading it in small sections at a time to make it last. There's so much to say but I don't know where to start. I know you're still hurt that I took TJ away when you needed him most. But if I could only explain so that you'd understand. I didn't take your boy from you for any selfish reason on my part. He so desperately wanted to see the lakes, and one last thing of beauty. Deep down, I think he wanted to be alone so he didn't see the sorrow in everyone's eyes while he came to terms with it. He didn't want to leave us. And he wanted to feel in control of his one last wish, and so I did what he asked, and I'd do it again too. Was he running away, or was he following his heart? This is the question I ask myself every day, and the same thing I have since done with my own life. I keep running, and nothing ever changes and it doesn't bring him back. But still I run.

What can we do, Mary, except hope to find peace? My life has been so empty without him and there's days where I wonder what the point of it all is, if you love so hard that the world is dull when that love is gone. But then I have these small euphoric moments over the smallest things, like the deliciousness of a pink frosted donut, birds flying at sunset, my friend Rosie's snort laugh, and it gives me hope that there is something around the corner if only I try to live in the moment . . .

But how can I? When the man I love is gone? Nothing can ever replace TJ.

Anyway, this is probably a rambling mess, but I wanted to reach out and tell you I'm sorry if the part I played in TJ's final time hurt you. I only ever wanted to do what made him happy. I hope you can forgive me as I am willing to forgive you.

I did bring him home, after all.

Aria xxx

Chapter Fifteen

Blois, Loire Valley

The next morning I'm up far too early because of everything on my mind. With coffee in hand I sit in bed, contemplating the long walk back to the camp I'd taken with Jonathan the night before. We'd edged around so many sensitive subjects that I'd been left confused as to what was really being said. So I do what any modern-day girl would and head straight to Facebook to stalk him.

When I open the app I'm surprised to find a friend request from the man himself. I accept it and I smile as I scroll through the pictures which are mostly book-related. There's a photo of his home library which is an enviable thing of beauty, a black room with floor-to-ceiling shelves and French antique furniture in rich, bold blues. There's a snap of him at a dog shelter which makes my heart pound a little quicker. He volunteers there as a dog hugger and ambassador for the *Adopt Don't Shop* movement.

A *dog hugger*! I never knew there was such a thing! There are lots of snaps of mixed-breed dogs who he walks when he donates his time. I wonder if that's what he does when he gets writer's block?

There's not many posts of people and it occurs to me that he really does live a very solitary life, unless he doesn't share online because of who he is, but somehow I don't think that's the case in this instance. I think, like me, Jonathan is truly lonely, having built up his career to the detriment of personal relationships. Didn't he say as much? He *gets lost to it* when he's writing, I can understand the pull.

Eventually I drag myself away from my stalking session and check my emails in case any book orders have come through. I stop short when I see TJ's mum, Mary, has replied and so soon. I click on the message:

Aria,

You'll consider forgiving me? For what exactly? I wasn't the one who spirited TJ away from everyone he loved. I wasn't the one who kept him from extra medical treatment which would have prolonged his time with us. I wasn't the one who said he was sleeping every time someone called. It was you who did all of this and I could continue on, Aria, as well you know. Have you ever considered that TJ might not have been in sound mind at that time? And yet you thought following his wishes was the best course of action – well, I'm telling you right now, it was not. It was the worst possible choice you could have made and that I cannot forgive. Perhaps it's best if we cease contact.

Mary

I swallow a lump in my throat. How stupid could I have been trying to make contact? Her resentment towards me is as strong as ever and I doubt myself again about the choices I made back then. When I think of my beloved TJ's last wishes, the fervent look in his eyes, the way he pleaded for the trip, I know in my heart I did the right thing. He *was* of sound mind, and he was adamant he wanted to visit the most beautiful place on the planet. In the end we were only gone a couple of weeks because of how quickly he deteriorated. It had happened scarily fast and in the end I took him home because I couldn't give him the proper care he needed and secretly I'd been terrified and wasn't ready to lose him. Back home, he *was* reunited with his family for the last few weeks of his life and they were a time of excruciating sadness for all of us. He refused to leave the van, refused to go into palliative care and I promised him no matter what – he'd die on his terms. And I fought for it. I fought for him. Wouldn't anyone do the same?

I did the right thing for TJ.

As I hug myself tight, wishing TJ was here, I wonder what he'd think of all of this, and what he'd tell me to do if he could send a message from wherever he is. My instinct is to flee (no surprise there) and grant Mary's wish of ceasing contact, but that's the cheat's way out and I know she deserves better from me. And I also need an apology from her. It all comes back, the messy falling out that we had when we should have been hugging one another, not arguing. She insisted on organizing his funeral, a drawn-out religious affair that wasn't TJ. It wasn't an ode to the man I loved and I told her so at the time. Where was the joy? I wanted his favourite songs played, upbeat songs as the slideshow of photos slid by, but Mary refused. I let it go. And in that slideshow, pictures from TJ's baby years, right up to adulthood, there was not one of me. Not a single one. Of course, I'd given the funeral director a plethora of pictures, TJ with his students, with his friends, with me. They didn't use one. Not one. And little did I know after the funeral, they'd cut me out of their lives for good.

But I know Mary's inherent goodness, I know her heart. And it's been long enough to know that hurt makes her speak such a way, and not anything else. TJ would want me to fix this, to be the bigger person. We need to repair our relationship in honour of the man we both loved with all of our hearts.

There's no time to reply now though and I need to proceed with caution and make sure I word my reply right.

I dress quickly and head to Rosie's van. By the river a few nomads are circled around a fold-out table playing cards. They give me a wave and yell out for me to join them. 'Later!' I promise.

I barrel into Poppy, mind scattered. 'Hey! Are you OK?' Rosie asks, searching my face.

I must look shell-shocked still, so I do my best to wipe the worry from my expression and give her a wide smile. I won't unload any extra stress on Rosie, not while she's sick. 'Yeah, I'm great. Sorry.' I shake my head. 'I spent too long reading, stayed up way too late.'

'Oh, it's just you looked so lost there for a minute,' she says.

I smile. 'No, no I'm all good.' My go-to lie for the last forever. 'Where's Max?'

'Changing after a run, he'll be back in a tick.'

Max knows a lot more French than we do so he can help translate at the doctor.

Within a few minutes he's back and we all squish in to the front of the Little Bookshop van. 'Maybe we should have taken my van?' he says, trying to negotiate a place to put his feet as boxes of second-hand books I picked up at a car boot sale lie scattered in the foot well.

'You'll live,' I say, feeling determined that today I will make things happen. There won't be any putting off of anything. Not on my watch. I'm surprised how calm Rosie and Max are, considering. If anyone was to worry, it'd be Rosie. Just when I wonder if I'm overreacting Rosie nods off, head against Max's shoulder and I know she isn't herself.

We arrive at the doctor's surgery and I softly shake a groggy Rosie awake. Inside, we take a seat and I fidget with a book, pretending this is just another day and everything is fine.

Beside me, with hands clenched, Rosie says, 'I'm feeling a little silly that you're both here when all I need is another nap and a slice of chocolate gateau. Can we cancel? If we leave now—'

'We're not cancelling.' My voice comes out harsher than expected and she reels back as if I've slapped her. 'Sorry, Rosie, but it's just better to nip these things in the bud before they blossom, you know?'

'What things?'

'Sickness things.'

Realization flashes across her face. She gives me such a sad smile my heart breaks in two. It brings it all back to the fore – the hospital visits where hope was lost, the way I tried to walk outside without my legs buckling from under me. The sheer and utter fear I carried inside me. I scrunch my eyes closed against the memories coming thick and fast.

'Oh, Aria. I'm not sick like *that*. I'd know it, I'm sure of it. You don't need to worry. Truly.'

I pretend to be confused. 'Better that we check you're not coming down with some kind of virus, or . . .'

Rosie latches on to my panic. 'God, you don't think it's some airborne disease, do you? Something I ate? Some kind of slow-moving poison?'

Max shoots me a look-what-you've-done stare.

We're saved by the doctor with an amiable face, who calls Rosie's name. 'Come with me, Max?' she asks him.

He nods and says, 'You want to join us, Aria?'

'No, no, you go.' *I'll just sit here and bite my nails down to the quick.*

They take an age. Years. Decades. I'm just about to go and bang on the door when they walk out, Rosie with a tearstained face, and Max wearing a smile so big it threatens to swallow him whole. I have no idea what to make of it.

'What is it?' I dash to her.

'I'll tell you in the van.'

I hold on to her arm as if she will fall at any moment. 'I'm not an invalid, you know. I *can* walk.'

'What did he say?' I ask in the quiet of the cabin.

Max takes her hand and gives it a squeeze.

With a shuddery intake of breath, she says, 'I'm pregnant. Little Indigo is coming well ahead of schedule without consulting us. I'm unprepared. *I'm not ready!* How can this be?'

I gasp and my entire body relaxes as if I've been carrying the weight of the world without knowing it. 'WHAT!' The word reverberates around the cabin of the van. I've never felt so happy in my life, so damn relieved.

Rosie's face is wan when she says, 'Right? I am meticulous, *meticulous* with note-taking on my body and its feminine functions. I can't believe I've overlooked such a thing. I mean, it beggars belief! I just cannot see how this could happen. I just can't.'

'Well,' Max pipes up. 'When mummy and daddy love each other very much—'

She clamps a hand over his mouth. 'Is that some kind of a joke, Max?'

It's too soon for jokes for the shell-shocked girl in front of me, even if it is pretty funny. Rosie's utter astonishment is something to behold so I try to rein in my joy but I'm sure it shines from my face anyway. I've always imagined these two as parents, it's almost like it is meant to be, just slightly ahead of Rosie's schedule.

'Are you happy though, Rosie?'

A stray tear winds its way down her cheek. 'Yes. I'm ecstatic. Scared. Bamboozled. Anxious. The doctor said I'm being bombarded with a range of hormones that are probably going to cause all sorts of mood swings and that's also why I've been so tired. He said the fatigue should pass by the third month. I've got a lot of research to do, that's one positive.'

'Max?'

He lifts her hand and kisses the top of it. 'I'm the happiest man on the planet. I'm hoping it's twins. Triplets, even.'

Rosie's face pales. 'Trust a man to say that! Let's not get carried away or anything will we, Max?' She shakes her head. 'Triplets, can you imagine? We need to think about this rationally.'

'Yes, rationally. The first thing I'm going to do is buy you the world's biggest notebook.'

'Aww,' I say. 'The perfect present for our mum-to-be planner extraordinaire.'

'I have to tell my folks, they're going to be grandparents again,' Max says. Max's parents have about ten or eleven children, some biological, most adopted, so their brood of grandchildren is already huge. His mum, Nola, sort of picks up people along the way – anyone who needs a hand, a mother figure, or just a straight-up confidante will find it in her. She's a total mother-of-earth nomad and we all love her to pieces.

The shock slowly begins to wear off and Rosie's expression becomes tender. She clasps Max's hand and says to me, 'Can we go back? I'm feeling a little queasy.'

'Sure.' I fire up the van and drive slowly as if I am transporting a newborn baby, which I suppose is not far off. I'm transporting a teeny tiny little jellybean that will grow into a baby.

'How was last night?' Rosie asks, as she rests her against the seat, eyes closed. 'I heard you went to Jonathan's author talk.'

'Oh yes, last-minute thing. It was fine, fine. Very informative.' One eye peels open.

'He's an exceptional talent. Fascinating to hear about the process behind the words.'

'Why are you talking like that?'

'Like what?'

'Like you're someone else.'

'Your hormones are making you hear things, Rosie.'

She laughs. 'Maybe you need a truth injection for your liar-betes?'

I shake my head. 'Fine, *fine*.' I swear Max to secrecy and then I tell her the whole sorry story and she clutches her (baby) belly and laughs, unable to form words.

'Gosh, Rosie it's not that funny!'

'Holy mother of tofu, it is! The thing with the shirt!'

I blush.

'So then what happened?'

'I told him a bit about TJ and then left him with Max.' Ran screaming from possibility, might be another way to put it.

'Wow, you don't normally tell anyone about TJ.'

I take a deep breath. 'I know, but it felt right. And I know he's not the type of guy to give me any throwaway lines about grief, you know?'

'If only you were single.'

'Shut up.'

'Some other girl is going to snatch him right up.'

The thought gives me pause. 'Probably. He'd make a good boyfriend for the right girl. He's always so attentive, you know, like the way he just listens, hangs off every word as if what you say is of the utmost importance.'

'Wow, what a monster. You're right to stay away from him.'

'Very funny. Don't think I'm going to let you get away with comments like that just because you're carrying my nephew in there.'

At that she bursts into tears. 'I'm OK,' she says, 'Don't mind me!'

Max and I bite down on laughter. Rosie is going to have to come to terms with the fact her body is in control and not the other way around. I hold the steering wheel with one hand and hers with the other.

'I think the patient needs a long hot shower and nap.'

She wipes at her face. 'And a slice of cake. For the baby.'

We laugh and the earlier tension I felt evaporates. I'm so glad it's happy news and not the alternative. It's probably not natural to think the worst like I do, but I just couldn't bear to lose anyone else, especially Rosie. Soon, there'll be a little baby in the mix! Everyone's lives are marching on, while mine has stopped on the end pages where TJ left . . .

Chapter Sixteen

Blois, Loire Valley

With our plans slightly skewed I head back to my van to absorb it all. Out of the corner of my eye I catch a glimpse of Tori, who by the looks of it is only just getting up now. The day has been interminable, so much has happened and it's not even lunchtime yet.

'Aria! Where have you been?'

Hands in pockets I join her. 'In town.' Damn it, we didn't discuss sharing the baby news, but I'm sure Max and Rosie need some time to digest it all before it gets around.

'Doing what?'

'Getting coffee.'

'But Rosie makes coffee.'

'So?'

'So why go pay for it?'

'Why not?'

'Urgh, it's like talking to a rock sometimes. Where is Rosie? And Max?'

'They're having a quiet day to themselves.'

'But I thought we were off to Bordeaux today?'

'Change of plans.' I shrug. 'Maybe tomorrow.'

She narrows her eyes. 'I don't get it. Rosie doesn't change plans.' She stabs the air with a finger. 'What's going on?'

'Stomach bug, I'm afraid. Rosie's got it bad. If I were you I'd stay well away. Highly contagious.' I shake my head as if the memory pains me. 'She's been up all night with it. Let's hope she feels better soon.'

Sure enough, Tori reels back. 'And she went and had coffee?'

'No, she went to the doctor.'

'Well, why didn't you just say that?'

'You asked me where I'd been . . . not them.'

With a roll of her eyes that she doesn't even try to hide she says, 'What about Max? Is he sick?'

'Head nurse today.'

She huffs and puffs like the big bad wolf. 'So that leaves me with you?'

I pull my mouth to one side. 'I'm fairly busy – those books won't read themselves.'

'Well, I expected a bit more, to be honest.'

'Sorry.' The very last thing I'd choose to do on a suddenly free sunshiny day is spend it with Tori.

'You want a Pimm's?'

I glance at my watch. 'It's a bit early for me.'

'Could you be any more boring?' Her mouth turns down.

'Probably.'

'Where's that other guy gone?'

It's my turn to narrow my eyes. 'Which guy?'

'The one who looks slightly lost, as if he's not quite sure how he got here. Cute in a very shy bookish way.'

Jonathan!

'Why?'

'Why what?'

'Why are you looking for him?' I keep my voice light.

She folds her arms across her chest. 'Well, who else am I going to hang out with? Why, Aria, is he off limits or something?'

128

I should have just denied knowing who she meant. 'Of course not. But I'm fairly sure he's gone. He was only here for an author talk for the one night.'

She tuts. 'Shame. I'd have liked to get to know him better. I joined them last night in Max's van after you rushed off, didn't you know?'

'Oh?' She's goading me and it's hard to keep my expression serene but somehow I manage, silently telling myself she's an immature child in an adult's body.

'Yes, Rosie had gone back to Poppy and you were probably reading about life rather than living it.' She lets out a giggle and I roll my eyes.

'You're probably right. I *do* have more in common with fictional people.' I give her a winning smile and take pleasure when I see her eyes darken.

She waves my words away. 'Anyway, we had a few beers, and I'm sure we made a connection.'

I lift a brow. 'Yet you didn't know his *name*?'

'We skipped past the small talk and went straight into the deeper stuff . . .'

I don't believe her but my blood pressure spikes, I'm sure of it. 'Sounds riveting.'

'It was. You know when someone is into you, well you probably don't, but he did this eye contact thing, this really intense sort of—'

I cut her off. 'Oh, that. He dropped his contact lenses at the author talk, says he's blind as a bat without them. Didn't he mention it?'

OK, that's a mean, horrible lie but I can't help it.

'No, I'm sure you're wrong.'

'I was there, I saw him on all fours. Patting down the carpet for the damn things. Why do you think I had to walk him back here? He couldn't see, the poor man. How does one lose two contact lenses at the same time? But I suppose he *was* doing a lot of blinking what with all the photos being taken, all the flashlights going off and all, famous man he is. In such *demand.*'

Her face drops and I know I've won this round.

'Well, it wasn't just the eye contact of course. It was everything. The air hummed with promise . . .'

'Right. Electrifying stuff. Anyway, I'd better push on, too much time in the real world sends me batty. Cheerio.'

She's already looking past me into the distance where German Van Lifers Otto and Jörg appear, walking back from the river, fishing poles propped against their shoulders. I give them a wave and then turn on my heel and flee. Why does the thought of Jonathan spending time with her annoy me so? It's not jealousy, he's free and clear to do whatever he wants. There's nothing between us, aside from a drunken kiss, right?

It's just that it's Tori. I'd hate to see him with a snake like that. Perhaps if we were to cross paths again, I could subtly warn him? But surely he's not likely to fall into the arms of someone like her? It's not really my business though . . .

Then I think back to what Rosie said about Tori not quite fitting in and trying to be someone she's not. She could very well be lovely under that surly, brash persona, but I doubt it. I think I've pegged her just right.

Normally I'd confide all this to Rosie but I don't dare disturb her with such trivialities today. And that's all they are – trivialities, right?

Back in my van I take out TJ's diary hoping to feel connected to him, that his words ground me to this earth. I feel like I'm in flux, floating and soon I'll drift away. It's a strange feeling, and I can't quite work out what's changed to make it so. Perhaps it's the new group, the new place. Everything seems up in the air, so changeable.

I'm so tired I just can't shake the feeling something is wrong other than this flu that just won't go. But I don't dare tell Aria. She'd frog march me to the doctor and I'll have to suffer a barrage of tests and all for what? To find out I'm low in vitamin B or something. Instead I take naps at lunchtime and hope my students don't sense I'm not quite right. Maybe we need a holiday. I've always wanted to go to the Lake District.

Aria can read a book a day while she's wrapped in my arms. I'll hug her when she cries (she always cries, happy tears she says, when the girl gets the boy) and we'll watch the moonlight shine on the water. That will be cure enough for me . . .

Chapter Seventeen

Blois, Loire Valley

Our trip stalls with Rosie's pregnancy news, but she won't listen to reason. She wants to head to Bordeaux as planned, albeit a week behind schedule to get there for the book, food and wine festival. I'm not sure it's such a good idea but I'm prepared to hear her out. A gaggle of Van Lifers and I have visited every garden, and chateau in Blois and the surrounding Loire Valley, Chambord being my favourite, but after a while they all blend into one and we make the joke, 'NABC!!' to one another which means n*ot another bloody chateau*. Maybe it is time to move on . . .

As I go to leave my van, I see a neatly wrapped package sitting on the step. A small envelope is tucked into it so I hastily open it, curious as to who it's from. Has Mary reconsidered?

A,

I found this little gem in a bookshop yesterday and I thought of you. Well, not that you're anything like Madame Bovary, of course, but I thought it might appeal to you, being a vintage edition (sadly not a first edition!) and quite beautiful. I love the scent of old books, the shape of them. The way their pages hold the essence of who came before as they patiently await the next step on their journey through many lives . . .

J

I smile and take a great big unladylike sniff of the precious tome, and it conjures memories of Madame Bovary herself. For some reason I haven't actually read the classic but I recall the themes of the novel. I picture her beauty, feel her desperation, her need for passion, for wanting more. I'm transported back to that era, and for a brief moment in time, I'm her, throwing caution to the wind and acting on my desires.

If only . . . I quickly send Jonathan a thank-you message on Facebook and tell him I can't wait to read it. I need to return the favour, but which book for the famous writer himself? While I walk to Rosie's van, I contemplate a French writer who might appeal to him . . .

'Knock, knock,' I say and enter her van.

'Back here,' Rosie's reply comes back softly. I move the pink curtain that partitions the living area from the bedroom.

'How are you feeling?' She's still slightly green around the gills but gives me a big smile.

'A little better.'

'Liar.'

She gives me a watery smile. 'You always can see right through me. I'm ready for the next part of the adventure. Bordeaux will be just the tonic.'

'But, Rosie—'

'No, honestly. Behind the wheel in Poppy I have a semblance of control, and the breeze blowing in will ease that fog I'm in.'

'What does Max say?'

'You'll convince him.'

I blow out my cheeks. 'Right, like that's a cakewalk.'

'It'll be fine. But let's share a pot of tea first? I'm starving but I don't dare eat in case it makes me sick again. Tea first. That should help settle my stomach.'

'Of course. Which tea?'

'Sense and Sensibility, maybe I will absorb some of that too.'

I grin. 'You're perfectly sensible. Sometimes, life just has grander plans.'

I bustle around Rosie's tiny kitchen which is still pristine even in her predicament. I balance the tea things and a tin of ginger biscuits and set them up on the end of her bed.

'I'm so sorry for holding everyone up,' she says, her face glum.

'Don't be, Rosie. What's a week or two here and there? It's all part of the journey.'

'Yeah, I know. But I still feel bad.'

'Please promise me you'll stop worrying? Van life is all about the unexpected and there's always bumps in the road, this one just happens to be a baby bump which makes it pretty bloody special, darling.'

'Thanks, Aria.' We sip tea and Rosie manages a few nibbles of the biscuit. 'It's still sinking in, I guess.'

'What happens now with the medical side of things?'

'Dr Benoit has given me a list of midwives to check in with along the route we mapped out previously. He's rang ahead and explained what he calls our *unusual circumstances*, so I feel confident I'll be in good hands, and of course I'll research them—'

'You mean investigate them as if you're an FBI agent.'

She giggles. 'Yes, if there's any sniff of malpractice, I'll find it.'

'I have no doubt. Will you head back to the UK to have the baby when it's time?' My heart sinks, thinking I might lose Rosie on the journey, just after I found her. I'd understand, of course, but I'd be lonely if she and Max parked up for the duration and settled into normal everyday lives.

'Yes, Max and I discussed it and we think that's best, maybe leave France around the six-month mark or so? We're not going to stop travelling, we're just going to be closer to home and healthcare. You'll come too, won't you?'

My heart lifts. 'Of course. I'll be with you every step of the way.'

Relief shines in her eyes too and I know she's probably felt the same as me, that we don't want to leave each other no matter how our circumstances change. 'I caught Jonathan arriving early this morning . . . must have been visiting Max?'

'I found a book from him on my step this morning.'

'Oh, that's it then. How thoughtful of him.'

'Yes,' I say, not being drawn.

'He's *such* a lovely guy. Such.'

'He is, isn't he? He friended me on Facebook and I noticed he volunteers at a dog shelter as a dog hugger!'

She gasps. 'He does not!'

'He does!'

'You've always wanted to volunteer at a dog shelter!'

I have but being on the road put limits on such things. And truthfully I don't think I could walk into a shelter and walk out without one of those little fur babies who need just one person to love them. Lots of Van Lifers have pets but it can restrict the journey because many campsites refuse to allow animals and also National Parks often ban pets in order to protect wildlife. It's a big responsibility when you don't know what tomorrow will bring.

'That cements it then! I shall marry the man!'

'People have married with far less in common than that!'

'Oh god, Rosie, I was joking.'

She gives me a puzzled look. 'Right. Well you should add it to your list.'

'What list?'

'Aren't you making a list of his attributes as you go?'

I stifle a laugh. 'No.'

'Well therein lies the problem. You, a romance reader aficionado, should know better. Did you want me to scribe it for you?'

I smile. 'No, Rosie, I'm good. I've got it all up here.' I tap the side of my head while I think I'd give anything to see Rosie's list about Max. I bet there are some doozeys on there.

'Anyway, back to our famous writer,' Rosie says. 'He had this dreamy look in his eyes . . . It made me wonder why?'

I can't shake the thought of him and it pains me so I anchor myself to the past and say, 'Not sure, maybe he had a full eight hours' sleep?' Her eyes twinkle and I know she's never going to let it go so I deflect to my next problem. 'Anyway, I emailed TJ's mum.'

'Wow, when?'

I explain what I wrote and when I sent it.

'Have you heard back?'

I nod, and tell Rosie all about Mary's reply.

'Wow, Aria, I'm really sorry it didn't go the way you expected but you shouldn't have to feel bad about following his wishes.'

'Yeah, I've always thought so, but the more time goes by I understand. She's his mum and she wanted him right by her side. I do understand. I still wouldn't change what I did, but I guess I can see why she feels as though it's all my fault. There's no one else to blame, TJ is gone.'

Rosie touches her teeny tiny belly, her eyes welling up. 'Yeah, gosh, what you both went through . . .' Her words freeze on her lips while she composes herself. 'You and Mary could still be a real support for one another. You both know best just how it feels to lose the person you love most.'

'That's it, isn't it? We could have been there for each other when no one else was.' Having someone to share the burden of grief with would have been life changing.

'There's still time, Aria.'

'Yeah, maybe. At first, I was angry but I put myself in TJ's shoes and I know without a doubt he'd hate to see us fall out for good. He'd hate that *so* much. So no matter what, I'm going to try and make things right.'

'Remember though, it's a two-way street.'

With a long sigh I say, 'I know. Anyway, get ready and I'll see what I can do with the pacifist about driving to Bordeaux.'

She grins. 'I'll have a shower now, and hope that a bit of a freshen-up will fool my body that all is well.'

I groan. 'I'll tell him you're being stubborn.'

'You're a gem, Aria.'

Chapter Eighteen

Blois, Loire Valley

'Where are you rushing off to?' Like my shadow, Tori is never far behind.

'Have you seen Max?' I ask.

She waggles her brow, insinuating something untoward. 'He's inside his van.'

'Is there something wrong with your face?'

'What?'

'Oh, nothing, it just looked as though you lost control with that eyebrow wibble-wobble . . .' Urgh, I hate how she implies things, as if Max would take one look at her.

'It wasn't a wibble-wobble!'

'My mistake. Max!' I bash on his van door.

'Come in, Aria.' I do and shut the door with a bang, happily closing out Tori's surprised face.

I find him in a yoga pose, looking deeply relaxed. 'Hey.'

'Hey, what's up?'

It's hard to reconcile big, tough Max as a yoga devotee. It seems so incongruous that he can shift his hulking body into such poses but he manages somehow. He's such an enigma, poor man gets judged on sight by his looks alone, but it doesn't take long to realize Max is a lot more than just a pretty face. And now he's to be a dad. My heart melts just thinking of Rosie and Max as parents. She's chosen well.

'Hey, Daddio. So Rosie's sent me here to browbeat you into submission.'

He shakes his head, his mane of hair catching in the prisms of soft sunlight streaming in. 'I don't think it's a good idea. Do you?'

'Bordeaux is what, about four hours or so away?'

'Yeah, give or take. I'm worried about all that driving and the baby.'

I lean against the doorjamb. 'Did she check with the doctor?' I ask and I damn well know Rosie would have had a notebook full of questions at her second appointment yesterday. The doctor would've needed a stiff drink after that kind of interrogation.

Max gives me a look that suggests I'm correct in my assumption. 'He said she'd be fine, it's not like we're driving in a jungle or anything, but still.'

'Aww, your protective daddy instincts have already kicked in. But if I go back and tell Rosie her new plan is off, I'm not going to hear the end of it. You can bet she's already made a new schedule including various baby doctors along the way.'

He sighs. 'She made it last night. I was sitting with her when she stalked them all online.'

I grin. 'So . . . she's not going to take any risks, that's not in her DNA. I think we should listen to the baby mama and let her lead us depending on how she's feeling. We know Rosie is not a risk taker. If anything, she's the exact opposite.'

He scrubs at his face. 'Right. It's just . . . I never thought I'd say this, but I have this overwhelming urge to fly us back to the UK and set up house. I know it'll pass, I know if I did that I'd feel like a caged animal before long, but it's just this all suddenly feels risky.'

'Because it's new.'

'Yeah.' He un-pretzels himself and stands, blocking out the filmy rays of sunlight. 'OK, if Rosie is keen and you are too then we can try for Bordeaux. We also don't want to let you down all the time if things change.'

I wave him away. 'I can sell books anywhere, and she's my best friend, Max.'

'OK. But it's still generous of you.'

'Yeah, well don't get too soppy on me now, Max. You've got a reputation to uphold.'

'I feel like you two are going to gang up on me a lot going forward.'

I pretend to be outraged. 'What!'

'She sent you over.'

I smile. 'True. Look she's got an influx of *the hormones*. Let's just do as she says.'

We laugh. 'It'll be easier in the long run. Hey, thanks for looking after Rosie the other week when Jonathan visited after his author talk. I'm certain he was disappointed he didn't get to have those drinks with you.'

I frown. 'No, he said he had drinks all planned with *you*.'

Max gives me a vacant look. 'Oh . . . he did? I must've forgotten.'

'You've got a mind like a steel trap, Max, from all that gingko biloba memory vitamin you're always preaching about, so don't try that with me.'

'Yeah, then you've got to ask yourself why he said such a thing . . .'

I fold my arms. 'Max, don't speak in riddles. Did you or did you not invite him for beers that night?'

He shrugs. 'Not *that* night. I wonder if the man might be smitten, is all?'

Was Jonathan nervous I'd say no to a drink after the event? I remember feeling stupid that I'd assumed he wanted to walk me home when really he'd organized a few beers with Max, and now Max is saying that's not the case? What is actually going on then? Jonathan probably didn't know how to act that night after the way I behaved at his author talk and then the subsequent walk home – to say I was all over the place would be an understatement.

Whatever it is gives me a nice warm feeling as if I'm not as invisible as I once thought. But of course, I can't tell Max that. 'Probably a bookworm thing.'

Back inside Poppy, I give a refreshed Rosie the news about Bordeaux. 'Thank you! We were at loggerheads.' She takes her notebook from her desk and grabs a pen, a to-do list of epic proportions coming this way!

'He's looking out for the baby.'

'Isn't he the best? Sometimes I think I'm going to wake up and find this is all a dream.' She writes the heading: MIDWIVES SHORTLIST PROS AND CONS.

'It's real life, Rosie and it's only going to get better.'

She casts her dreamy eyes to the window. 'I feel like I've been asleep for weeks. What's been going with you lately?'

I sit on the edge of her bed. 'We've toured the Loire Valley and visited every chateau known to personkind. I *really* want my own chateau one day . . . I've read a tonne of historical books on the area and I'm currently *in love* with a very suave man who resides in London but of course travels the French countryside when the mood takes him.'

The pen falls to the floor as she slaps a hand to her mouth. 'I knew it! Max told me that Jonathan is head over heels for you, but I wasn't to mention it. Did you see him again since the author talk? You said you'd made friends online but I didn't realize things had progressed so fast!'

I double blink. 'What . . .?'

She searches my face and then realization hits. 'Oh . . . god! You meant you're in love with the guy in the book you're reading, didn't you? *Don't tell Max or Jon that I told you!* Bloody hell, I must have that affliction they call baby brain already!'

I bite down on my lip unsure of what to say. 'Did he really say that?'

Her eyes glaze and she stiffens. 'I . . . don't . . . know . . .'

Laughter gets the better of me. 'Don't turn robot, Rosie. It's OK, truly. I'm just a bit bamboozled by it and I wonder if he meant someone else. If you ask Tori, she says he was giving *her* signals.'

She scoffs. 'No, Max was quite clear about it. Jonathan is madly in love with our resident bookworm but he suspects you're not ready for love and he doesn't want to rush things. And as for Tori, Max told me she was one step away from throwing herself on the poor guy. Looks like you've got a competitor.'

My pulse speeds up. Probably because deep down I'm competitive, there's no other explanation for it. 'Well, I'm not saying this out of spite, but he and Tori are not a good match. They just aren't.'

'Could it be the green-eyed monster talking?'

I make a show of being offended by such a suggestion. 'I hardly think so.'

'Mm-hmm.'

'What does that even mean?'

'I've lost my train of thought,' Rosie says, zoning out for a second. 'Can you fall in love with the dreamboat so we can have a double wedding, already?'

I let out a scoff but can bet that Rosie has got a notebook stashed round here with double wedding plans, *just in case.* 'No, I bloody well cannot. Are you getting married?'

'Not until you are.'

I giggle. 'So that's a never then.'

'Never say never.'

'Never.'

'Troublemaker.'

'I am so too.'

'Please don't tell Max I told you! He'll never tell me another secret again!'

'Lips are sealed. I still think Jonathan might have been referring to someone else.' I don't know what it is that makes me say these things, maybe it's that same need to hide, to run, so I don't have to make any scary decisions.

'Yeah.' She rolls her eyes. 'Because there's a million Arias out there. This is your typical slow-burn romcom trope and I'm just waiting for you to recognize what's right in front of you.'

'Oh, you're using my own lines against me now?' I say, grinning. 'And you're right in front of me . . .'

She waves me away laughing. 'Not literally right in front of you.' She catches the sarcasm late. 'Oh, you minx. You'll do anything to try and distract me when we talk about Jonathan. Don't think I don't see what you're doing.'

'*Moi?*'

She throws a cushion at me. 'You're the worst. Now pick that up so I don't have to.'

I laugh and place the pink cushion back in the centre of her bed.

Back in my van I take the little diary and pull a rug over my legs. I need to reconnect with my husband, because no matter what I tell myself it stills feels strange to have these pangs of worry that I'm doing something wrong just *thinking* about Jonathan in such a way.

We found out the terrible news today. There's no hope, you could see that reflected in the doctor's eyes, in his sad smile. Imagine having to be the bearer of such news? I felt for him. My shock set in and I didn't know what to say to Aria as she sat silently next to me, her hands shaking. I never imagined it would be cancer, or maybe some part of me did and I knew instinctively it wasn't fixable . . . That explains the strange dreams, the sudden necessity to write the diary. How can I leave this darling girl? Already I wonder who she'll be without me. Will she remarry, will she have someone else's children? I know she must start over, my girl is a hopeless romantic and needs love like she needs air to breathe. It's impossible to accept this is my fate. But I must gather all my courage and help her for the tough roads ahead. I never want to leave her . . .

What kind of man finds out he's dying and thinks only of his wife and what the rest of her life might entail? He was so adamant about planning what came next for me. It must have broken his heart into a million tiny pieces. Just reading this breaks mine all over again. Maybe the old adage is true: that some people are just too good for this world?

I'm suddenly glad for the pop-up roadside stall we've got planned for this afternoon. I'll be too busy to think. I'm still lying on my sliver of bed when Laurent knocks on the door with a bang and wanders in.

'Ooh la la, were you sleeping?' He raises his hands in apology for barging in, but we all do the same thing. If you want privacy as a Van Lifer, you lock the door!

I sit up. 'No, no, I was just chilling out.'

'We're going to check out Château de Cheverny before we set up for the roadside stall. Do you want to come with us in Violetta's van?'

'NABC,' we say at the time and laugh. 'What's one more to add to the list?'

I give the diary a quick kiss and place it back in the drawer, glad to be focusing on Violetta's nail-biting driving skills instead of my heavy heart.

Chapter Nineteen

Blois to Bordeaux

I awake to a Facebook message from Jonathan:

My pleasure, and in no way was I ever assuming you were like Madame Bovary 😉 *I chose the book on scent alone, even if that makes me sound like I have some kind of weird book-sniffing fetish (which I don't!). Well of course, I do sniff books, but doesn't everyone? What if you don't though, then you won't understand, and now I've gone too deeply into this and next minute you're going to dub me some weird name . . . Book-Sniffer Weirdo, or BSW for short. It's OK, I get it. Anyway, I'm rambling. Glad you liked it. J x*

I clutch the phone to my chest and laugh. I am a book sniffer from way back so I totally get it, but he doesn't need to know that just yet.

You sniff books? WTF! From this moment on you shall be called WBSD (Weird book-sniffer dude) and I'm going to have to warn people to hide their books when you're around . . . A x

The drive from Blois to Bordeaux is a pretty one, green and lush as far as the eye can see. As we get closer to the town itself, vineyards point the way. They're so graceful, the vines in their neat symmetrical rows.

Me and the other Van Lifers spend the next couple of days playing tourist, taking it in turns to sit with Rosie as she does her best to hang on to her sanity, not liking it one little bit that she's a hostage of the tiny little being inside of her who is wreaking havoc with her health. She had to share her news with the nomads because there was no hiding the fact that she hadn't been well and we were way behind our proposed schedule.

Whenever I return I go straight to her van and show her photos of the magnificent sights we've seen like Place de le Bourse and the water mirror, the world's largest reflective pool, stunning at night with the Palais de la Bourse mirrored on the water.

I tag along with Violetta and Laurent and visit the Quincoces Square in the centre of Bordeaux, a twelve-hectare garden where many festivals are held over the year. Rosie sends me on a culinary mission to find Bordeaux famous Canelés, a small pastry filled with rum and vanilla custard centre, and a thick caramelized outside crust. I take a box back from the patisserie for her when they assure me they're safe for pregnancy, that the rum is cooked away in the baking process. Rosie is pink-cheeked with joy as she tastes the delectable treat.

Bordeaux is a vibrant city, and we could spend weeks exploring, but work calls. While we made decent money at the fete and the small roadside stalls along the way, most of us Van Lifers are haemorrhaging through it with all the campsite costs, entry fees, long lunches, French wine and cheese and fuel and transport. Rosie isn't able to work so I want to make sure I have extra in case she needs it, even though I'd have to battle her to accept it. Max is working longer hours for the same reason but neither of us mention it, we just stash away what we can so we have a buffer when it's needed.

Back in my van I take some arty pics of books to sell and upload them on social media. I wonder if I can include some of Laurent's poems as a bundle deal with a book and also help him in the process. Isn't life all about unique selling points? I make a mental note to find him later and ask. Before I close the laptop down I decide to reply to TJ's mum having spent a few weeks considering what I'll say . . .

Dear Mary,

I know you're heartbroken and the world will never be the same without TJ in it. I know this, because I feel the very same as you. If you need someone to blame, then go ahead and blame me. I have strong shoulders and I'll willingly wear that burden so I don't tarnish TJ's memory and argue with his beloved mum. But before I let it all go, I wanted to tell you how your actions made me feel, as you pointed out how mine made you feel.

Yes, I drove TJ off into the sunset, as per his wishes. Yes, I agreed when he said he didn't want any more medical intervention aside from pain relief – what could I do, Mary? I railed, I screamed, I begged, but all that did was steal the light from his eyes, so I had to do what he wanted. And I'd do it again too.

And yes, if he was asleep when you or anyone called, I didn't rouse him. You didn't either when we came home. You said he needed the rest. We both knew he had no fight left.

If anything, Mary, you should be happy that he had a wife who loved him as much as I did and who, despite my own wishes for him, went along with his. It was his life, his choice, and what could I do but allow him to choose how it would end?

It broke my heart when he refused more treatment. It almost killed me knowing there was no hope, but for TJ's sake I reined it in so his last memories of his time on earth weren't all of me sobbing and shouting at the sky, pleading with a god I don't know to let my husband stay. I would have swapped places with TJ in a second. He was bound to do great things here and I still can't understand why. Why him? He had so much to give.

After he left, you cut me from your life as if I was nothing to you. You were like a mother to me so you can imagine how devastated I felt. Suddenly the phone went unanswered, the front door remained closed. Of course, I escaped. Who wouldn't? What was left for me there, but sadness?

So, excuse me, Mary if I ask for your forgiveness in exchange for mine but I think I'm damn well owed it. Don't you? Don't forget I lost the love of my life, my entire reason for being too.

Aria xxx

* * *

We've come up with a plan. Aria's bought this rusty old van and we're off to the Lake District. I've always wanted to see it and if I don't go now there will be no time left. This thing is aggressive and there's nothing they can do. My family have insisted I start treatment, begged, cajoled and pleaded. But the treatment won't kill it, so what's the point? It'll make me ill and reduce the quality time I have with Aria so I've said no, much to their disappointment. But Aria understands. She knows I have to do this my way. End my life on my terms. So off we go . . . in a little campervan where we can cuddle in the cool nights before I have to let her go . . .

And here I am in the same little van, in a foreign country, living my best version of life without TJ. He'd be proud of me, I think, for continuing the journey. Following the open road and never putting roots down. He loved his job as a teacher, and was especially passionate about helping disabled kids reach their full potential. He got so much joy out of seeing developmentally delayed students set a goal and go for it. He used to come home and tell me about his students and how proud he was that they never gave up. That's why his family had been so shocked that he wouldn't even try treatment, TJ wasn't the giving up sort. But he knew the facts and he was never going to look at 'the thing' with rose-coloured glasses. It had been an impossible time and looking back I'm almost breathless wondering how I managed to get through it knowing I was going to lose to him but trying so desperately to be enough for him in those final weeks.

* * *

A couple of days later we're soaking up the French sunshine at the Bordeaux Wine, Food and Literature festival. Vans line one side of the park and little pop-up tents face us on the other side. My mouth waters at the scent of so many types of food. On my first lap around the grounds I try buttery garlic snails much to Rosie's disgust. They are delicious, but I do have to close my mind to the mental picture of the little slug.

'Oh, god no,' Rosie says, turning away hand over her mouth. 'I just can't. You're a disgrace, Aria.'

'Sorry!' I say, not sorry at all. If you could smell the divine garlicky butter in the air you'd cave in and try them too. I wink at the girl and say, '*Merci!*'

We amble on buying locally made butter, and a range of cheeses. 'I can't eat most of these anymore,' Rosie says, flicking to a page in her notebook that reads: Foods to avoid. And underneath in her elegant handwriting are far too many foods for a former Michelin-starred chef to stop partaking in.

'Pregnancy is such a minefield! It's a wonder any children are born. You can't have this; you can't do that. It's like the mother guilt starts at conception,' Rosie huffs.

'Don't let the patriarchy get you down. Just be sensible, you know how to do that inordinately well.'

She blows out a breath. 'Yeah, you're right. When it comes to safety, who knows better than me?'

'No one . . . so relax into it and soak it up, Rosie. This is a really special time. Your body is growing a tiny human!'

'And the tiny human wants food! I need a baguette so I can basically eat my body weight in that salty French butter!'

'An impromptu picnic, why not? Anything else take your fancy?'

'We may as well check out the charcuterie pop-up, though I'm sure that's not allowed either. Maybe olives will curtail the cravings. Although I'm sure they're not actually cravings they're just an excuse to eat . . .'

'Roll with it,' I say. My mouth waters picturing all the cured meats on offer. 'Let's have a look. Maybe they have some rotisserie chicken, that's allowed, I'm sure, as long as it's fresh.'

Back at my van, I spread our feast out on the table and hunt high and low for a knife sharp enough to cut the crusty bread. 'Just tear it,' Rosie says then she insists I have her share of wine that a French viticulturist from across the park gifted us. If this is how the French live every day, I want in.

But I pretend to be sensible and say, 'I've got to get through the madness of a festival. I can't be seen with red wine for lipstick.'

'Why not? It hasn't stopped you before.'

I fill the glass and tip it to her in a salute. 'True and I suppose I'm only appreciating the spoils of Bordeaux.'

She nods solemnly. 'They'd be offended if you didn't. Who comes to Bordeaux and doesn't drink Bordeaux?'

'You just like saying Bordeaux.'

'*Bordeaux.*'

We eat in companionable silence, delighting in every home-made morsel. On the long list of things I love about France, their enthusiasm for what they eat is at the top. Not only do they love eating, but their food is produced locally, methods discussed dissected and passed down the line traditionally. Nothing is ever just a tomato, or just a wedge of cheese. They want you to know about growing conditions, family recipes, and I love that delight in the everyday food they consume. Food is revered here, meals times savoured. There's no dashing about with a sandwich in hand. Meals are taken at the table, with friends and family and enjoyed over a lengthy amount of time – and wine is always on offer, otherwise what's the point?

I unwrap the wedge of blue cheese we bought and only wish Rosie could sample it. It's her favourite but a no-go for pregnancy.

'You've got a customer,' Rosie says. 'I'd better make myself scarce.'

Rosie hasn't opened up her teashop since we left Blois. The smells of some types of food send her over the edge and she's decided to take a few more days off and see if her stomach settles. She's feeling more energetic, so hopefully it won't be long until she can eat a proper meal and not have to worry about what might make her ill. It's so strange to see Rosie eating dry toast and crackers, because she loves cooking and pouring her heart and soul into every dish.

'Stay,' I say. 'They can fit in here too.'

She doesn't say a word but I know what she's thinking.

'Well, if we breathe in.'

So it's a tight squeeze? I can't say no to any books, and I usually buy them as I go. It's been a little trickier to replenish my stock in France, but not impossible. Tomorrow I'm off to another car boot sale where a lot of English books are on offer for virtually nothing. They should tide me over for the French Riviera leg and not hurt the coffers too badly. Plus who doesn't love car boot sales? I'll probably come back with a box full of things I don't need and a head shake from Rosie.

'*Bonjour*,' I say to the newcomer, a girl in her mid-twenties, who gives off a bookworm vibe by the way she eyes up novels as if choosing what *not* to take to narrow it down.

'*Bonjour*,' the tall girl says. 'You have an impressive collection.'

'*Merci*! I can't say no when I go on book-buying sprees, even with the lack of space.'

'It must be hard to sell them too.'

I smile. 'Yes, always.'

She takes her time and searches every rickety shelf, making a pile of books to take that is so high I begin to worry how she'll carry them all. Rosie puts the kettle on to boil but stops suddenly, hand going to her mouth. 'Excuse me,' she says and dashes outside back to the safety of Poppy. I wonder if the scent of blue cheese is too much for her delicate belly.

'What's wrong with her?' the girl asks in that direct French fashion.

I debate with what to say, but it's not as if it's a secret now.

'She's pregnant – morning sickness comes and goes at all hours of the day.'

The girl nods. 'It must be hard for her travelling like this.'

'It is at the moment, but it'll pass. Once you get the travel bug the thought of living inside four walls is a depressing one. I don't think she'll ever go back to that life, despite what she feels like now.'

She arches a brow. 'You make this lifestyle seem very romantic. But I'm sure there's times where you still feel lost, *non*?'

'Literally and figuratively!' I laugh. 'But that's just life, right?'

With a flick of her long mane of dark hair she says, 'Right. And you get to spend your days admiring views like this and reading. Maybe *I'm* choosing the wrong path?' She smiles. I'm not sure what the pull is but I seem to earn strangers' confidences in the Little Bookshop of Happy Ever After. Maybe it's the warm cosy vibe of the van, the comfort of being surrounded by books. Whatever it is, people often tend to confide in me, probably knowing I'll be moving on soon and their secrets are safe with me.

I contemplate the newcomer and wonder what she means about the wrong path. Love? Isn't it what drives us all? But I stick to what I know for now. 'As long as you read you can escape anywhere though. You can travel around the world; all from the comfort of your own home.'

'My boyfriend says I spend too long reading.'

Aha, and there it is. I bite my tongue to stop the words escaping but crafty little things slip out anyway, 'You might need a new boyfriend. That would be a deal breaker for me . . .' *Spends too long reading*, is there such a beast!?

Laughter escapes her. 'You know, I've been thinking just the same.'

'Does he not read?' *Could it be possible?*

She shakes her head. 'No, he does not! He spends hours at the gym staring at himself in the mirror. We're so different.'

'But opposites attract?' But I'm not convinced. A man who says his girlfriend spends too long reading sends alarm bells ringing but maybe that's the bookworm in me. I can't be impartial to such a thing.

'Maybe we're too opposite. How do you know when you're settling for someone or if you're trying to compromise?'

I motion for her to sit down at the little book table. She folds her lithe frame into the small spot and slicks her long black hair over a shoulder while I finish making tea and hand her a mug.

'When I'm confused about my love life . . .' *What love life, Aria?* ' . . . I put myself in the shoes of a heroine and think: what would they do? Is this just an obstacle I have to climb to reach greener pastures or is this a deal breaker? Does that make sense?'

She grins. 'That makes a lot of sense actually.'

'So if you think like that, what does your heart tell you?'

Through the rising steam of her tea, she contemplates. 'I think he's not the one for me and I'm settling for second best hoping he'll change, and he probably feels the same way, but we're stuck in a rut and don't want to hurt each other by speaking the truth.'

'Love is so hard, but when the right guy comes along you'll know it.'

'And until then I've got my books.'

'A holiday in *Romancelandia*.' I smile.

She lifts a shoulder. 'What better place to be if I'm waiting for Mr Right for a while since Mr Right Now isn't working out so well. What about you, do you have a hero who goes on these grand adventures with you?'

I fix my eyes on hers. 'I did have once, but he . . . passed away. So now it's just me.'

'I'm sorry to hear that. When did he die?'

I blow out a breath. 'Almost three years ago.' Look at me being open and honest with people. It feels strangely refreshing not to pretend my life is one big road-tripping party on wheels. 'And I promised him I'd never love anyone again.'

'So you bury yourself in books?' She tilts her head as if trying to read me, my story.

'It's starting to feel that way, like I'm drowning in my own sorrows. At the time I thought I'd never be capable of loving anyone else, but now I'm not so sure, but a promise is a promise.'

A frown mars her smooth forehead. 'Did he agree with you?'

'No, he told me I'd fall in love again, he could "see" it. But he was heavily medicated at the time.' Why am I confiding so much to this stranger? *Because the entire world is in love! Because it feels right!* Maybe the magic of the Little Bookshop of Happy Ever After is working on me too?

'Medicated or no, he wouldn't say such a thing if he didn't mean it,' she says gently, her French accent more pronounced as we delve into sadder topics.

I cluck my tongue. 'But what if no one ever lives up to him? I mean, how can they?'

With a shake of her head she says, 'But what if they do, but in a different way? No one will replace him, they'll just take up another piece of your heart.'

I consider it.

We sip our tea in silence, both lost to the thought of what might be . . .

Aria Summers finds that being self-exiled to the land of singledom is not all it's cracked up to be. Her loneliness is ever present being surrounded by loved-up couples aplenty who are all moving on swiftly with their lives. Marriages are being proposed, babies are being made and Aria suddenly feels a little left behind . . . but she made a promise to her husband and who rescinds a promise to a dead man? She vows to stay true but what if Cupid has other ideas . . .?

* * *

'I'm going into town to hunt out all the glorious *bibliothèques* and bookshops, do you want to join me?' I ask Rosie who holds a cold compress to the back of her neck in an effort to cool down. French libraries are next level, a home for books that more resemble a grand chateau with their rich wooden shelves and antique furniture. So different to the stark libraries back home.

'I'd love to, Aria but I don't feel up to it. I'm sorry!' It's hard seeing Rosie so sick. I want to help her more but don't have the first clue how. Dr Google says lots of rest and relaxation is key, so I figure with us noisy nomads out of her hair she can at least nap in peace.

'Don't be sorry. I'll spend the entire day getting lost in dusty stacks of books so it's probably better you stay here and rest up. Message me if you need anything, I'll find Wi-Fi in town.'

'I will. Enjoy.'

I head into Bordeaux in my van, taking in the old town which is so different to Rouen and Blois but equally beautiful. These towns all have their own historical charm and I fall in love with them as I go. Bordeaux has a plethora of bookshops and libraries and I'm determined to visit as many as I can. The French love their literature, they revere writers and artists so much that they're worshipped, even those long dead.

I find a place to park and head to *Librairie Mollat* on rue Vital-Charles. According to my guidebook it's the oldest independent bookshop in France and is also one of the biggest. Inside is a brightly lit, book lover's wonderland and I relish the fact I have plenty of time on my hands to explore.

There's something about French books; they whisper about secret worlds in a language I don't understand but want to try and decipher. My search continues and I find a photographic book about Château de la Brède, a gothic castle where famous French philosopher Montesquieu wrote his books. 'Ah . . .' a man in a linen trouser suit appears. 'You found it.'

'Sorry?' I say and take a look behind me to make sure he's not talking to someone else.

'Have you visited the chateau yet?' He speaks as if we're old friends, and it's quite disarming.

'No, not yet.'

'You must.' He speaks perfect English with only a slight French inflection. 'It's only twenty-five kilometres from here.'

'Then I must.' And I wonder if it is on Rosie's list of haunted chateaux to avoid. From the photographs inside the book, it definitely dives off that vibe!

He smiles. 'You sell books?'

'How did you know?'

'I can sense a like-minded soul.'

I give him a wide smile. 'I'd have picked it on you too.'

'*Oui*. We know these things.' He taps his nose as if it's a secret we share. 'I hope you enjoy your time in Bordeaux.'

'*Merci*.' I smile as he walks away, charmed by such an interaction. Back to the shelves, I hunt out the English section and see if a book jumps out that I can gift to Jonathan. As soon as I see the famous title I grin. *Vagabond* by Collette. A story about Renée, artist and dancer who lives the wandering life and must choose between that and the man she has feelings for. It strikes me how similar it is to our lives, yet he's the creative and I'm the wanderer. Perhaps I'll buy two copies . . .

After I leave, with a spring in my step that only book buying can do, I head back to my van and make my way to the chateau.

I almost drive into a tree as the beauty of the place completely distracts me. There's a moat, a real-life moat! I park up and head inside and take the tour, stopping longest in what was the library room. It has a stunning curved ceiling made of chestnut wood and the room has that particular perfume of old books, a sort of yesteryear scent that makes me want to curl in front of a fire and do what I do best. Read.

After a long day I drive back to camp, and I find myself so mired in loneliness it quite steals the breath from my lungs. It strikes me I had no one to share my day with. No one to gasp over books beside, no one to traipse through the chateau with, and no one to sit with me now over a pot of tea and biscuits and plan tomorrow. I miss that.

In my van I curl up with the ghost of my husband and read.

The Lake District is what I imagine heaven must be like, and I'll know soon enough. I try to hide my pain from Aria but she senses it. My body hurts, and my heart is broken for what I'm losing: life with this beautiful book nymph. So I switch my thinking around. Our time together may be over soon but the best things can't last forever, that's what makes them so special. I know I've loved her with every breath and I'll love her with the very last one too.

Chapter Twenty

Bordeaux

We pack up and ready ourselves for the drive to the South of France the following day. Rosie's schedule has us leaving at precisely 9 a.m. tomorrow, so I spend the afternoon pottering about in the Little Bookshop van, stashing away loose books for the drive ahead, Taking note of what I need to reorder and what I can discount to move on.

I join a game of soccer on the sprawling green lawn before getting annoyed that the Italian guys are so much quicker than me. 'I'll give you the ball for a kiss,' Guido says, smiling as he toes the ball towards me.

'Sure,' I say, waiting for him to wander over. When he does I pretend to lean in and when he closes his eyes ready for the smooch, I quickly kick the ball away and run after it laughing.

'You tricked me!' He grins.

'You hot-blooded Italians, all you ever think about is kissing!'

Laurent pipes up, 'It's called *French* kissing for a reason, it's not called Italian kissing, is it?'

I shake my head; these sorts of cultural debates can go on for hours. I leave the boys to it and find a more sedate way to pass

158

the afternoon. Bingo with Dede and his gang from Indonesia is just the ticket. They're on a break from the cruise ship they work on and are revelling in van life, squished together in one van. They pull out tents at night and sleep like the dead, the noise of the campgrounds not a bother to the young guys. They have the biggest smiles and are always laughing and joking. Once I lose a few rounds of bingo I say my goodbyes and promise to come and find them before we leave for good. Who knows, maybe I'll run into them on a cruise one day? I hope so, I'm going to miss their beaming faces.

Bordeaux has been a blast but the beach calls and Rosie is intent on following her pre-planned route. Over summer there's a lot of events in the French Riviera we can pop-up in and Max has gotten approval for us which eases the usual bureaucratic paperwork headache. It will take the pressure off if we can bank some much-needed funds too.

Night falls as we sit by the fire. The nomads are coupled together listening to Max strum a guitar while someone croons a love song. I feel like I've stumbled into a real-life *Love Island* and didn't get the memo! There is not one solitary figure in the group aside from me. And for one tiny moment I wish that Tori was around so at least I wouldn't be so obviously the only singleton. Who knows where she is, I haven't seen much of her of late. A good thing . . .

Violetta and Laurent are a mess of arms and legs as they entwine themselves together. Lorenzo sits with Gaia in his lap. Rosie is next to Max, staring dreamily into his love heart eyes. And about six million other couples are in various states of *conscious coupling*.

It's as if there's some kind of magic in the air but I'm immune to it. Space is what I need. Surely there's other people out there without a significant other, I just need to find them.

I tap Rosie on the knee. 'I'm going to take a wander into town and grab a drink.'

A line appears between her eyes. 'I've got drinks, what do you want?'

'It's OK,' I reassure her. 'I just want to stretch the ol' legs.'

She slides the blanket off her lap. 'I'll come with you.'

I slide it back on. 'No, no, you stay here. I'm just going to meander.'

'OK,' she says, and I note the relief in her eyes. She's still so tired and is counting down the days until she feels more energized.

In town a small wine bar called *Cancan Bordeaux* catches my eye. It's got a cool saffron-hued laidback vibe and is just what I need tonight. It's bookish for a bar, with old, wrinkled leather chairs and a wall of books stacked in disorderly piles – the perfect space for me to while away some time.

I take a small table in the back and plan to drink a few glasses of vin rouge and feel sorry for myself. So what if everyone's shacked up? Some people would say I had the most envious life, wouldn't they? Free and in control of my own destiny.

A glass of red appears and I thank the bartender. An elderly gentleman comes over and sits beside me, nodding a hello. He's wearing a suit that has seen better days, but makes him look smart nonetheless. Please god don't let him ask me on a date. He is old enough to be my grandfather and I will probably say yes since the entire planet is in love! The bar is empty so maybe he's lonely just like me?

'Why aren't you out with all the others?' I'm surprised when he speaks in a cockney English accent.

'Which others?'

He points in the direction of the busier end of town. 'At the party down at the campsite.'

'Oh. I wanted to get away from them for a while.'

He takes a sip of wine. 'So you are one of those nomadic folk?'

'Guilty. I'm the single one. The cat lady.' OK, I don't have cats, but I really should. Lots of them that can alert Rosie when

I finally keel over and die at a hundred, still the only unattached one in the group.

'I don't know about no cats, but seems to me like you're a little sad. I could be wrong, I often am.'

I sigh. 'Is it that obvious?'

'You're slumped over your glass like a bar fly, as if you've got all the troubles in the world. Now what would they be? A trouble shared is a trouble halved or some nonsense like that.'

I manage a half laugh. 'Well, all my friends are basically having hot, passionate young people sex, while I'm alone reading by candlelight, eating ice cream straight from the tub.'

'And what's wrong with that? If I could still eat ice cream, I'd eat it straight from the tub.'

'You can't eat ice cream?' What a tragedy. An injustice!

'I'm so old my nerves are on the outside of my body these days, I can't eat *anything* the way I used to.'

The description makes me laugh. 'I wouldn't go that far.'

'It's true. But I can still quaff a few of these' – he points to his glass of red wine – 'every night so that's something. As for the hot, passionate young people sex, I wouldn't know about that, can't remember that far back, but surely you've got men lining up?'

'Just how many wines have you had?' I say half seriously.

'Not enough.'

'No, there's no men, there's no line, except the ones appearing on my face as I age disgracefully.'

'That's the spirit.' He gently nudges me shoulder to shoulder. 'What brings you to Bordeaux?'

'The name's Neville. I'm here with my grandson, one last hurrah, you know, before my toes curl up and I leave this mortal coil.'

This strange elderly gent has a dry sense of humour and I like him a lot. 'I'm Aria. So where is this grandson of yours?'

'He's over there.' He nods to the bar where I see another man in a suit, his back to me . . . but I would recognize that body anywhere.

My jaw drops. Jonathan must have been to the loo or something because I didn't notice him when I walked in. But how adorable is it that Jonathan has asked his grandfather to join his book tour! It's exactly the kind of thing TJ would have done, and not for the first time I think the two men would have really liked each other. There's a lot of similarities in the way they put others first with their big, empathetic hearts but it's more than that too. They remind me of each other, but I can't quite put my finger on why – or am I just dreaming up such a thing?

Neville pipes up, 'Maybe you can have hot, passionate young people sex with him?'

'Pop! Wash your mouth out!' Jonathan looks downright scandalized as he walks over, wine bottle in hand. 'Aria, what a nice surprise.'

My heart skips a beat and I'm sure I'm blushing.

'And I'm sorry,' Jonathan says, his cheeks flushed. 'I'm not sure what's got into him.'

I give him a wide smile. 'No, no, it was me who suggested it, not him.'

When Jonathan's mouth falls open I have to retrace our dialogue until I realize he thinks either A: I propositioned his Pop or B: I want hot, passionate young people sex with anyone who offers. Both not ideal.

'I meant, erm . . . it was just a joke we were making. No one is having any sex with anyone.'

'What a darn shame.' Neville laughs. 'Problems of today's youth could be fixed with—'

Jonathan plonks a hand over his Pop's mouth. 'You can see I get my uh – imagination from Neville here.'

I grin. 'Ah, he's the best. You're lucky to have him.'

He sits beside Neville and stares into my eyes, which renders me mute. 'Very lucky. Pop thought he'd join me for the Bordeaux book events but I lost him sometime soon after we arrived.'

'All that talk about books,' he says, his eyes rolling upwards. 'Sends me to sleep after a while.'

Jonathan grins. 'As you can see, he's my *biggest* supporter.'

'And then there's the fans, hanging off him like he's Kenny Rogers, I feel like showing them the pictures where he's sucking his thumb and throwing the world's biggest tantrum, and it wasn't that long ago if you get my drift.'

'And he's my most *loyal* confidante, keeps me humble.'

I laugh at their rapport and the jokes that bounce between them.

'Well, I needed to see it for myself. His mother's always going on about Jonathan this, Jonathan that and he was never around, you know? Back in the day that meant they were in the service of Her Majesty. It was suspicious like and I would have bet money he was in prison. In fact I did bet and so to avoid paying up here I am.'

'Here we are.'

Neville winks at me and downs the rest of his wine. 'I'd better leave you young folk to it. The days of me falling asleep at the bar are long over.'

I stand and give him a loose hug. 'It was nice to meet you, Neville. I hope you enjoy your last hurrah.'

'All the better for meeting you, my dear.'

'I'll walk you back to the hotel,' Jonathan says.

Neville put a hand to Jon's shoulder to sit him back down. 'I'm a big boy, and I can find my own way. Don't you go leaving this pretty little thing on her lonesome or you'll come back and find her married to someone else.'

I shake my head and laugh. We give him a wave as he walks heartbreakingly slowly from the bar.

'He's such a character,' I say. Mary pops into my mind and the way she changed almost overnight after TJ's death, her once proud upright posture gone overnight, replaced by stooped shoulders as if her sadness actually weighed her down.

'He sure is. He's always been that way. When he said he wanted to come with me on tour, I wasn't sure if he'd have the stamina but he has. He's been out walking every day seeing the sights, and ends the evening with a few glasses of red. Jokes aside, it's been wonderful to share this special time with him. He's not doing so well health-wise, he won't elaborate of course, but says this is his last holiday and he's going to go out with a bang. I hope he's wrong, I hope he's got years left, but Pop isn't one to exaggerate, he's the tell-like-it-is sort.'

It strikes me that like TJ, Neville is living out the end part of his life exactly how he means to, no matter the physical cost to him. And he chose to spend that time with Jonathan which says a lot about what kind of grandson he must be. 'I hope he's wrong too and he gets the chance to heckle you at many more book tours.'

'Let's drink to that.' We clink glasses and now the jokes are over and awkwardness descends.

'How is Rosie going? Max told me the good news.'

I smile, conjuring Rosie's face when I catch her staring into the ether, the realization she'll soon be a mother. It's such a lovely mental picture of my very best friend. 'Still feeling queasy at every turn, but she's reconciled herself to motherhood now and is enjoying the prospect of a baby on the horizon.'

'It must have been a shock for them, but I can see them as parents somehow.'

'Yes, can you imagine it for Rosie? A shock for anyone but for Rosie that's next level scary. They'll make it work, Max comes from a family who grew up on the road so I'm sure they'll adapt fast.'

'They'll be OK, they have each other. What about you, do you want to have children?'

The question takes me by surprise as it did when Rosie asked me not so long ago. Just how does everyone expect me to make these mythical children? A spell, an incantation? 'I did, once. What about you?'

'Yes, definitely. I look forward to long summers abroad, building sandcastles, ice creams melting down sticky arms.'

'And what about the kids, what will they be doing?' Deflect with humour, don't picture his future Kit Harrington-esque beautiful dark-haired children with lovely manners and shiny white teeth and sandy feet.

He laughs and the sound makes my stomach flip. He's so lovely. He's the geeky book boy who grew into his looks, the stuff of every bibliophile's dream with his dark locks and smooth beautiful skin. He really is the epitome of modern-day hero. Sensitive, caring, reliable and destined to be around in five, ten, twenty years.

'Oh!' I say remembering his gift and the one I have for him. 'Weird book-sniffer dude, thank you so much for the book. You're right it did smell good! But I'm conflicted about the character Madame Bovary. I'm not sure I like her, although I liked the story itself very much.'

'It's such a strange tale in that respect. You want her to have her heart's desires but she is always dissatisfied. And to what end? It's always interesting to me to read about love that doesn't work, when I've just written about love that does. True love, not the pretence of love for gain of some sort.'

I love his love of reading! It's so rare to find someone to untangle books with. 'Exactly. It's not love she's interested in really, is it? It's her base desires coupled with a materialistic bent. And . . .' I stop myself before I fall into an hour-long monologue. 'Anyway, I found you this' – I rummage in my bag for his gift – 'and thought it you might like it.'

He gives me a wide smile when he sees it and takes a great big sniff. 'Smells delightful, like adventure is just on the horizon!'

'Doesn't it?' I say grinning.

He gives me a wide smile. 'Collette. *The Vagabond*. Why do I feel this is going to remind me of you?'

I lift a shoulder and smile back. 'OK, I bought two copies because I thought the same! We can read them together and . . .' Oh god. 'I mean at the same time, and compare notes.'

'Reading them together sounds wonderful. Thank you for thinking of me.'

'Just returning the favour.'

We sit in an awkward silence for some baffling reason. We're just two bookworms talking books, what's there to be worried about? But I know, of course I do. Jonathan is the whole package, the looks, the personality, the bookworm, the big heart, the wistful soul. And I want to act, I do, but I don't know if I can. If I should.

'I lost you there for a second,' he says, touching my elbow to bring me back from reverie.

'Sorry, I . . . lost my train of thought.' And then it comes crashing back when Tori of all people swishes into the bar as if she's on a catwalk, flicks her shampoo commercial hair and narrows in on us. Dammit. *Not now!*

When she sees me her face drops. 'Are you OK?' I ask. 'You look like the curried egg sandwich you ate at lunch is on its way back up.'

She throws me a dark look and retorts, 'Aria, I didn't know you were coming to our date. Third wheel *is* your style though.' She laughs it off as a joke and leans past me, to kiss Jonathan's cheek.

'Date?' I turn to him and catch something indecipherable in his eyes. He didn't want me to know! 'Well, don't let me stop you. I was just leaving.' I take an unladylike chug of my wine and then throw down some euros on the table. 'Enjoy, won't you?'

I'm up and out of the bar fast, because for some tragic reason I feel like I might cry and the last person I want to witness that is Tori. Surely they're not dating? Tori has the personality of a wet tea towel! But what it does make me realize is that what I'm feeling for Jonathan is real and what do I do about it? What would TJ think? And what about Mary? She'd despise me even more if she knew I was even considering such a thing. I go back to my van and for once I don't read, I fall into a deep sleep and have murky dreams.

166

Chapter Twenty-One

Bordeaux to Nice

We say goodbye to Otto and Jörg as they play pétanque in the cool of the morning. The German Van Lifers are heading back the way we came so we've swapped suggestions about campsites and where to find the cheapest beer. We've only known the guys for a brief amount of time but they've stolen into our hearts already. They're just young lads taking life as it comes and enjoying time on the road and what that has to offer with whatever funds they can muster by finding jobs fruit picking or labouring. One day soon they'll go home and settle down for university and this will all be a distant but fond memory.

The remaining nomads are still snoozing but most are following the same direction as us and will catch up eventually. We wish the lads well and offer the same assurances that one day soon we will meet again, when I know most likely we will not. It always makes me a little sombre, leaving people behind like that.

As I chug along the beautiful Mediterranean coastline my heart is heavy. So what if Tori and Jonathan had a date? I'm not the couple police. And I told him in no uncertain terms I wasn't moving on from TJ, so why would he wait? But it hurts and I'm conflicted. I need to debrief with Rosie and make sense of it all.

Max pulls into a car park. There's a sign with directions for a short walk to the best vantage point to view the Mediterranean Sea. I indicate to follow him and see that Rosie is not far behind. It's been a long lonely drive despite the beauty so I'm keen to get out and be with my friends. Tori chose to stay a few extra days in Bordeaux and I can imagine why. Jealousy roils in my gut at the fact she'll probably meet Pop Neville too and joke around with him like I did. It annoys me for some reason. When I catch myself thinking like this, I know I'm losing the plot. Note to self: crank the music for long solitary drives so you don't drive off a cliff when you can't see the road for your tears! Maybe I'll adopt a rescue puppy. I can speak baby language to my fur baby and I'll know I'll never be alone.

A rescue animal is not a *bad* idea. Or I could stop at shelters and hug *all* the doggies and then I can go back to my van and feed my *food* baby . . .

Aria Summers yearns for love but has sworn off it and so the days became longer and lonelier than ever before. It doesn't help that the entire population of the planet has coupled up and driven off into the sunset leaving Aria driving never-ending roads to nowheresville. She pictures herself in the future, surrounded by rescue dogs, maybe the odd bird or two, and a tub of ice cream so big she can dunk her head in it when things got bad—

Wait—

Aria Summers has sworn off love but that doesn't mean she can't have a happy fulfilling life, right? She has great friends, a unique lifestyle and the chance to change it all if only she listens to her heart. She needs a sign, something from above to guide her and show her the way, but doesn't that sort of thing only happen in fairy tales? Writer Jonathan knows a thing or two about love stories, he pens them after all. Perhaps he's the man who might rewrite Aria's story if only she gives him a chance . . . ?

'Urgh,' I say to no one. 'Now I'm officially talking to myself? Could things get any worse?'

'Boo!' Rosie startles me, pushing her face in the window. 'Who are you talking to?'

Hand on heart I say, 'My future rescue puppy.'

She frowns. 'Well, ah, it's good to prepare I suppose. Get out of the car, I've got a raspberry milkshake with your name on it.'

'You're feeling better?'

'I am. Must be the Mediterranean air.'

I ease out of the van and take in the view while I stretch the kinks out of my body. The light here is different somehow, the sky is bluer. Can that be? Even the air seems fresher, like it could cure all that ails. I take a deep breath in and feel it flow through me, awakening my senses.

'I never want to leave,' I say.

'We say that everywhere.'

Max wanders over, flicking his mane of leonine hair. 'Are you girls OK if I head into town? I need to refuel and grab some supplies for the street festival before we go to site.'

Rosie gives him a quick hug. 'We're fine.'

Max roars off in his van and we take chairs from the back of Poppy and set them up to get the best vista of the sea. While Rosie sorts the milkshakes, I slap together a couple of cheese sandwiches and slather on her homemade mustard pickles.

We hand each other the spoils and sit down. 'So before you take a mouthful of food, tell me why you hid in your van all morning,' she says.

'*Moi?*'

'Don't try to out-Rosie Rosie.'

'I . . . don't . . . know . . . what—'

'The robot, really?'

I laugh. 'OK, well last night I was just minding my own business when . . .' I fill her in on the story, meeting dashing old Neville, and Jonathan, and then Tori's Hollywoodesque entrance.

'She said I'm used to being the third wheel! I tell you what, I *so* wanted to throw my glass of red wine at her shampoo commercial hair.'

She bites down on her lip but a smile escapes. We've both had visions of revenge against Tori but haven't wanted to stoop to her level . . . or something. I'd be quite happy to, but Rosie advises me against it. 'Why would she be so mean?'

'That's just Tori,' I say. 'You don't see the half of it.'

Rosie lets out a long sigh. 'Yeah, I know I don't, she's not brave enough to fall foul of Max all of a sudden, that's the only reason she's all sweetness and light to me. Don't worry, I know she's as slippery as an eel under all that. I haven't forgotten.' Rosie takes a slurp of her milkshake. 'Nectar from the gods.'

I follow suit. 'Fresh raspberries?'

'Fresh *organic* raspberries.'

'Picked by the silky soft fingers of innocents?'

She laughs. 'Yes. But back to matters at hand. I'm surprised they set up a date. Jonathan's not one to jump from one girl to the other, far as I can tell. I'm sure she's making it up.'

'Well, he didn't exactly jump from me, since there was no me.'

'OK, let's pretend for the sake of your own pride there was no you and him, but remember he told Max he was smitten with you, why would he say that and then go on a date with Tori? It doesn't make sense.'

I shrug. 'I don't know!'

'Why don't you ask him?' she says.

'As if! What if he *is* dating her?'

'Then you'll say wow, congratulations, I hope you'll be very happy together.'

'OK, what if he says he's *not* dating her, then I'm really stuck.'

'Why do you care who he's with? Aren't you up there in your spinster castle with your friendly bats for company?'

I sigh and sip my milkshake to buy time. 'I don't know why.

I've been asking myself the same thing the entire drive here. It doesn't make any sense, and yet . . .'

'If I didn't know better, I'd say you might be falling for the guy, horrible monster that he is.'

'But what if he's dating *Tori*? I don't think I could even consider someone who wants to date Tori.'

'Aha!' she says triumphantly. 'You do admit to considering dating again, yes?'

'No. Yes. No. I don't know.'

She cocks her head and gives me her mummy look, the soul-searching *I know you* gaze that is surely going to stop her child in their tracks when she pulls it out of her arsenal. 'What's happening with the diary? Is TJ helping?'

It's like she summons him. My beautiful gap-toothed husband with his impossibly curly hair and lovely rangy body.

I close my eyes against the sun. The fresh spring air ruffles my tresses and sends a rash of goose bumps down the length of me almost as if someone is giving me a sign they're still around. The thought makes me smile and catches Rosie's attention. 'What?'

'Nothing.'

'Why are you smiling like a loon?'

Will I sound crazy telling her that from the afterlife my dead husband is ruffling my hair with the French breeze just as I'm talking about potentially allowing myself to have feelings about another man? 'I just get this sense sometimes . . .' My words dry up, suddenly I feel exposed saying such private thoughts even to Rosie.

'That TJ is here?'

Holy mother of metaphors. 'How did you guess that?'

She shrugs. 'Sometimes I just know things.'

'It's crazy, right? Ever since reading his diary it's like he's close, off in the distance just out of sight. I used to pretend he was in the next room, you know, so I wouldn't have to face reality.

But this, this has been different. This feels real, somehow. Like I magicked him here.'

Her gaze drops in contemplation. 'Not crazy. When my dad died I had this little bird that would fly to my flat window every morning before work. For six weeks this bird sat outside my window twittering away as I got ready for work. I knew it was a sign from my dad that he was OK, that I had to try and move on with my life, you know all that guilt and turmoil I carried about it. One day it wasn't there, and I felt so sad, but also that it was sort of a message to pull my socks up and try and live in the present, not be so mired in the past.'

'That's so beautiful, Rosie.'

'It reminds me of this. Have you thought maybe TJ is trying to tell you something?'

I have, and I've wished so hard for it. 'Like what?'

She shrugs. 'That's for you to work out.'

'It's almost like he's coming to say goodbye . . . like it's time to move on.' I whisper, because the words hurt as they fall from my lips. 'The diary brings him right back to the fore, but in the gentlest of ways, as though he's giving me permission, almost ordering me to start again. God, he was amazing. I know everyone says that about someone they've lost, but he really was. I wish you could have met him.'

She throws an arm around me and gives me a squish. 'I feel like I have from what you've told me about him. He was the best and there's no forgetting that. But it's a process, Aria. And the only way to get through it is to keep moving forward.'

'Yeah, but you can't outrun grief. That's a major design flaw with it.'

'So why try and outrun it? Why not face it head on?'

I wait a beat. 'That makes a lot of sense, Rosie. But it's easier to run than to face up to the fact he's not coming back and I'm *not* OK with that.'

She throws an arm over my shoulder. 'It's OK to feel like that.

It's really unfair that he died so young but that doesn't mean you'll ever forget him or what you had, even if a new man comes along. It's not like TJ suddenly gets wiped from your memory.'

The turquoise sea and the gentle rolling of the waves slow my heart rate down and I find a level of peace I haven't had for so long, especially discussing such weighty subjects as these. 'Yeah, deep down I know all of this but I made a promise to him that I'd never love anyone again and here I am just three years later considering it. I can't help feeling bad about it. And I wonder if our roles were reversed would he do the same, and I don't think he would.'

Her big eyes widen. 'You can't know that. You've read *a million* love stories, Aria, you know love can change the world, so why not let a little into yours?'

'I'm getting there, Rosie. I'm definitely getting there. I'm coming to the end of the diary entries and I know it doesn't have a happy ending, but maybe there'll be some sort of closure for me.' My eyes are glassy, knowing that whatever comes next is going to hurt but maybe it's all part of the healing process and I have to face it.

After an hour more in the blissful beauty of the French Riviera, we pack up and head to the campsite to meet Max. I have a lot to think about . . .

* * *

We arrive at the campsite which is jam packed with Van Lifers and holidaying families who are following the sun. There's a trampoline set into the ground and the child in me runs straight over to it.

'Oh my god, Aria,' Rosie admonishes. 'You're sure to break a leg on that death trap and then how will you drive?'

I laugh as I *boing* high into the sky, drawing annoyed faces from the kids who topple over in my wake. 'With the other leg!' I call out to Rosie.

She shakes her head and goes back into the safe confines of Poppy. Violetta turns up and runs over. 'Wheee!' she says joining me, telling the children something in rapid-fire French that has them scuttling away.

'What did you say to them?' I ask.

'That there's a troll underneath and if they haven't paid the fee they'll get gobbled up!'

I gasp. 'You're so mean!'

'But we have the trampoline to ourselves, *non*?'

I shake my head and steel myself for someone's *papa* or *maman* to come storming over. We're always getting into tiny spots of bother as Van Lifers. Usually it's about the level of noise, and the fact we keep odd hours.

We attempt somersaults and tuck jumps until we can't catch our breath and sure enough a man with fire in his eyes comes stomping in our direction. Violetta grabs my hand, 'Time to go, *chérie*!'

It's so absurd that I laugh as she drags me along. 'Time for a drink?'

'Yes,' I say out of breath.

'Let's take a walk down the *Promenade des Anglais*. I have a friend who works in a bar there . . .' Code for: drinks will be cheap. We head down the main beach in Nice, the prettiest expanse with palm trees running the seven-kilometre promenade. With the rustic ochre and pastel buildings as a backdrop it's got an almost Havana vibe about it.

'Laurent is leaving after the summer,' she says breezily.

'Leaving to where?'

'Australia.'

'Without you?'

She turns to me and smiles. '*Oui*. It was only ever going to be a summer romance.'

'Aren't you sad?' She looks anything but.

She shrugs. 'Not really. We've still got a few weeks left. And then I will find another lover for the autumn.'

My eyes go wide and she laughs.

'I told you, Aria, I'm not like you. I believe in love but I'm also happy to let it go. Why have one man when you can have them all.'

'I'm scandalized.'

'No, you're British.'

I laugh. 'As long as you're happy.'

It occurs to me that true love means different things to different people. Maybe Violetta's true love is herself and that means letting go when the time is right.

* * *

We have to leave this nirvana soon. I can feel my life ebbing away. The cocktail of painkillers is having adverse effects and I don't want Aria to have to handle it all on her own. She's asked if we can return home and of course I said yes. I'm not leaving the van though. That way I can pretend we're still here, still have time. One day soon I'll drift off with her in my heart, in my mind, the memory of the lake a stunning backdrop to her beautiful face, and that's what I'll take with me when I go. She's on edge, she's trying so hard to be strong for me, but I can see it. I can feel it. If I could wish for one thing it would be that she doesn't put her life on hold after I've gone. I want that laugh of hers to reverberate around earth, I want her to follow her heart, and have big dreams and do what makes her happy. Everyone wants to be in Aria's spotlight so I hope she doesn't let it dim. I wish she'd promise me that . . .

Remembering that day turns my heart inside out and I let out a sob. The diary falls from my hands and a picture slides to the floor. I bend to pick it up; it's me in half profile in the back of the van at the Lake District. I hadn't been aware of TJ taking it – I must've been so lost in thought. You can see the grief in the planes and lines on my face. He knew, it was right there to see and yet, I thought I'd hidden it so well. I'd pretended we were just going home and medical help would buy us another year, two even. Maybe forever if the miracle I wished for was answered.

But I knew in my heart we only had weeks to go, if that. And I was trying to summon the courage to look into his eyes and let him go. But I couldn't. I didn't want to admit it to him that I knew it was almost time. I wanted to join him. I wanted to leave this life if he wasn't in it. But I knew he'd hate that more than anything. So I did the next best thing and made him a promise that I'd never love anyone else. And he told me it'd break his heart if I stopped living. One of us had to live and soak up the joy of life and I'd been chosen. How I screamed, railed at the universe to take me instead.

Chapter Twenty-Two

Nice

Nice is a romance novel come to life, from the bright blue of the skies to the pebbles on the sand and the gorgeous olive-skinned Europeans with barely any clothes on. I sit on a deck chair on a patch of road outside of the Little Bookshop van, sunglasses on, novel in hand only taking the occasional break to people watch and imagine what brings them here. I feel downright translucent compared to them with my lily-white complexion so I'm hoping the sun turns me a shade browner and not *Scarlet Letter* red.

While I'm slathered in sun cream, the locals are like descended gods, slick with some kind of oil that highlights their every muscle or curve. Life is so unfair. I'm straight up and down, nary a curve in sight. The only muscles that are marginally defined are my biceps from holding books upright for lengthy periods of time and I'm quite proud of that actually.

We're set up for a street party and from my perch I can see the beach and it's calling me in a seductive manner: *take a swim, Aria.* I'd be crazy not to. The party officially opens in an hour so I have plenty of time to take my white body and throw it into the ocean.

Swimsuit on, I grab a towel, sling it over my shoulder and then go to Rosie's van and find her at the helm in her happy place. The kitchen. The fresh Med air has done wonders for her. 'What are you making?'

She looks up with a smile. 'I've made popsicles – guava and lime mojito, pina colada, and key lime pie.'

I'm thirsty just thinking of them in this heat. 'I'll have one of each when they're set.'

'Of course. Where are you off to? The water?' she says it as if I'm about to jump into the burning pits of hell.

'Yes, want to join me?'

Wiping her hands on a tea towel she says, 'I'll fry, I'll turn lobster out there. I'll—'

'Put some sun cream on, mama bear, and get moving.'

Rosie is even paler than me if that's possible. She has white-blonde hair and the most glorious luminous skin. We stand out among all the beautiful bronzed bodies, that's for sure.

'OK, but let me lather up first. Max is out surfing somewhere, his life in the hands of the deep blue sea.'

'We're all going to survive, Rosie.'

She crosses her fingers as if she's not quite sure we will and goes behind the partition to her bedroom. While I wait for her I check out the vans parked lengthways up the street. Looks like it's going to be a fabulous multicultural festival which are my favourite kind. There's a Greek food van called Taramasalata and their sign advertises a plate-smashing event in the afternoon. Further on there's TaiDin Dumplings, Creole Soul Food, Croquembouche . . . just to name a few. I can see I'm going to roll out of the street festival a little heavier than I came.

'Looks like we've got a lot of research to do,' Rosie says, joining me and pointing to the pop-up food vans.

'I love how you call it research and not gorging ourselves silly on cuisines from around the world.'

'Well, everyone knows the calories don't count if it's research.'

'Of course. And you're eating for two.'

'So I'll have double then.'

We hit the sand and take off our flip flops. 'Where's Tori?' I ask, suddenly realizing I still haven't seen hide nor hair of her a week later, and wondering if that's a good or bad thing.

Rosie spreads her towel out and dithers with a response. 'Well . . .'

'Come on, Rosie just say it.'

'She sent me a Facebook message, but you know you can't believe everything Tori says.'

'They're dating. He's proposed. I'm now the sole resident of Alone town, population: one. They're going to buy a mansion in LA and make beautiful tanned babies and have a nursery full of ethically sourced wooden toys.'

Rosie throws her head back and laughs. 'Well, not exactly. She says they went on the one date, the one *you* were actually present for and since then she hasn't seen much of him because he's very busy doing author-y things, but she's there for the times he needs to unwind. And I told her that's complete BS and if she's going to stir the pot for no reason other than to make trouble then she won't be invited to wander with us ever again.'

'You told her that?' Rosie avoids confrontation like it's exercise. Her two pet hates.

'Yes.'

'And what did she say?'

'She said sorry. She said she had feelings for him but so far they haven't been reciprocated.'

Wow. A quiet thrill runs through me but I'm about to melt in the heat. 'Let's get wet.'

I race into the water and dive in, while Rosie edges uncertainly on the shore as if the ocean might swallow her whole. 'Come on, Rosie. It's water, not acid!'

She rolls her eyes and takes delicate steps forward, gasping when the cold water hits her ankles. 'I have to acclimatize myself.'

'I'll be out before you get in!'

Eventually she wades in, gasping and panting like a little old lady. 'Golly, this is why I'm more of a "feet firmly on the earth" type.'

'It'll be good for you, good for the baby.'

She gives me a wide smile joining me in the deep. 'It's all falling into place. I don't want to jinx myself but I finally feel like I belong, that I'm right where I'm meant to be. Even being pregnant and so far from home doesn't seem as problematic as it once would have. Can you imagine if this happened to me a year ago? It would have been breakdown city central.'

'You've come such a long way, Rosie.'

She nods, fanning her arms in the water. 'Golly, I had so many hang-ups, still have plenty of course, but they don't hold me so far back.'

'Van life, the tonic for all that ails.'

'It truly is. What if I'd stayed in London once Callum had moved on with Khloe with a K?'

On her birthday a year previous, Rosie's husband Callum announced he was leaving her for the Chef de Partie at the restaurant he worked at. Not long after, when the divorce was still pending, she found out Khloe was pregnant with Callum's baby, the baby conceived when he was *still* married and living with Rosie. It had hit her hard and she escaped into van life mostly because she had no other option and she wanted space from the toxicity of the London culinary scene where everyone knew everyone's business, including Rosie's. But then Max happened and Callum was just a slimy step on the road to true love.

'I don't think you were ever destined for that life, Rosie. It never made you happy.'

'No, it didn't. That was a *shell* of a life. And now I have Max, and I wonder what I ever saw in Callum.'

'Gotta kiss a few frogs first, right?'

She grins. 'Right.'

I kick my legs and lie on my back and float, eyes closed to the sun. 'You know, Rosie, I've been thinking, maybe being alone the rest of my life isn't such a good thing. I feel myself retreating further into my books, spending more time alone. I worry one day I'll look up and there'll be no one there. Just me, the van and the endless view . . .'

Rosie turns on her back and floats beside me. 'I can see why you made the promise to TJ. It must have been such a devastating time but even he didn't want that for you. You're the bubbliest person I know, and for you to be alone goes against the grain of who you are.'

'It wasn't just the promise I made though, it was his last words.'

'What were they?'

'*Until we meet again.*'

She's silent for a while. 'So you think that if you move on, whatever chance you have of connecting on some other realm will disappear?'

I bite down on my bottom lip while I consider a response. 'It sounds ridiculous out loud. But yes. What if that means I forfeit the chance to be with him again, in the next life, in the afterlife, any life . . .'

'It doesn't work that way, surely, Aria. He's your first, spell-binding love and if there's anything after here, he will be there waiting for you, just like he promised.'

'It's silly, but at the time it felt like the truth, like he had this incredible *knowing*, and it's what I hold on to, it's what got me through that first impossible year.'

Rosie's teeny tiny belly sits just out the water. She's only three months along. I imagine the size it will grow to and picture her in other bodies of water as we go, her bump getting bigger and bigger.

'Aria, there are no hard and fast rules about grief and the stages after that. When I say listen to your heart I mean *listen* to it. It's not just a cliché, it's an actual step in the next process

181

of grief. You know there's stages – anger, denial and all of that – but then there's the steps, like when you gave away TJ's clothes, and stopped looking at his picture a hundred times a day, before moving it into a drawer so it didn't hurt so much. Eventually once all those steps are trudged up, the next one can be opening your heart to someone new.'

I hadn't thought about it like that.

'Let some sunshine in to what's been a really dark place for you. But you can only do that if you stop letting guilt drive you.'

'I just don't know how to stop feeling that guilt, though, Rosie, that's the thing.'

She swirls her arms out and back in. 'Trust me, I know that feeling well. When my dad died I was consumed by it, right up until Mai did that bizarre and beautiful face reading thing where I thought she was possibly trying to steal my soul. I realized that guilt was only holding *me* back and it had absolutely no effect on *anything* else. Guilt wasn't going to bring my dad back so I could make amends, get that forgiveness I so needed. So what's the point of holding on to something so toxic and letting that drive your life? There's no point to it, especially if the person is long gone from here. And I *had* something to feel guilty about. You don't. There's a big difference.'

'TJ really wanted me to make a new life without him. Marriage, the kids, the whole shebang. That's pretty amazing considering.'

'You need to hold on to that when you feel that guilt creep back.'

I take a deep breath in and exhale all the angst and feel lighter, floating in the Mediterranean like some kind of sea goddess. 'I'm so lonely all the time. I'm literally surrounded by *happy campers* and I've got a million friends yet I feel so alone. I want to change that.'

'Then what's stopping you?'

'Well, his mum for one. Imagine how much she'd hate me if she found out I'd moved on with someone else?'

'I'm sure she'd be happy for you, Aria. You need to lay it all out on the line for her. Emails won't do – you need to speak on the phone. I think you need to give her more credit. Remember at one time you were like a daughter to her.'

And I was. We took girl trips away together, just me and Mary. We had once-a-month movie dates.

'Yeah, I just can't help worrying.' I kick my legs to stand.

'So what are you waiting for? Speak to Mary and then tell Jonathan how you feel.'

After an age I say, 'So I guess I have to tell him that maybe . . . what? I don't even know how to do this anymore. I'm broken!'

'You're not broken, you're rusty.'

We laugh and swim back to shore.

* * *

The street festival is a jovial affair. There's a band playing reggae music on the sun-bleached street, and how can you not be happy when there's reggae music? It's one of life's simple joys. I dance along as I help Rosie serve – her popsicles are a crowd favourite.

When we've caught up with the queue I go back to the Little Bookshop and help customers find long-forgotten books, getting dusty alongside happy sun-pinked tourists who've flocked to the outdoor party. The vibe is incredible and it's a reminder why we live this way. I never want the day to end.

A few hours later, the crowds thin so Rosie and I take our chance to try some international cuisines. Taramasalata and the vans closest to us are still pumping orders so we continue on until we find a quieter vendor. Thai-tan has a range of spicy food on offer so I fill up on larb as we walk while Rosie hunts for something with less chilli.

'What are you craving?' I ask.

'You won't believe it.'

'Pickles?' Isn't that the usual thing women crave for some inexplicable reason.

'No.'

'Erm . . . a big juicy cheeseburger?'

'No. I'm craving one of Max's bloody live forever smoothies or whatever he calls those abominations.'

'No!'

She drops her head in mock shame. 'I know. Why, why, WHY!'

'The baby has half his DNA, that's why!'

With a slap to the forehead she says, 'Yes, of course, I didn't think of that.'

Rosie has protested every step of the way with Max's foodie lifestyle; how the two have dinner together is beyond me when they eat the very opposite. If Rosie had to give up sugar, I think she'd give up air, whereas Max finds it the work of the devil. *Ah, sweet love.*

'Well, let's go get you some food that you can drink, eh?'

'What's to become of me?' she moans holding her head in her hands while I stop and buy a tray of mini tacos. 'Extra jalapeño, please.' The vendor heaps a mound on top and I give him my thanks. 'Without you sharing, I'm eating double. You sure I can't tempt you into a bite of one of these bad boys?'

She glances at the stuffed tacos and her face turns puce.

'That's a definitive no then.'

'I hope I'm not turning . . . *vegan!*'

I laugh at poor Rosie's expression. As a former Michelin-starred chef, she finds the whole premise of veganism problematic and yet her diet is distinctly heading that way. 'Blame it on the baby. Once little Indigo pops out I'm taking you to a Tex Mex joint and we are going to eat our body weight in bad food, topped off with a decadent dessert so huge you'll need two spoons to go at it.'

'OK, I'll mark it in my calendar.'

Max is doing a roaring trade; it's the right weather for fresh icy juices. When he sees Rosie he stops everything and comes around the counter to hug her and check she's OK. *Oh, that man!*

'Yes, all good, I'm just a little hungry.'

Max's eyes glisten with triumph but he doesn't rub it in. 'Do you want the ginger smoothie to settle your stomach?' His expression turns tender.

'Fine.'

She will never get over having to admit Max's food is medicinal. Ever.

He blitzes up a smoothie with all sorts of wholesome nutrients and explains to the waiting crowd that Rosie is the love of his life and they're expecting their first child. The patrons oooh and ahhh collectively while Rosie turns the same colour as the strawberries he adds to the concoction.

'I've made plans to catch up with a friend at Répondre in Monaco tonight. Will you both join me?'

'Sure,' I say. 'What do you think, Rosie?' She takes the proffered smoothie.

'Yes, good plan. It'll be good to get out now that I'm feeling better. Let's head back to work to replenish the coffers so we can spend it on overpriced drinks.' I laugh at her honesty. The French Riviera is known for its glamour and that comes at a high price, including the be-seen-at bars and clubs that we usually tend to avoid.

She gives Max a chaste kiss on the cheek but he grabs her into a bear hug and holds her for an age. I love that Max wears his heart on his sleeve and isn't afraid to show it.

'So tonight,' Rosie says, 'what should we wear?'

'It's only a casual drink with one of Max's friends, right?' Surely Max wouldn't choose a place that we need to dress to impress?

She is focused on her smoothie, mixing it with her paper straw. 'Yeah, but we're in Nice, we have to look *nice*.'

'I see what you did there but we're going to Monaco.' Where royalty live!

'OK, well stop by when you're done for the day while we wait for the road to open and we can discuss the merits of the two dresses I own, yeah?'

She laughs. 'You'd look good in a potato sack.'

'Too itchy.'

She laughs and it's not until I'm back at the Little Bookshop that I wonder if there's not more to this innocent catch-up drink than I gave them credit for . . .

Chapter Twenty-Three

Nice

As the street festival winds down, I check my Facebook page for any orders. Laurent's five-euro poems have gone down a treat, matched with Mills and Boon book bundles, I've been selling them quicker than he can write them. I'm happy to see another handful of orders, so I make note of the books to find and send Laurent a message to let him know I need more poems. Once I've caught up on the work side of things, I check my personal Facebook page and find nothing from Jonathan, but see a message from Lulu and Leo to Rosie and me. I click on the message:

Hello from sunny Cornwall, darlings!

We've got some fabulous news and wanted to share it with our favourites before splashing it about on the world wide web for all and sundry to read. Yesterday Leo and I ELOPED and it was the most beautiful day confessing our love with only the bright orb of the sun as our witness. Sure, it's soon, but when you meet your cosmic soul mate there's no point waiting, right? We hope you like our very first picture of Mr & Mrs StarTribe. Yes, we've chosen ourselves a new surname that reflects us as people . . . now to apply to deed poll. How mundane but these things must done if one is to have a passport . . .

Has the entire world been infected by Instalove? They're a spiritual match made in heaven and we did envisage this but how time is racing on for those in the land of *l'amour*.

The photo highlights their radiant, blooming faces and my heart tugs. You can tell just by their smiles how truly in love they are, with their whole happy, hippy lives ahead of them.

There's a tap on the door and Rosie peeks in as she hears my squeal. 'What is it?'

I point to the message and she reads, gasps and puts her hands to her mouth. 'Already! Oh, put a fork in me, look how happy they are!' She promptly bursts into tears. 'Sorry, it's just—'

'It's OK, Rosie. I get it.'

She sniffles and snuffles and tries to compose herself. 'It's as if they are love personified, aren't they? I hope it lasts forever.' She stops. 'Oh, god, sorry, Aria, I didn't mean it like that. I just meant, I hope they always feel the same as they did yesterday . . .'

I rub her back. 'I know, so do I. It's OK.' And I really mean it. 'I hope their love spans decades and they get to grow old together, surrounded by a big family of StarTribes who grow their own food, attend full moon parties and never lose their sense of adventure.'

'The hormones, golly, one minute I'm laughing, the next I'm sobbing over the smallest things. We'll let their good news sink in before we reply. So what are you waiting for . . .? Show me this magnificent wardrobe of yours then.'

That's the thing about van life, there's not a whole lot of room, especially in this bibliophile paradise, hence things like clothes storage are on the bottom of my practicality list.

'Ta-da!' I say, pointing at two dresses draped on a coat hanger wedged between books. 'This little number I like to call "frolicking in a field of flowers".' I gesture to a flowy summery number adorned with yellow roses. 'And this of course needs no introduction being the obligatory little black dress suitable for any occasion.'

With a finger to her lips Rosie considers them as if I'm going to strut the red carpet at the Brit Awards, or something.

'Why the sudden interest in my sartorial taste?'

She tries to play the innocent but our Rosie is a hopeless liar. '*Moi?*'

'Cue the French . . . What is it, Rosie? Some blind date with an out-of-work trucker with a seventies-style moustache to get me back in the game?'

'Where do you come up with this stuff? Honestly.' She laughs. 'No, I'm trying to Frenchify us both, simple as that.'

'Nothing is ever as simple as that. Tell me the truth.'

She darts a glance at the floor and her arms stiffen.

'Bloody hell, Rosie, what is it? Not a blind date?'

'Of course not! Imagine the safety logistics of that – it would take me months to figure it all out.'

Folding my arms, I wait her out.

And I wait.

'Fine.' She sighs, loud and theatrically. 'Apparently Jonathan is going to be there.'

'So the friend we're having drinks with is Jonathan? Why the secrecy?'

She sighs. 'In case you bailed. But now I've bloody well told you so you can't bail.'

'I won't.'

'Promise?'

'Promise.'

'We'll just let off some steam, you with a tropical cocktail, me with a mocktail.'

'OK. So floaty floral dress it is?'

'Hell no. It's the mighty tighty LBD with a killer pair of heels.'

'You're incorrigible.'

'I try. We're ready to drive to the campsite if you are?'

'Ready as I'll ever be. I might just throw myself in the sea one last time.'

'OK, I'll finish tidying and we can leave in convoy.'

She leaves me with a peck on the cheek.

* * *

The campsite is a set on the side of a cliff with the most magnificent view of the water and blue skies that span for days. It's a tight, small camp, but we manage to squeeze in, probably due to Tori saving us a space. I guess my begrudging thanks are in order.

Hand over my eyes to stop the glare of sun, I find her sitting around a table with some nomads I've not met before. 'Thanks for saving us a spot.'

'Well, of course. Friends, aren't we?'

I can't discern any malice in her voice. Maybe she's learning to live a little more Zen?

'Yeah, friends.'

'Are you coming tonight?' she asks.

'For drinks, yeah.'

Her eyes sparkle with challenge. Maybe she hasn't done an about-face just yet. 'Brill, Jonathan's going to be there too. I haven't seen him in at *least* a day, so don't mind us, will you?'

'Mind you what?'

'You know.'

'Tori, can't you just be honest with yourself for one day? What do you get out of acting like this? There's nothing going on with you and Jonathan and there never was. I seriously don't understand why you alienate people by stirring up trouble, and for what?'

She double blinks in surprise but soon enough her eyes darken.

I continue, 'We're all offering a hand in friendship to you, Tori. You might want to think about what a real friend is.' With that I walk away, finished with her and the game-playing.

A long shower cools my blood. I get dressed, apply make-up and straighten my hair to a shine. Earrings on, great big chunky bracelets and I'm almost ready to go. Lastly, with an apology to my feet, I ease on my patent black heels that are so high I can almost see the Eiffel Tower from here.

There's a knock at the door and I say yeah as Tori pokes her head in. What now?

'Hey,' she says quietly. 'You look great.'

I narrow my eyes waiting for the punch line.

She laughs. 'I suppose that sounds insincere?'

'What can I do for you, Tori?'

She shrugs. 'I had a think about what you said, and I guess you're right. You know about the friendship thing. It's just . . . have you ever been so madly in love with someone and they don't even know you exist?'

I stand silent, not knowing where this is going. Is it musician Axel she claimed she couldn't live without, or Max or Jonathan she's set her sights on this time?

'Well, I have, and I can tell you it's no fun. I guess, I've acted like a brat in the sense that because I didn't get my own way – the boy that I loved – I tried to ease my heartache by latching on to the next man who came along, like Jonathan. Except he wasn't the slightest bit interested as you probably know.'

I nod. 'I know.'

'I have this horrible premonition I'm going to be alone my whole life and I acted like a fool. It's just I'm not like you and Rosie. I don't fit in, I never have. And I always seem to alienate people just like you said.'

'So why act the way you do?'

'Probably some kind of misguided defence mechanism. I've never had many friends and I thought van life would be the answer to that, but it's been just the same. Axel was the first guy I loved and my first real friend on the circuit, but even he left without any fanfare.'

'But you never told him how you felt.'

She squirms. 'I couldn't bear to be rejected by him.'

I sigh. 'Try being honest in future, Tori, not just with Axel but with everyone and I think you'll find things will change.'

'I'll try. Look, I'm really sorry if I messed things up alluding to all of that with Jonathan. He's so dreamy you can't hold it against me for trying, can you?'

'Again, it's an honesty thing, right? Making up a fake date is pretty sad, Tori.'

'I'm cringing just thinking about it.'

'Well, you're forgiven on one condition.'

Hope shines in her eyes, and for the first time ever it seems genuine. 'What?'

'You have to tell Axel how you feel and see what happens.'

'By text?'

'Sure.'

'What if he—'

I cut her off. 'What if he feels exactly the same?'

She grins. 'Wouldn't that be amazing?'

'Go do it now before you change your mind.'

She gives me a hug and dashes off. Tori is so young, so naive in many ways, and it feels good to forgive her for her actions that only served to make her look foolish.

After one last look in the mirror I go to Poppy and grab Rosie. 'Oh, wow, Aria. Golly. I don't know what to say!'

'Too much make-up?' We hardly ever get the chance to get dressed up so I've gone all out.

'No, not at all. You look like a catwalk model. I didn't realize that your legs go all the way up to your armpits. Hot tamale!'

I laugh. 'You look beautiful too.'

'Let's find Max and get this party started.'

We drive to the swanky area and park up a hilly street. I find it highly amusing that we're all dressed up yet practically fall out of an old rusty van that none of the millionaire residents in this area would ever dare set foot in.

At Répondre Max wraps a protective arm around Rosie and then throws the other around me making me smile. 'You're such a gentleman,' I say, thankful Max picks up on so many things most men wouldn't. I'm a little jittery but push the nerves away.

We order cocktails (Black Rose for me) and a mocktail (French Kiss) for Rosie and find a seating area big enough to fit us and our tardy friends.

Before long Tori arrives in a leopard-print strapless dress that could do with a few more inches in length but she gives me a friendly wave and I return the favour.

'I hope she doesn't drop anything,' Rosie says and laughs behind her hand.

Max's friends Camille and Lucas arrive and introductions are made. Again, I feel like the odd one out but Rosie sidles over and sits next to me, giving me a reassuring pat on the leg.

'God, this place is beautiful,' I say. 'I can see why all the fabulously wealthy people flock here.'

'No, it's because of tax exemptions. It's a right royal tax haven!' Rosie says. 'That's why they live here, not just because of the view.'

'Lucky doers.'

'Yeah, but imagine having to drive those corniches every day. No. Thank. You.'

The three corniches are these impossibly tight roads on the side of the cliffs with the best view of the Med. Tour buses barrel around them as if they're as wide as a highway which makes driving our vans on the other side a hair-raising experience. It's not so hard to imagine Grace Kelly fatally losing control on the Moyenne Corniche. The three corniches provide a heart-in-throat drive and none of us are keen to drive them again. 'Yeah, not the most fun I've had in the van, that's for sure.'

An hour or so later Jonathan arrives and I'm lulled by the view and the long day (and OK, the cocktail helped) and I wave to him natural as anything. As if I don't care. Because I don't.

He grins and it lights up his lovely author-y face. He's wearing his specs tonight and it gives him a bookish air that is hard to resist. But I must. At least for now.

'It's lovely to see you looking so bright again, Rosie. Pregnancy suits you.'

'It's a wonderful excuse to eat at all hours of the 'day now my stomach has settled.'

193

He laughs. 'And how are you, Aria?' I go to take a sip of my drink when he says, 'Had any hot, passionate young people sex yet?'

The cocktail duly leaves my mouth in an unladylike spurt and covers me and Jonathan's lower half.

'No, not yet,' I choke, trying to wipe my face while giving thanks my dress is not white. I take a napkin and dab uselessly at his chino clad legs. Unfortunately, he is wearing beige, now smeared blackberry in places. He waves me away as if it's no problem like he gets drinks spat at him all the time. 'What about you?'

'Not yet either.'

I stop dabbing as it's only spreading the stain and it also feels a little weird, his *naked* body is just under that fabric. 'Waiting for the right moment?' I ask with an arch of the brow.

'Waiting for the right girl.'

I raise a brow. 'Where's Pop?'

'He flew home after Bordeaux. It hasn't been the same without him.'

'I bet. How's he feeling?'

'Honestly he looks strong as an ox.'

'I'm glad to hear it.'

Jonathan's eyes lock with mine for an age but I know I can't act on my feelings, not yet.

An hour later, I stand and say my goodbyes. 'Why?' Rosie says. 'We can all leave together soon.'

'I'm zapped from today and one more cocktail and I'll be asleep.'

'Jonathan can drive you back, I'm sure.'

I don't give him a chance to respond.

'No, no, I'm all good, I'll grab an Uber. There's something I have to do actually.' I feel the truth in my words and I realize what's been stopping me from moving on, not just with relationships but with my whole life and I've got to fix it before any change is possible.

Chapter Twenty-Four

Nice

When TJ's family disowned me after he died, completely ghosted me as if I was someone so easy to let go, I didn't think I'd ever forgive them, especially Mary who I'd been so close to. TJ's dad had always been a cold fish, and with Mary leading the charge, he duly cut off contact with me while Mary inspired the rest of the family to do the same. When the first anniversary of TJ's death came around I reached out to them, hoping to share the heart-breaking day with people who'd understand, but they refused and then stopped answering the phone. I spent that day curled up in bed watching our wedding video on repeat, drowning my sorrows with red wine and then vodka. Not the healthiest way to reflect on the man who set my world on fire.

My biggest grapple had been what did I owe them after they way they'd treated me? But now I know. And I need to do what's right. Not only for TJ but for me too. It's time to make peace. I dial the familiar number, remembering when I'd call them just because.

'Hello?'

I take a deep breath. 'Hi Mary, it's me, Aria.'

There's a long silence before she says, 'Aria,' almost reverently.

'It's been such a long time.' I search her voice for reproach but there's none, instead she just sounds a little low, as if she's exhausted.

'Three years,' I say.

'Feels like a hundred.'

'Yeah.'

'I'm existing on autopilot.'

Goose bumps prickle my skin in recognition. 'It doesn't seem to get any easier like the books say.'

In some ways it gets harder because the longer you're alone the more you realize he's not coming back. It's not a nightmare you'll wake from. There's no deal you can make with god. There's nothing you can do.

He's gone forever and ever.

When she doesn't reply I say, 'Look, Mary, I wanted to clear the air between us. I . . .'

'I know, Aria. I do know. I'm sorry I haven't replied to your last email. You certainly gave me the talking-to I needed.'

I'd expected anger, stern words, not this . . .

She continues, 'I've been trying to find the right words, and they just won't come.' There's a long silence. 'I wasn't at my best back then, and I regret a lot of the things I said to you. Did to you. Trust me, I know I wasn't being fair. But part of me will always wonder if he'd still be here now if he'd at least *tried*. I don't think I can ever fully forgive that – taking that hope away – but I know it was his choice, I *do* know that now. It breaks my heart wondering what might have been, you know? And why you couldn't convince him to do what was right. I think about that every day. Every single day.'

'I understand,' I say, as my eyes go bright with tears. 'And Mary, if I thought the treatment would have worked, there's no way I'd have driven him away; you know that, right?' The prognosis had been dire; the oncologist didn't sugar-coat it. Treatment would have bought him a few more months, but to what end?

'I know. But I wanted my boy with me.'

The strong bonds of motherhood. Had I been insensitive to her needs? It's so hard to look back at that time and make any sense of how I could have pleased them both.

'I feel horrible about that, Mary. And he wanted to be with you all too. But he desperately wanted to see the Lake District, one last thing of beauty. He wanted that quiet to come to terms with facing the end of his life.' I swallow a lump in my throat, remembering his face, the pain and sadness in his eyes replaced by something greater, something miraculous. For one lonely moment I'd thought maybe it was a healing place and he'd soak up the vibe and return whole – cancer-free. I was willing to believe anything back then if only I could keep him. 'That place lit him up from within. The van was a godsend, I set him up so I could open the back doors as he lay there, just the mirrored lake for company.'

'He always wanted to see more of the world, and I see you're doing that for him,' she says, her voice raspy with tears.

I take a tissue from the box and dab at my eyes. 'I can't seem to settle, Mary. I don't know my place without him. There's days where I feel adrift as if I'll float away and it won't matter a damn. But I've made a really good friend in another nomad called Rosie; without her, I don't know where I'd be.'

'She sounds nice. You need a friend like that. I wish I had some answers, but one thing I do know is that you can't escape grief. It will chase you down, stand right behind you like your shadow, darting this way and that, just when you think you've dodged it. All you can do is move on. There's still time for you, Aria.'

I picture her as she was when she loved me as a daughter-in-law, her hair in a neat bob, rouged cheeks, and eyes brighter than her age suggested. But when I saw her last, the light had gone, and her cheeks were hollowed, she'd looked a decade older. I wonder if she's recovered or if death indelibly changes those who are left behind?

'Hear me out,' she continues. 'This is why I've struggled to return your email. It's hard to find the words to say what my heart feels and still be fair to my son. But I figure if the roles were reversed and TJ was here instead of you, I'd be having the same conversation with him. If you let grief win, you'll *never* find solace in this world. You'll have all these amazing opportunities that will pass you by. People will come into your life but if you're not open to them, you're going to end up alone, a withered shell of that sparkly, joyful girl who walked into my life all those years ago, nose pressed in a book even back then.'

'It's only been a couple of years, Mary, and I struggle with the thought of it all.'

'Three years, Aria. He'd want me to ask: Are you happy?'

Am I? There are days Rosie and I are doubled over clutching our bellies and howling with mirth. Or those times I'm sitting in her tea van eating a slice of cake the size of my head, delighting in every spoonful. But when night falls and I'm alone in my Little Bookshop van that's when it hits me anew and the darkness finds me again.

'I miss him so much,' I say, my voice breaking and the tears falling in earnest. 'There's no one like him and no one can ever live up to him.' Jonathan briefly pops into mind and I close my eyes against it.

'We all miss him. But it's what we do with our life now that matters.'

'I didn't expect we'd have this conversation,' I say.

She lets out a small laugh, a glorious sound and I can't help but smile. 'I've replayed our last argument over and over again, and I hate myself for it. You were going through just as much as me, and I didn't take it in to consideration. And cutting you off and all the awful things I did – he'd hate me for it. But I needed someone to blame, and I know that's not right. I'll always be upset he went away, but I can see why he wanted to go. I can see it was him driving the idea and you *as always* doing what you thought best for my boy. I'm really sorry, Aria, that we weren't there for you when you needed us most. I'll always be ashamed about that. I was just so angry and you were an easy target.'

The apology is enough for me. That we've made amends takes a weight off my shoulders. 'I'm sorry too, Mary, for the things I said and did but regrets are such a waste of energy. I'm so glad we talked.'

'Is there anyone in your life?'

I hesitate – it's TJ's mum after all – but I figure honesty is the best policy. 'There's an inkling of attraction with a guy called Jonathan. But I've had a hard time even thinking about someone new.'

'These things always sound so clichéd, but I know my boy and I know he'd have urged you to live your life fully, Aria, and that means being in love again, as impossible a notion as it is to contemplate.'

'I didn't expect you'd be encouraging me in that respect.'

She takes a moment to respond. 'He's not coming back, Aria. All we can do is make the most of what time we have left. For me, it's not so much, for you, it's an eternity.'

'Yeah.'

'What does the diary say about it?'

'You didn't read it?'

'No, I'd never break his trust like that. And I'm only sorry it's taken this long to send it.'

'Don't be sorry. To be honest, I don't think I could have handled it any sooner, I wasn't ready for it. It's full of little anecdotes and things he wants to do and see, and then it turns darker with the diagnosis and what he wanted me to do after he'd gone.'

'So why don't you respect his wishes and follow them?'

'Could it be so simple?' Why don't I stop running and listen to my husband's wishes for me just like I listened to his last wishes for himself?

'The diary is his last goodbye, Aria.' *Until we meet again.* 'All he wanted was to know you'd smile again, and you *promised* him that too, didn't you?'

'Yes, I did.' I'd totally forgotten about that. Smiling again seemed like an impossibility at the time.

'So make good on that promise.'

'I will, Mary. I promise I will.'

Chapter Twenty-Five

St Tropez

The next day we take a slow drive from Nice to St Tropez. The gang check in to a campsite perched on a cliff while I make some excuses and leave to be alone for a bit. I drive aimlessly for a while, until I realize what I must do. Windows down, the breeze whipping my hair back, I get some clarity for the task ahead.

I park and walk the *La Ponche* quarter until my feet hurt, and ruminate about life and love and everything in between. It feels good to be outside and pounding the cobblestones trying to make sense of things. What I've learned is there's no rule book, there's no one way to grieve and it doesn't diminish what TJ and I had if I entertain the thought of loving a new man. I'll always feel that spark of guilt, but that's OK, right? It just means my love for TJ is ever present. It's inside of me and it always will be. But I'm allowed to strive for happiness too.

From my bag I take the diary to read the last entry. I want to read it while I'm bathed in sunlight, not in the gloom of the van, so I make my way past the docked yachts to the beach and find a spot on the sand.

With one last look at the bright blue of sea before me I swallow a lump in my throat, and open it to the last passage. His hand-writing is jagged and messy, as though he didn't have much strength left. Taking a deep breath, I steel myself for this one last message and am surprised to find this one is written directly to me.

My darling girl, each breath brings me closer to the last I'll take so I want to leave you with this. If I had one wish, it would be that you enjoy every minute of the rest of your life. Don't second guess yourself. Follow your heart. Make mistakes. Drink all the wine and dance on tables (I can picture this already and it makes me smile). Hug a koala. Travel far and wide. Trust people based on instinct. And never, ever look back. Live outside of your comfort zone.

You've made my life on earth a joy and now it's time for you to start afresh. Do that for me. The road ahead for you is a long one, so make it count, my beautiful girl.

I love you more than words can say xxx

Tears run down my face as I sit and absorb the words. How I love that man. His generous heart, his loving soul.

He's right, and he's been right all along. Opening my heart again won't damage what we shared. But it might help to ease the pall of sadness that's plagued me since he left. My husband was always the clever one and I should have listened to him when he tried to tell me back in the Lake District. But I wasn't ready back then. The diary was misplaced for three years for very good reason and as strange as it sounds, I think TJ sent it to me when I needed it most and not one moment before.

I'm ready to love again. Or at least entertain the idea of it. And Jonathan is the man for me, the one I want to read side by side with and take long walks and discuss romcoms with, because whatever I pursue it will be have to be at a long, slow pace and if he's the right person then he will understand that. And somehow I think that he is. Whatever magic that is in play here has made me sure of that.

I kiss the diary once more and hug it to my chest. *Only parted until we meet again, TJ my love.* I wait for a butterfly or some other sign that he's here like you read in the books but none come and that's because he *is* here, he's with me in my heart, and my soul and he always will be. Already, I know I won't read this diary again. I'll put it in a special place but now it's time for me to say goodbye to that chapter of my life and start the next as per his wishes.

As I walk back to the van I marvel at so many happy faces, so many people in love and feel hopeful that soon I might be one of them too. I won't have to hide behind a smile anymore because it'll be real.

When I get back to the new campsite I find Rosie's van and park beside her. I knock on her door and fall in, the tears starting again.

She looks up alarmed. 'Are you OK?' Her gaze drops to the diary. 'Oh. You read the last passage?'

I nod.

'Sit, sit. I'll make some tea.'

I duly sit and wait for Rosie as she hurries to make tea and serves me a slice of cake so large it has its own postcode. 'How do you feel?' she asks.

I go on to explain what it said and how I felt, that I'd let him go with his final words. 'Only because I know it's not forever,' I say. 'TJ will be waiting for me just like he promised, and he will always be in my heart. And it's OK to want to chase happiness.'

'Of course it is. And hasn't everyone told you so, but you had to believe it for yourself.'

I sip my tea trying to get a handle on all these emotions fluttering inside. 'Yeah, I guess it's that long, lonely process that only you can go through. It sort of feels like I'm coming out the other side and isn't it bright and sunshiny here?'

'I'm so happy for you. You deserve to start again, Aria, whatever that entails.' She gives me a big hug and holds me while I cry.

'I need to find Jonathan and tell him how I feel and see if there's anything there.'

'He's in St Tropez too.'

'I thought the tour finished yesterday?'

'It did. He's writing his next great novel from some rental he's got for the rest of the summer. Methinks it's just because he knows we're in the French Riviera for the season, but what would I know?'

'Really?'

'Really. And there's more news.'

I put a hand to my heart. 'What is it? I don't think I can handle much more today.'

'Musician Axel has arrived and declared his undying love for Tori.'

'He has? Wow, that's fabulous news.'

Her mouth hangs open and I realize I haven't had time to tell her about Tori's confession and subsequent apology.

'What?'

'I hope she finds happiness, I truly do.'

Rosie raises a brow. 'You're being really good, forgiving her after what she's done.'

I shrug and fill Rosie in about the deal Tori and I made. 'And she was the catalyst in some respects. If I hadn't felt threatened when she was around Jonathan, I probably wouldn't have acted at all. But when it looked as though I might lose him before I even had him, well that got my attention.'

'So, now we've nutted out all the plot holes in your life, what are we going to do about the romance?'

'I'm going to find Jonathan and invite him for drinks in the van and then I'll see how I feel . . .'

'Wow, fancy.'

'Well that's the best gauge of character, right? Whether he can handle my book babies.'

'And your clutter?'

'Hush your mouth!'

She grins. 'I love your book babies no matter how much dust coats them.'

'You're a liar.'

'I am.'

'OK, so what do I wear and where do I find him?'

'Show me your casual wardrobe,' she says, heading next door to my van. 'I think it's best you're just your beautiful carefree self, going forward.'

'You mean dishevelled, don't you?'

She grins. 'Yes. Bookworm sprite.'

We settle on an outfit of cut-off denim shorts and a T-shirt that reads: *I have no shelf control*. 'OK, maybe I'll text him: ISBN thinking about you . . .?'

She stares at me like I've lost the plot. 'Have you been sniffing books again? What's gotten into you?' Rosie pinches the bridge of her nose as if my lame jokes inspire headaches. Which to be fair, they probably do.

'I *do* feel like I've been on a book-sniffing bender!'

She shakes her head. 'Bookworms, a breed of their own.'

'You know it.'

'I do know it.'

'I see what you're doing.'

'What?'

'Delaying the inevitable.'

Shoot. 'OK, I suddenly feel nervous. What if he thinks I've got too much baggage? What if—'

'What if the sky falls down? We'll deal with it as it comes and you're only inviting him over for a drink, right? Keep it simple. Get dressed and don't text, that's such a cop-out. Go to his villa and invite him over.' She jots down his address on a slip of paper.

I nod. 'God, OK. You make it sound so easy.'

'It's not bloody easy, but nothing that's worth it ever is.'

'Fine.'

She kisses me on the cheek and her eyes well up. 'Oh god. I have to go before the waterworks begin in earnest. But I am proud of you, Aria!' She leaves with a sob and one hand on her belly.

I throw myself in the shower and then wear my everyday clothes, not bothering with my hair or make-up. Instead I spritz on perfume and take my phone for directions and go.

Aria Summers thought that putting love on the backburner was a sure-fire way to honour the love of her life, TJ. But when a long-lost diary appears, it turns every belief Aria had about life, love and friendship upside down. Can she follow her heart and the open road, or is love a one-way street?

Chapter Twenty-Six

St Tropez

I get to his villa which is more like a castle etched into the hillside and something royalty would stay at. It stops me in my tracks. I'm not a fancy sort who swans around with Côte d'Azur millionaires, and for a second my enthusiasm falters. Then I centre myself. I'm not marrying the man, I'm merely going to invite him for a drink. He might not be the swan-around type either. He hasn't appeared that way so far. And I know not to judge a book by its cover, right?

I ring the bell and wait. After an age the door opens and he's standing there in denim jeans and a T-shirt that reads: *ISBN thinking about you.* It's all I can do not to double over and lose it laughing. If this isn't a sign then I don't know what is.

'I like your shirt,' we say in unison.

'Thank you.' Again together which provokes laughter.

'So,' I say, 'Rosie told me you're holed-up here for the summer?'

He grins, his lovely author eyes crinkling like stars. 'Got the mad urge to write, you know how it is.'

'I get it. So hey, would you like to come to my van for drinks tonight? If you can bear to leave your writing, I know what it's like to be in the zone. Well from a reader's perspective.'

'I'm ready now, if you are?'

Holy mother of the bride. 'I was born ready.' Oh god, Rosie turns robot and I turn stupid. 'That's to say, no time like the present.'

He grins and it lights up his handsome face that is all so new to me. His eyes are dark blue, flecked with hazel and I wonder if I'll be the one who loves this man next?

'Give me two secs,' he says and dashes back inside. When he returns, he's holding a bottle of fancy champagne and a book.

'Are we celebrating?' I ask.

'Why not?'

'And the book?'

He gives me a sheepish look. 'I don't like to go anywhere without one.'

I laugh. 'You're my people, no two ways about it.'

'I feel the same about you, Aria.'

I'm not sure what to say so I walk to my van and he falls into step beside me. 'I was hoping you'd give an author talk for the Little Bookshop of Happy Ever After. I know you're much in demand and everything but it would just be an intimate affair.' *Maybe just us . . .*

'I'd love to.'

'Well, come and visit and see what you think first.' Jonathan has spent time in the van before, way back when, but things have changed and I want to make sure we gel before I make any decisions about moving forward. My book babies are my life, and the way I live will never change. I'm not sure how a man could even slide into life with me, but I suppose if it's meant to be, it will be.

He hops in the van and we chug along the sun-drenched streets of St Tropez, squinting against the sunlight that fills the cabin. Silence falls and I think we both can gauge nervousness in one another.

'What's the book?' I say falling back to the safety of what I know.

'*After He Left.*'

My eyebrows shoot up. 'You've read the whole series?' A series based on a woman losing the love of her life one wet, wintry day when he stepped out to save a child who slipped on the road.

He blushes. 'I wanted . . . I wanted to know more about how that sort of tragedy felt.'

It dawns on me. He is doing his own version of research into grief, the same way I would through fiction. 'And what did you learn?'

The campsite comes into view, and I see a bunch of nomads in a circle having a continental picnic. My favourite kind where everyone contributes whatever they can and it's usually a feast of weird and wonderful from so many cultures.

'What did I learn?' he asks, rubbing at his chin. 'Well, the person left behind will never really be the same but they'll grow, become a new version of themselves, slightly battered and bruised but stronger for it, even if they can't recognize that in themselves.'

'Huh.' I park my van and shut off the engine, contemplating it all. 'You're right, I think.' I want to lighten the mood so I give him a dazzling smile, and say, 'Would you like to attend your first nomad picnic? You might have to throw your fancy champagne into the mix, that's all.'

'I'd love nothing more.'

I get the feeling Jonathan is the patient sort and happy to give new experiences a go too. Maybe it's the writer in him and this is all potential book fodder or maybe like me he's trying to open up to the world more, step from the shadows of loneliness. And I can appreciate that, while I've spent the last three years hiding behind laughter or a smile when inside I was dying, he lived behind his words and used them to blot out the world.

I jump from the van and close the door with a bang. Jonathan takes the champagne and his book and joins me. We approach the group and Rosie stands and gives me a hug. She's changed into a long flowy dress that highlights her tiny bourgeoning baby bump.

'Hey Jonathan, how are you? Want to join us for a picnic?'

'I'd love to,' he says and hands her the champagne. 'I promise there'll be another one of these just as soon as you're able to toast to the health of the baby.'

She laughs and kisses his cheek. 'That sounds mighty fine. Until then I'll stick with my kale juice or whatever it is Max insists I drink.'

'Come and sit,' I say and laugh because it all feels a bit culty. My nerves jangle as if I'm bringing a new member to the tribe, which I suppose I am.

Max wanders over, guitar in hand, singing Michael Jackson's 'Earth Song' quietly to himself. When he notices Jonathan he abruptly stops. 'Hey, man! How's things?' He shakes his hand.

'Great, got myself that little villa and have settled in for the summer. You'll have to come and visit.'

Little villa? How humble the man is! It's a bloody great big castle that overlooks the sea. Is he downplaying it for our sake or does he truly not care about such things? I'm sure it's the latter and I get the feeling Jonathan would be just as happy in a little campervan, or is that wishful thinking . . .?

'Yeah, sure,' Max says. 'We're here for a couple of weeks, a month maybe. Rosie has an ultrasound coming up and a few appointments so we'd rather have a base for a while at least.'

'You guys can always come and stay with me.'

'Nah, man we'd get in the way of the writer at work. We're cool here. But we'll come and visit for sure.'

We sit on the velvety grass and I introduce Jonathan to the other Van Lifers, some like Violetta and Laurent who've been with us since Rouen (who he already knows, I remind myself), and others like Claude and Emily who we've only just met. Plates of food are passed around, from French cheeses, fresh bread to open cans of sardines and pungent anchovies. Packets of crisps, slices of sun-warmed tomato – it's anything goes.

'Excuse me,' I say and go to my van to grab something to add to the mix. All I can find is a gourmet box of chocolates from a local *chocolaterie*, so I give them up to the greater good and console myself that I still have Rosie on hand for any sweet treats I might crave.

Laurent plonks himself between me and Jonathan. 'How's the latest book doing? I see it advertised everywhere.'

'It's been my highest seller to date. I think there's something refreshing about writing romance, although my publisher took some convincing.'

I realize I haven't read his backlist yet and I'd just presumed they'd all been the same genre. 'What did you write before?'

'Thrillers. Espionage.'

My mouth falls open. Some Internet stalker I turned out to be. I'd been so distracted by his puppy photos I hadn't got much further than that. 'What? That seems so incongruous.' He has never struck me as the manly man sort, I can't see him writing explosions and tough burly characters somehow. To me, he's more poetical. Deep. The type of guy who writes about love and makes you rethink every notion you had.

He runs a hand through his hair. 'I know, but I had that brand built up over a decade of writing and it was hard to shy away from it. My publisher thought *The Quiet of Loneliness* would be the death knell for me but I had to write it, I felt the story in my bones, you know? I had to take the risk and write it, even if it damaged my career in the process.'

'Why take such a gamble?' I ask. 'Couldn't you have written *The Quiet of Loneliness* under a pseudonym?'

He's quiet for an age and everyone around me drops their gazes to the green of the grass. It's like they all know a secret and I struggle to make sense of what's going on.

'Well?' I ask, miffed at the change in the group.

He coughs, clearing his throat but bookworm extraordinaire that I am, I know that's a tactic to buy time to think of a response.

Rosie joins me and stares into my eyes like she's trying to hypnotize me. What am I missing here? She blinks rapidly and I start to worry she's had too much sun or something. With a long, weary sigh she says, 'Perhaps Jonathan wanted the book *widely* read.'

'Well, of course. Wouldn't every author?'

'Widely read by people who he *admires.*'

'Yeah?'

'People who are *voracious* readers . . .?'

I shoot her a blank look.

'Voracious *romance* readers. Who might have recognized his author picture on the back cover?'

Me? Is she referring to me?

'You wrote it for me?' I whisper, wishing that the bunch of sunburnt nomads were suddenly anywhere else but here.

If flushing were a sport, Jonathan would be a gold medallist. 'It was inspired by you. That time we met at the music festival.'

How could I not see it when it's so *obviously* us. A fictionalized version of us with our messy pasts. Now I know why I felt so confused at the author talk in Rouen, like the novel was speaking directly to me because it *was* speaking directly to me! I'd just been too closed off from the world and all it offered up to make sense of it.

'Wow, I didn't realize . . .'

'I hope you don't mind,' he says. 'I find inspiration everywhere but I've been endlessly intrigued by you.'

Endlessly intrigued.

'No, I don't mind. But how did you know about my past?' Of course it wasn't a direct retelling of my life but it had been similar enough with layers of loss and heartbreak.

'I didn't. I only found out about TJ when you told me. It came about because of the haunted look in your eyes. I knew there was more there so I expanded on it.'

I'm quite lost for words. It's probably one of the most romantic things anyone could do. Pen a love story about someone so she finally gets her happy-ever-after despite her tumultuous past. He hadn't sugar-coated it. He hadn't taken away anything from the love she'd lost before. If anything, he'd made that character – TJ's character – front and centre of the storyline. Somehow he'd known, he could read it in my eyes and he'd translated it into a thing of beauty. Of acceptance. Of healing. And new beginnings.

The group chatter away to themselves, trying to look as if they're not hanging on our every word, of which they do a terrible job. I'm still stunned and don't quite know what to say. In truth, I'd felt that first zap of longing with Jonathan at the same time way back when at the music festival the year before but it had terrified me. And to think he'd felt the same and we'd managed to find one another again despite both of us leaving it to fate.

'That's a lovely gesture.' Gesture? I can't think of the right words. I'm not sure who to be in this situation.

He waves me away as if a hundred-thousand-word novel about the art of redemption, forgiveness and longing is nothing. A walk in the park. 'I only hoped you'd read it, that's all I wanted.'

'And then we had a chance meeting like they did?'

He laughs. 'I didn't expect that. And I was more shocked when you said you were going to France and I was about to do the book tour here.'

'Why didn't you say?'

He shrugs. 'I didn't get a chance.'

I think back to the kiss and then my sudden departure. He knew he had to tread softly even back then. 'I suppose not.'

'I'm open to the idea of fate, and when you kept being thrown in my path, I wondered perhaps if it wasn't showing me the way.'

I'm not sure where this is going and in front of so many people. He must read awkwardness on my face because he says, 'Would you like to go for a walk?'

I nod and stand, dusting grass from my shorts.

We say our goodbyes and everyone pretends to be surprised we're leaving.

'Sorry,' he says. 'I didn't mean for it to be a group discussion.'

'It's OK. It gets around any way; the walls have ears when you're a nomad.'

He takes my hand and it feels natural so I don't overthink it. I don't compare him to TJ. I just be.

'I know you've had a rough time. I won't make demands on you. I won't ask for anything except to be in your life, if you'll let me. And if that means us reading by candlelight, that's fine by me.'

It's like he can read my mind. Didn't I say my great big fantasy was us reading by candlelight and that was that?

'Would that really be enough for you?'

He turns to face me, his eyes bright with happiness. 'Yes, of course.'

'But you're really hoping I read some erotica or something and then have this burning desire and rip your clothes off, right?'

He throws his head back and laughs. 'Well, I wouldn't say no.'

Chapter Twenty-Seven

St Tropez

We do exactly that. Well, not the hot, passionate young people sex part. Not yet. But we head back to my van and we talk for hours. There's so much to learn about him. He's similar to me though, so that when the words freeze he lunges for his book, just as I do the same.

For a while we read by soft candlelight. I keep snatching glances at him and find he's doing the same and we let out an awkward giggle and go back to our books.

I have this overwhelming sense that I've done this before, or felt this before. Is it how new love begins? *Is it the retreat of loneliness?*

I reread the same page for what feels like the hundredth time before I close my book.

'Tea?'

'I thought you'd never ask.' He grins.

I take the canister from the shelf and open it to find a note folded into a small square.

Don't be mad but the tea I've been working on is called Love Potion . . . I might be wrong but I think it's worked? A word of advice, take the chance, kiss the boy. You only have so many days

in this wonderful journey called life so why not follow your heart?
Love, Rosie xxx

That alchemist! I knew there was more to the tea than she let on. That and the fact she only made a pot for me and wouldn't let anyone else share it. She might call us hippies but what does that make her? Brewing a tea that she believes is a love potion is right up there in my eyes!

I bustle around the kitchen wondering how one kisses one these days without it being clunky. I think back to my romances and how my strong take-charge heroines do it.

Option A: Take the book from his hands and fling it across the room to get his attention.

No, too intense and what if the book got damaged? He might think I'm about to hurt him or something. Far too dramatic.

Option B: Ask him.

No, that's just plain weird. No spontaneity.

Option C: Sidle over and pretend to trip thus landing in his lap, faces pressed close together.

Yes. No. Maybe. It's how it's done in the books, right?

I take the tea to the table and pour two cups. The aroma of rose permeates the air and sends a charge through me (Rosie and her love potions!). Jonathan shifts in his chair and shoots me a look full of desire. That girl has a gift, no two ways about it.

I hand him a cup with shaky hands. He takes a sip and I wait for it to work its magic.

He murmurs to himself and then says, 'What's in this tea?'

'Oh . . . tea leaves.' *Tea leaves, really, Aria!* 'And umm, rose petals. Why, do you like it?'

'I love it.'

Time is a wasting so I take the tea from him and put it back on the table. 'It needs to cool down,' I say when he shoots me a puzzled look. Just as I'm about to faux trip over and land in his lap he stands up and we bump heads. 'Sorry,' we apologize at the same time. Heads pressed together. 'I was going to . . .'

216

'I meant to . . .'

'Well, we're here now,' I say.

'Yes,' he says and cups my face with his hands. I know he won't make the first move; he's promised me he'll take it slow but suddenly I don't want to waste another minute.

I close my eyes and press my mouth against his, delighting in the sweet scent of rose on his lips from the tea. I kiss him like he's the first person I've ever kissed and all thought goes from my mind. He kisses me back gently as if I'm fragile. The room spins as desire takes over. As far as kisses go this one is better than the books. I drop my hands to his jean-clad hips and pull him against me, I want to feel him, make sure he's real and never let him go.

After an age we draw apart but hang on to each other hands. 'Wow,' he says, grinning. 'And I thought reading together was going to be the highlight of my day.'

I laugh. I've got a lot of living to do and it starts with him.

'Reading is pretty wild, you have to admit.'

'Super wild.'

'What's next?'

'For us?'

'Yes.'

'You tell me, Aria. I'm happy to go as slow or as fast as you need.'

As much as I want to rip his clothes off, I know that's lust taking over. I need to take my time and make sure I'm not doing anything rash that will send me back to the dark place I've been stuck in.

I let my body do the talking and press my lips against his. He feels new and wondrous and like a little bit of light is shining where there were shadows before. Breathless we pull apart. 'Come back to the villa for a swim,' he says.

'OK.' I pack a small bag and grab some books and we head over to the castle on the hill.

Chapter Twenty-Eight

St Tropez

I splash water over him so he dives deep and grabs me around the legs pulling me under with a screech. When we run out of air we burst upwards laughing, our faces angled towards the sun.

I wrap my legs around his waist and he walks to the edge of the pool.

'Where are we going?'

'To rehydrate,' he says. 'I've got a bar stocked up there and only a few weeks to get through it.'

'Do you know how to make cocktails?' I ask as I lean my elbows on the edge of the pool.

He gives me a look that suggests I'm obtuse for asking such a thing. 'Of course! Name your poison . . . as long as it's a mojito.'

I laugh. 'A mojito it is.'

He makes our cocktails, throwing bottles of spirits in the air while I cover my face and screech when he almost drops them. 'I'm a little rusty, that's all.'

'You haven't had a bevy of women to make cocktails for?' I half joke.

'Nope. You're the first.'

'Why, Jon?'

He shrugs and comes back with our drinks which we sip while sitting on the edge of the pool. 'I don't see the point in settling for someone who doesn't set your world on fire, you know?'

'Really?'

He nods. 'Really. And the writing life, well it's not exactly conducive to finding love.'

'So why me, why now?'

'Aria, do you really not know?'

I shake my head.

'When I met you at the music festival it was as if time stopped, the rest of the world became a blur and all I wanted to do was listen to you talk. But before long the night was over and I knew you weren't ready. I didn't know what your past entailed but I could gather it held you back and that I needed to be patient.'

I remember he'd given me a chaste peck on the cheek and I'd reeled back. 'I wasn't exactly open to it then.'

He gives me a half-smile. 'I sensed it and I thought I'd never see you again. But even if I didn't, I felt happy I was still capable of those feelings that had been so dormant after my marriage ended.'

'Why did it end? You said you grew apart . . .?'

He takes a long sip of his drink. 'We were childhood sweethearts, so she was there every step of the way when I was a hopeful but destitute writer getting rejected time and time again. When I got my first lucrative book deal we were ecstatic. I'd been at the point of almost giving up. You can't sustain that kind of life and be married. There's bills to pay, mortgages to dream about having. Then suddenly being plucked out of the slush pile and offered inordinate sums of money, well . . . I felt this intense pressure though to live up to the hype. The first book did really well and then the second book the words wouldn't come.'

'Second-book syndrome?'

He grins. 'The worst case ever.'

'So what happened?'

'I locked myself away and rewrote the thing so many times, in the end I couldn't make sense of it. I felt like a failure. I had imposter syndrome. I felt that the first book was a fluke and all these people were going to be disappointed in me.'

'I can imagine the pressure. It sounds like a horrible thing to get mired in.'

He nods. 'Louise, my ex-wife, couldn't understand it. She wanted me to just write the damn book and move on to the next. But I couldn't send it in, not like that, a jumble in my mind. I decided to go away, get as far from everyone as I could and maybe I'd find clarity there. I rented a little shack in the foothills of the Scottish Highlands. It was the happiest I'd ever been. Just me and the roaring fire for company and I started the book anew.'

'How did it go?' I find the life behind the words so endlessly fascinating but I bet his story doesn't have a happy ending since his marriage didn't survive.

'Great, better than great. The words flowed almost as if someone else wrote them and I felt intensely as though the story was right. I stayed away a few months, only sporadically calling Louise, probably selfishly, because I was so in the zone. So connected to the story, the characters that I didn't want to lose that laser-like focus with mundane things like what party I'd missed and who was seeing who. Louise had fallen into that glitzy lifestyle that goes with the sudden onset of money and the girl I once knew was gone.'

'She changed that much?'

He shrugs. 'Overnight. We were so much happier when we struggled to pay the rent week to week. But I digress. Eventually I went home, ready to send the book in, feeling on top of the world. I'd done it, I'd beaten the second-book demons and I felt like I could breathe again.'

'But . . .' I knew there was a big *but* coming.

'Louise was nowhere to be found. She came home a few days later –she'd been on holiday with a group of friends and one of them just happened to be my so-called rival, another author who wrote in the same genre as me, who debuted at the same time with similar success. He'd managed to write his second book well before me and that too had rocketed up the charts.'

'She was with him as in with him *with* him?' *How eloquent you are with words, Aria!* Face palm!

Jonathan's face remains open with nary a hint of the hurt he must've felt. 'Yes, with him *with* him,' he laughs. 'Romantically involved, at least on her part. She got the shock of her life when she found me at home as they walked in, him attached to her like a second skin.'

'Did he do it because he wanted to get back at you being so-called rivals?'

'Partly, and just because he could. The rivals thing meant nothing to me. So we released books at the same time? Who cares? But he did. You might know him.'

He shares a well known name and I gasp. 'But he's married!'

'Louise obviously thought he was the next rung in the ladder but she got it wrong. He's a serial philanderer and dropped her soon after.'

'Did you take her back?'

He shakes his head no. 'I couldn't. She wasn't even remorseful really, she was more concerned about the lifestyle she didn't want to lose. Whatever we had was dead and buried. It hurt though, it hurt a lot. She was a completely different girl to the one I'd fallen head over heels with as teenagers. But people change, right? Looking back, we were so young, with this sudden fame thrust on us. All this money when we'd had none for so long. It's bound to happen.'

I raise my brows. 'You're pretty forgiving; I don't think I could be in the same circumstances.'

He takes his sunglasses and pulls them down against the glare of the afternoon. 'It took a while but I'm not one for grudges, they don't serve any purpose.'

'What's she doing now?'

He bites down on his bottom lip. 'She's with another writer.'

'Who?'

He whispers the name in my ear and laughter gets the better of me. 'But he's got to be twice her age!'

'Three times.'

I slide closer to him. 'Thank you for sharing that with me.' It makes sense, his hesitation in finding someone new. How could you trust anyone after that? Once again I thank my lucky stars I had someone as genuine as TJ.

'I wanted you to know why, that's all. Sometimes I struggle with my writing and I have to hide out, I have to do it my way, which is to disappear and I know that can be a dealbreaker.'

I bump him with my shoulder. 'Well, you're talking to a nomad here, someone who is used to escaping when things get tough.'

'Maybe we're the perfect match?'

I lean over and kiss him just to be sure. 'Maybe.'

Chapter Twenty-Nine

St Tropez

The sun sinks for another day and the air cools. I've been hiding out at Jonathan's villa for a couple of weeks and I know Rosie is missing me. I'm missing her too.

'I should probably think about heading back to the campsite,' I say reluctantly but knowing I must. We both need time to think things through and what might come next if anything. He's still a bit of a puzzle to me, even though he's been nothing but open and honest.

'Will you come back soon?' he says, his eyes sparkling with hope.

'Sure, if the invitation is open.'

He takes me in his arms and buries his head in my neck. I'll never get used to the buzz he gives me. Never.

'I don't ever want to let you go,' he says. 'But I know I have to.'

'You can get some writing done.'

'There's that.'

We say our slow goodbyes and I leave, feeling a pull of loneliness when he's out of sight.

Back at camp Rosie comes running out as soon as she hears

my van. Her face is awash with relief. Poor girl has probably pictured my grisly death in myriad of ways, despite me texting her daily to try and put her mind at ease.

'I'm alive!' I crow and jump from the van.

She envelops me in a hug and I feel her tears against my arm. 'Are you OK, Rosie?'

'Yes, yes, these are happy tears. I'm not used to you being away for so long, it was hard to know what to do without you.'

'Aww, Rosie I missed your sweet face.'

'Has he declared his undying love for you? Asked for your hand in marriage? Tell me everything!'

We sit on the little deck of the travelling tea shop and I spill the beans leaving nothing out.

'And with sex, you know the old saying goes: it's like riding a bike, you never forget so don't be nervous about it. Maybe you just need to get back on the bike if you get my drift?'

I mock slap her arm. 'Rosie!' I feign being scandalized. 'It's not that. OK, well maybe it is a small part of it. I'm sure it'll all come back to me, but it's that I want to make sure we're on the same page. I'm almost certain we are, but something holds me back. He's been the perfect gentleman which helps.'

'What's holding you back? You didn't *actually* order that chastity belt, did you?'

I laugh. 'No, no, I didn't, I've been using sheer willpower alone. I guess it's the usual nomad curse. If I start something how can I sustain it when he lives in St Albans and I live at no fixed address? Long distance relationships are hard, but love on the road is downright impossible.'

'Have you discussed this with him?' She tilts her head.

'No, it's still too new. It might freak him out. It freaks me out thinking so much into the future about such serious things.' We have both tiptoed around talk of what's next, but it's been right there, just below the surface.

'What do you think he'll say if you did put the question to him?'

I make a face. 'That's what I'm afraid of. What if he asks me to move in with him, move back to the UK? As much as I know I've used van life as a means of escape at times, I still love it and nothing would make me give up the journey. It's who I am, it's what I love. And I don't want to have to choose.' Just like the lovers in Collette's *The Vagabond* . . .

'Has he hinted at that?'

I squirm. 'Well, no. He hasn't put any pressure on me at all.' My heart bongos as another thought hits. 'Maybe he's not interested in long term?' Love can be so messy! 'Is this just a summer fling for him?'

She scoffs. 'As if. Listen to yourself, Aria!'

'It hasn't come up and I don't want to bring it up. I don't want to ruin what we have which has been so much fun. I feel like a carefree teen again, swimming all day, kissing a boy, sleeping after lunch. Reading all hours. It's been downright magical.'

With a smile, she says, 'It's exactly what you need. But summer will come to an end soon enough so you'll have to bring it up eventually.'

I nod and run my hands through my hair which could do with a cut. My coppery locks have been bleached by the sun and are now a shade lighter. 'We're not staying here all summer though, are we? We're off in another week.'

Van life gives and takes just like that.

Rosie toys with her necklace. 'We can stay if you want?'

We can't. I need to go back to the circuit as ever to bank much-needed funds and I know it would make Rosie break out in hives if she had to change her plans. It wouldn't be fair on them especially when she's got doctor's appointments scheduled as we go along.

'No, we can't stay. I'm not going to be one of those girls who gives up everything as soon as a man walks into her life.'

She tuts. 'I hardly think that's the case, Aria. You're giving yourself some time to see if Jonathan's the guy for you, that's all.'

I fold my arms above me and think. 'Yeah. But we're not changing our plans.'

She lifts a hand. 'I can switch a few things around if we need to. I'm not *that* rigid.'

I give her a squeeze. 'I know, Rosie. But let's wait and see. It's been a revelation being with Jonathan but real life has to come crashing back eventually. If it's meant to be, it will be.'

'You bloody hippies. Honestly. You're going to make me go into early labour, I swear it.'

'That reminds me! How did the ultrasound go?'

She grins. 'Want to see the pic?'

'Of my first nephew, of course!'

She looks shifty for a moment and I ask. 'What?'

'That's the thing.' She laughs and it lights up her face. 'Little Indigo isn't making an appearance just yet.'

'What?'

She dashes off and returns with a grainy black-and-white ultrasound picture. A perfect little baby lies there and my heart explodes with joy. 'Aria Rose has totally messed up the schedule and decided she's coming first.'

My eyes go wide and I shriek with joy. 'Aria Rose! *It's a girl!*'

'It's a girl,' she confirms, beaming.

I give her a loose hug, careful of her ever-swelling belly carrying my namesake. 'This is so exciting! We're going to have to hunt out the cutest little clothes.'

'No need. Sharia has made me a bunch. She got to sewing as soon as she heard. She's made little Aria Rose an entire wardrobe of high fashion, and it's all matching which really helps my OCD side of things.'

Sharia is a friend from London who has a pop-up van selling homemade eco-friendly children's clothing from hemp fabric. 'That's so sweet of her!'

'I know! She sent me a bunch of pictures of everything she's made but I told her to hold off posting them as we'd be back eventually.'

'Good plan. Gosh, I kind of can't imagine being back in the UK after being in France for so long. It gets under your skin, this beautiful country.' I'd miss it, that's for sure. But is it the start of more adventures to come?

Rosie tucks a tendril of hair behind her ear. 'I'm looking forward to Christmas in London, and then I think we plan the next sojourn. Greece? Spain?'

As ever Rosie and I are on the same level despite our very different personalities. She's my soul sister, and it strikes me that we wait all our lives for such people to fall into our path and how lucky am I that she's here? 'Do you think things will change when you have the baby? What if you suddenly decide you want the house, the car, the picket fence, the dog named Scooby? PTA meetings? Imagine the other mums with you at the helm!' I laugh in spite of it all.

She considers it for a moment. 'Part of me always worried that might be the case when I first started this trip, but now I know home is where my family are. And that's you and Max and little Aria here.' She taps her belly. 'Travelling with a baby will definitely have its challenges but I'm not alone. I have you, I have Max, I have my beloved Poppy, what else do I need?'

She's right. Of course she's right. Life doesn't need to be lived one way. It can morph and change and be lived on our terms, our way. This makes me think of Jonathan and how he can fit into my life and I into his. *It can be done.* We just have to figure out the nuts and bolts of it.

'I have to go . . .' I say to Rosie.

'Oh?' She shoots me a look that says she understands.

'I need to tell Jonathan how I feel and see if he feels the same.'

Her face breaks into a wide grin. 'Go, *go* before you change your mind!'

Chapter Thirty

St Tropez

I find him sitting in silent repose, book open against his chest, eyes closed. Asleep? I tiptoe towards him and am startled when he says, 'Back so soon?'

'I thought you were asleep.'

'Nope, quietly contemplating life.'

'Me?'

'You're part of it.' He grins.

'And what did you come up with?' I scooch in next to him and lie on my side.

He takes a deep breath. 'I was going to ask you the same thing. You leave in a week, right?'

'Right.'

'So?' He arches that lovely brow of his.

'You first.'

He smiles and traces my lips with a finger. 'It's hard for me to go first, Aria, because I made you a promise that I'd go as slow or as fast as you want, so I don't want to scare you away.'

'Try me.' I need to know he feels the same. That this isn't just some mad summer Instalove that will fizz out like flat

228

champagne. I need the fireworks, the declarations, I need the happy-ever-after. I need it to be like the books.

'OK. If you insist.'

'I do.'

'I've been in love with you since the moment I first saw you, even maybe a minute before when I had this strange feeling, this sense of déjà vu that my life was about to inexplicably change and then there you were.'

We all know romances are a guide to life and this proves it!

I don't interrupt but my heart beats double time.

'I've only known love once before but it was a different kind. Maybe first love is another beast, maybe childhood sweethearts are born from something more innocent, I don't know. All I know is, this burgeoning relationship of ours is all I can think about. It's not just the way you make me feel, like I'm in a daze, my heart won't stop pounding. But like it could develop into a thing of wild beauty. We're both similar at our core. We both need that solitary time but . . . when we met it was as though I recognized you. Like I'd been waiting for you my whole life and there you were . . .'

I smile a smile of gratitude, one of recognition. Maybe we'd both be each other's saviours? The person who came next and fixed the break in our hearts. Didn't we both deserve that?

'I feel the exact same way about you, Jonathan, and I think that's I why I pushed back as soon as I met you. It was scary that someone could make me feel such a way when I'd promised TJ my heart was only reserved for him, no matter what he wanted for me.'

'And I wouldn't ever question your love for him.'

I smile. 'I know. But I guess I had to get to that place myself. When the time was right. And it's right now. But what does that mean for us? How do we know this is real, that this is going to work? I'm a nomad, Jonathan, and I can't give that up.'

'And I'm a writer.'

'So . . .?'

'I can do that anywhere.'

'You'd stay with me?'

'If that's what you want.'

I go to hug him. 'It's what I want more than anything. The beginning of our very own love story.'

'Spoiler alert, I know the ending because I've waited a *lifetime* to feel like this.'

'What's the ending?'

'*And they lived happily ever after.*'

'Well, you *are* the writer . . .'

He leans over and kisses me, stealing the breath from my lungs as the warm Côte d'Azur breeze ruffles my hair. There's no outline for real love, there's no way to plot what comes next, all we can do is listen to our hearts and trust that Cupid has a plan for us. I know everything will fall into place because deep down I sense TJ has orchestrated this man to come into my life and fill the space he left behind. Jonathan's arms encircle me and I kiss him, the kiss of a thousand promises . . .

If you want to be the first to hear news about the new Rebecca Raisin book, sign up to her newsletter here: b.link/signupRR

Acknowledgements

Thank you to my fabulous editor Abi Fenton for everything you do! And to all the HQ staff behind the scenes that help shape/share/design and promote our books – I may not know who you are, but your work doesn't go unnoticed, so thank you.

A huge thanks to all the lovely book bloggers and reviewers that live and breathe books just like Aria. Legends, all of you!

Many thanks to my mum for always proof reading for me, always with a time limit attached. If there's any errors in this book, feel free to put some of the blame on Mum (only joking!).

Lastly, thank you for picking up this book! I hope you enjoyed the sojourn to France and loved living like a Van Lifer for a little while.

Read on for an excerpt from
Secrets at Maple Syrup Farm

Chapter One

With the beeps, drips, and drones, it was hard to hear Mom, as she waxed lyrical about my painting. Her voice was weaker today, and her breathing labored, but none of that took away from the incandescence in her deep blue eyes.

Wistfully she said, "Lucy, you have a real gift, do you know that?" She patted the white knitted hospital blanket. "Look at that sunset, it's like I'm right there, stepping into the world you've created."

I sat gently on the edge of the bed, doing my best to avoid the wires that connected my mom to the machine. These days her hair hung lank—the wild riot of her strawberry-blonde curls tamed by so many days indoors, head resting on a pillow. I tucked an escaped tendril back, and made a mental note to help her wash it later.

"You're biased. You have to say that," I said, keeping my voice light. Beside her, I cast a critical eye over the piece. All I could find was fault. The sun was too big, the sky not quite the right hue, and the birds with their wings spread wide seemed comical, like something a kindergartner would do. When it came to my art, I still had a way to go before I felt confident. Mom was the only person I showed my work to these days.

"Hush," she said. "I could stare at this all day. If I close my eyes I feel the heat from the sun, the wind in my hair . . ."

That's why I'd painted the picture. She'd been suffering quietly for so many years, in and out of hospitals, unable these days to pack her oversized backpack and follow her heart around the globe. She'd been a wanderer, always looking to the next city, a new host of people, a brand-new adventure . . . but her diagnosis had changed all of that. Even though she never complained, I could read it in her eyes—she still yearned for that freedom.

My mom, a free spirit, looked out of place in the gray-white room. She needed sunshine, laughter, the frisson of excitement as she met other like-minded souls, nomads with big hearts and simple lifestyles. The painting, I hoped, would remind her of what we'd do when she was home again. A short road trip to the beach, where I'd sketch, and she'd gaze at the ocean, watching waves roll in.

"Honey, are you working a double tonight?" she said softly, her gaze still resting on the golden rays of sun.

I had to work as many shifts as I could. Our rent was due, and the bills mounting up, just like always. There were times I had to call in sick, to help Mom. We lived paycheck to paycheck, and I was on thin ice with my boss as it was. He didn't understand what my private life was like, and I wasn't about to tell him! It was no one's business but my own. I kept our struggles hidden, a tightly guarded secret, because I didn't want pity. That kind of thing made me want to lash out so I avoided it. When I had the odd day off, I tried to make up for it by covering any shift I could. We needed the money anyhow. "No," I lied. "Not a double. I'll be back early tomorrow and I'll take you out to the rose garden."

She gazed at me, searching my face. "No, Lucy. One of the nurses can take me outside. You stay home and rest."

I scoffed. "You know the nurses won't take you all that way. You'll go crazy cooped up in here."

She tilted her head. "You think you can fool me? Not a double, huh?" She stared me down, and I squirmed under her scrutiny. "Don't worry about me. I've got plenty to do here." She waved at the table. "Sudoku, knitting, and . . ." Laughter burst out of us. The Sudoku and knitting needles were a gift from the lady in the bed over, who'd been discharged earlier that morning. When I'd walked in, Mom's face had been twisted in concentration as she tried to solve the puzzle of numbers. The yarn lay on her lap, knotted, forgotten. She didn't have the patience for that kind of thing, not these days, with her hands, her grip, unreliable at the best of times.

With a wheeze, she said, "There are not enough hours in the day to waste boggling my brain with knit two, purl one, or whatever it is."

I laughed. "I could use another scarf or two. Who cares if you drop a few stitches?" A million years ago Mom had taken up knitting for a month or so, producing with a flourish a bright pink sweater for me to wear to school. She'd been so damn proud of it, I hadn't had the heart to point out all the holes from dropped stitches. She knew though, and looped a pink ribbon through them, and said, "Look, it's all fixed with a belt." I wore that sweater until it fell apart, knowing how much love she had poured into every stitch. It was one of her foibles, taking up a new hobby with gusto, and then dropping it when something else caught her eye. It was a sort of restlessness that plagued her, and she'd skip from one thing to another without a backward glance.

She gave me a playful shove. "I'm not the crafty one of the family, that's for sure. That's reserved especially for you. Would you put the painting by the window? I'm going to pretend we're at that beach, drinking fruity cocktails, and squinting at the sunshine."

"We'll be there in no time," I said, knowing we wouldn't. It was January, rain lashed hard at the window. Detroit in this kind of weather had a gloominess about it; it cast a pall over the city, almost like a cloud of despair. It was different than other places in winter. Sadder.

I leaned the painting against the rain-drizzled glass, its colors too bright for the dreary room, but maybe that's what she needed—a bit of vibrancy to counter the gray. The bleak city was not our first choice, but rent was cheap enough for us to afford on one wage. It pained me to think of the places we'd lived when we'd both worked. I'd loved the sun-bleached streets of Florida, and being blown sideways in the woolly weather of Chicago. Those were happier times, when we disappeared for weekend escapades. Home for me had always been where Mom was, as we squished our too-full suitcases closed, and moved from place to place.

Stepping back to the bed, I pulled the blanket up, and settled beside her, checking my watch.

"Before you head to work, I want to talk to you about something." Her tone grew serious, and her face pinched.

"What, Mom?" I inched closer to her.

She cleared her throat, and gave me a hard stare. "I want you to make me a promise." She held up her pinkie finger.

"OK," I said warily. I'd promise my mom anything, she was the light in my life, but I sensed somehow this was going to be different. I could tell by her expression, the way she pursed her mouth, and set her shoulders. The air grew heavy.

"I mean it. You have to promise me you'll do as I ask, and not question me." Her lip wobbled ever so slightly.

I took a shaky breath as my mind whirled with worry. "What, Mom? You're scaring me." It was bad news. I was sure of it.

She shook her head, and smiled. "I know you, Lucy, and I know you're going to struggle with this, but it's important to me, and you have to do it, no matter what your heart tells you."

"I don't like the sound of this." I stood up, folding my arms, almost to protect myself from what she might say. I stared deeply into her eyes, looking for a sign, hoping against hope it wasn't something that would hurt.

"Trust me." Her face split into a grin. "I want you to take *one year* for yourself. To travel . . ." She held up a hand when I went to interrupt. "Hush, hear me out. Tell your boss tonight—you won't be coming back. Then go home and pack a bag, go to the station, and get on the first bus you see. The *very first*, you hear me? Let fate decide. Find a job, any job, save as much money as you can. I thought you might apply for that scholarship you've dreamed about at the Van Gogh Institute. You can stay with Adele in Montmartre. She's excited by the prospect."

Shock made me gasp. *Take a year for myself?* The Van Gogh Institute? I couldn't think. I couldn't catch my breath.

There was no way. But all I could manage to say was: "You spoke to Adele about this?" Adele was my art teacher back in high school. We'd kept in touch all these years. She was a mentor to me, and the best painter I knew. I'd left school at just fifteen, and only Adele knew the reasons behind my hasty exit. I hadn't been there long enough to make real friendships. She continued to teach me art on Saturday mornings, cooped up in our tiny apartment. I don't know if she saw something in my work or felt just plain sorry for me.

For years she arrived punctually every weekend, until a friend offered her a spot in her gallery in Paris. Saying goodbye to her had been heart-wrenching, but we kept in contact. She badgered me to share my work, and I sidestepped her gentle nudging by asking her about Paris.

"Adele's all for it," Mom said. "And before you go saying no, she agrees you should apply for the scholarship. It's time, Lucy. Your work is good enough. *You* just have to believe in yourself."

The Van Gogh Institute was a prestigious art school, notorious for being selective about their students, and far too expensive for me to ever have considered. Each year the school was inundated with scholarship requests, and I'd never felt confident enough to try for a place. Besides, I couldn't leave Mom. She needed me more, and whatever ambition I had with my art would have to wait.

241

"The deadline for entries this year is the last day of April," Mom continued to urge me. "So you've got a few months to decide. Maybe you'll paint something even more wonderful on your jaunts. You'll be spoilt for choice about which ones to send for the submission process." The room grew warm, as so many emotions flashed through me. The thought of sharing my work filled me with fear. I'd tried hard to be confident, but people staring at it, and judging me, made my heart plummet. I shook the idea firmly out of my mind before it took hold. Me leaving for a year? There were about a thousand reasons why it just couldn't happen.

I narrowed my eyes. What Mom was suggesting was just plain crazy.

"Mom, seriously what are you thinking? I can't leave! I don't understand why you'd even suggest it." I tried to mask the hurt in my voice, but it spilled out regardless. We were a team. Each day, we fought the good fight. It was us against the world, scrambling to pay bills, get medical treatment, live for the moment, those days where she felt good, and we pretended life was perfect.

She took a deep breath, trying to fill her lungs with the air she so desperately needed. "Honey, you're twenty-eight years old, and all you've seen these last few years is the inside of a hospital room, or the long faces of the patrons in that god-awful diner. That isn't right. You should be out with friends, or traipsing around the world painting as you go—not working yourself to the bone looking after me. I won't have it. Take one year, that's all I ask." She gave me such a beseeching look I'm sure I heard the twang as my heart tore in two.

"It's impossible." I summoned a small smile. "Mom, I get what you're saying, but I'm happy, truly I am. Any talk of leaving is silly." She must see? Without my work at the diner there'd be no money coming in. Rent, bills, medical treatment, who'd pay for all of it? And worse still, there'd be no one to care for her. How could she survive without me? She couldn't. And I doubted I could either.

242

"Your Aunt Margot is coming to stay. She's going to help me out, so you don't need to worry about a thing."

My eyebrows shot up. "Aunt Margot? When's the last time you two spoke?" Aunt Margot, Mom's older sister, hadn't struggled like my little family of two had. She'd married a rich banker type, and wiped us like we were dusty all those years ago after she tried unsuccessfully to curb Mom's travel bug. Aunt Margot's view was Mom should've put down roots, and settled down, the whole white picket fence, live in the 'burbs lifestyle.

According to her, Mom traipsing around America with a child in tow, working wherever she could, was irresponsible. There were times we moved so often that Mom homeschooled me, and Aunt Margot couldn't come to terms with it. If only Aunt Margot could see how much life on the road had broadened me. I'd learned so much and grown as a person, despite being reserved when it came to my art. We didn't need the nine-to-five job, and the fancy car. We only needed each other.

A few years ago, Mom tried to reconnect with Aunt Margot, their fight festering too long, but she didn't want anything to do with us nomads. Mom still didn't know I overheard them arguing that frosty winter night. Aunt Margot screeched about Mom breaking a promise, and said she couldn't forgive her. Mom countered with it was her promise to break—I still have no idea what they were talking about, and didn't want to ask, or Mom would know I'd been eavesdropping. But it had always made me wonder what it could have been to make two sisters distance themselves from one another for so many years.

For Mom to reconnect with Aunt Margot now meant she was deadly serious. Somehow, I couldn't imagine Aunt Margot living in our tiny one-bedroom apartment. She wouldn't lower herself. I'd sort of cooled toward my once doting aunt, after hearing her spat with Mom. She'd been judgmental, and narrow-minded, for no good reason.

"We've been talking for a while now. We've really mended

the bridges." Mom tried to rearrange her expression, but it was farcical, her smile too bright to be believable.

I squinted at her. "Really? Now who's messing with who?"

She threw her head back and laughed. "Well, we're on speaking terms at least. And she offered to help so you could go away for a bit. So I don't want to hear any more excuses. Got it?"

Stepping back to the bed, I hugged her small frame, resting my head on her shoulder so she wouldn't see the tears pool in my eyes. How could I tell her I didn't want to go? Leaving her would be like leaving my heart behind. Plus, accepting favors from Aunt Margot . . . We'd never hear the end of it.

Mom pushed me back and cupped my face. "I know you're scared. I know you think it's the worst idea ever. But, honey, I'll be OK. Seeing you miss out on living, it's too much. The young nurses here gossip about their weekends and all the fun things they manage to cram into each day, and then there's you, the same age, wasting your life running round after me. Promise me, *one year*, that's all. Can you just imagine what you'll learn there with all those great teachers? Just the thought . . . just the thought . . ." Her eyes grew hazy as she rewrote my life in her dreams.

I knew to grow as an artist I needed proper training, but that was for people who had lives much more level than mine. My day-to-day life was like a rollercoaster, and we just held on tight for the downs, and celebrated the ups when they came. But Mom's expression was fervent, her eyes ablaze with the thought. I didn't know how to deny her. "Fine, Mom. I'll start saving." Maybe she'd forget all this crazy talk after a while.

"I've got some money for you, enough for a bus fare, and a few weeks' accommodation, until you land a job. It's not much, but it will start you off. You can go now, honey. Tomorrow."

"Where'd you get the money, Mom?"

She rested her head deeper into the pillow, closing her eyes as fatigue got the better of her. "Never you mind."

My stomach clenched. She'd really thought of everything. Aunt

Margot must have loaned it to her. And I knew that would come at a price for Mom. There'd be so many strings attached to that money, it'd be almost a marionette. There was no one else she could have asked.

When I was in middle school my father had waltzed right out of our lives as soon as things got tough, and since then not a word, not a card, or phone call. Nothing. That coupled with our lack of communication with Aunt Margot, a woman who cared zero about anything other than matching her drapes to her lampshades, made life tough. But we'd survived fine on our own. We didn't take handouts; we had pride. So for Mom to do this, borrow money, albeit a small amount, and have Aunt Margot come and rule her life, I knew it was important to her—more important than anything.

"I just . . . How can this work, Mom?" I folded my arms, and tried to halt the erratic beat of my heart.

Just then a nurse wandered in, grabbed the chart from the basket at the end of the bed, and penned something on it. "Everything OK?" she asked Mom, putting the chart back and tucking the blanket back in.

"Fine, everything's fine, Katie. My baby is setting off for an adventure and we're excited."

Katie was one of our regular nurses—she knew us well. "That's the best news I've heard in a long time, Crystal!" She turned to me. "And, Lucy, you make sure you write us, and make us jealous, you hear?"

I forced myself to smile, and nodded, not trusting my voice to speak without breaking.

Katie checked Mom's drip, fussing with the half-empty fluid bag. "We'll take good care of your mom, don't you worry about a thing."

"Thanks, Katie. I appreciate that," I finally said. She gave us a backward wave, and said over her shoulder, "Buzz me if you need anything." Mom nodded in thanks.

We waited for the door to click closed.

"What you're asking me to do is pretty huge, Mom." My chest tightened even as I considered leaving. What if Aunt Margot didn't care for Mom right? What if she upped and left after a squabble? How was Mom going to afford all of this? Did Aunt Margot understand what she was committing to? So many questions tumbled around my mind, each making my posture that little bit more rigid.

"It has to be now, Lucy. You have to do it now; there's no more time."

My heart seized. "What? There's no more time!" I said. "What does that mean? Have the doctors said something?" I wouldn't put it past Mom to keep secrets about her health. She'd try anything to spare me. Maybe the pain was worse than she let on? My hands clammed up. Had the doctors given her some bad news?

"No, no! Nothing like that." She tried valiantly to relax her features. "But there'll come a time when I'll be moved into a facility. And I won't have you waste your life sitting in some dreary room with me."

My face fell. We'd both known that was the eventual prognosis. Mom would need round-the-clock care. But the lucky ones lasted decades before that eventuated, and Mom was going to be one of them. I just knew she was. With enough love and support from me, we'd beat it for as long as we could. Her talk, as though it was sooner rather than later, chilled me to the core. There was no way, while I still had air in my lungs, that I would allow my mother to be moved to a home. I'd die before I ever allowed that to happen. When the time came, and she needed extra help, I'd give up sleep if I had to, to keep her safe with me. In *our* home, under *my* care. Going away would halt any plans of saving for the future, even though most weeks, I was lucky to have a buck spare once all the bills were paid, and a paltry amount of food sat on the table.

"You stop that frowning or you'll get old before your time. I've got things covered," she said throwing me a winning smile. "I'll be just fine, and Margot's going to come as soon as I'm out of here. Don't you worry. Go and find the life you want. Paint that beauty you find and I'll be right here when you get back. Please . . . promise me you'll go?"

I gave her a tiny nod, gripped by the unknown. I always tried to hold myself together for Mom's sake, but the promise had me close to breaking. Dread coursed through me at the thought of leaving Mom, the overwhelming worry something would happen to her while I was gone.

But getting back on the open road, a new start, a new city, just like we used to do, did excite some small part of me. We used to flatten a map and hold it fast against a brick wall. I'd close my eyes and point, the pad of my finger deciding our fate, the place we'd visit next. That kind of buzz, a new beginning, had been addictive, but would it feel the same without my mom?

Dear Reader,

We hope you enjoyed reading this book. If you did, we'd be so appreciative if you left a review. It really helps us and the author to bring more books like this to you.

Here at HQ Digital we are dedicated to publishing fiction that will keep you turning the pages into the early hours. Don't want to miss a thing? To find out more about our books, promotions, discover exclusive content and enter competitions you can keep in touch in the following ways:

JOIN OUR COMMUNITY:

Sign up to our new email newsletter: hyperurl.co/hqnewsletter

Read our new blog www.hqstories.co.uk

🐦 : https://twitter.com/HQDigitalUK

📘 : www.facebook.com/HQStories

BUDDING WRITER?

We're also looking for authors to join the HQ Digital family! To find out more, check our website here:

https://www.hqstories.co.uk/want-to-write-for-us/

Thanks for reading, from the HQ Digital team

If you enjoyed *Aria's Travelling Book Shop*, then why not try another delightfully uplifting read from HQ Digital?